Bandicoot

NOVELS BY RICHARD CONDON

Bandicoot
The Abandoned Woman
The Whisper Of The Axe
Money Is Love
The Star Spangled Crunch
Winter Kills
Arigato
The Vertical Smile
Mile High
The Ecstasy Business
Any God Will Do
An Infinity Of Mirrors
A Talent For Loving
Some Angry Angel
The Manchurian Candidate
The Oldest Confession

OTHER BOOKS

And Then We Moved To Rossenarra
The Mexican Stove

Bandicoot

Richard Condon

THE DIAL PRESS
New York

Bandicoot, concerning Captain
Huntington, is the companion
novel to *Arigato.*

Published by
The Dial Press
1 Dag Hammarskjold Plaza
New York, New York 10017

Manufactured in the United States of America

Second Printing—1978

Library of Congress Cataloging in Publication Data

Condon, Richard.
Bandicoot.

I. Title.
PZ4.C746Ban [PS3553.0487]   813'.5'4   77–17195
ISBN 0–8037–0447–X

For Captain Huntington's Good Friend
STANLEY MARCUS

BAN–DI–COOT *(Bandicota indica)* The wanderer of the Australian outback and forests; family Peramelidae. Can burrow as fast as a man can dig; constantly on the run from predators.

Mammals In Our Lives (Gertrude Garfunkel)

1

Captain Colin Huntington, R.N. (ret.) stood at the arched entrance to the office building in St. Martin's-le-Grand, waiting for his solicitor to appear, as the dome of St. Paul's bloomed at his left. He watched with detachment as A. Edward Masters got down from the taxi under a high-brimmed bowler hat. Masters waved and called out, "Sorry you were early, Colin. Hideous place to stand about. Good show I am prompt."

There was no waiting to see the most senior legal partner, Basil Schute's own solicitor, Michael Sissons. They were ushered into Sissons' office and, without delay, the reading of Schute's short will began. It named Captain Huntington as sole heir to an estate which would be worth slightly more than £5,000,000 after death duties had been paid.

"When will I receive the money?" the Captain asked directly.

"I should say ten months' time," Sissons replied.

"Oh, easily ten," Masters said. "Possibly eight."

"But that won't do at all," the Captain said. "I am in need of a rather large sum of money right now."

"Not a possibility," Sissons answered. "Not a chance in the world."

"Last night," the Captain shuddered, "I incurred a gambling debt of more than thirty-seven thousand pounds."

1

"Let me go round and talk with them, Colin," A. Edward Masters said.

"Thank you, Edward, but no, thank you. My credit line in gambling casinos all over the world is involved here. The debt must be paid."

"Nothing can be expected from this quarter before ten months' time," Sissons said.

"This is all a very morbid experience for me," the Captain said, projecting malaise as he rose to his feet. He shook hands with both lawyers and left the office.

He entered his house in Farm Street through the tradesman's entrance and went into the office of his cook, Juan Francohogar, a sober-to-somber Basque who was judged by his peers to be one of the ten greatest cooks in the world. Francohogar was a man of great height, made taller still by the two-foot-high, fluted *toque blanche* he wore to ventilate his head.

"You are pale, sir," he said, speaking Basquaise French.

"I feel somewhat colorless, actually," the Captain answered in French flecked with the accents of Bordeaux. "I need hearty food. Perhaps you could contrive something with pasta. There is something cryptosexual about pasta."

"If you insist," the great cook shrugged.

"Shall we start with a buttered truffle?"

"At what time, my captain?"

"Early, please."

"Eight-fifteen *alors.*"

"Just right." He walked with dread to the lift.

After a warm bath he was massaged by his wife's podiatric maid in the presence of Steinitt, his man, and Winikus, the West Cork butler. His wife was in Maracaibo inspecting her family's guano simulating plants.

After the massage he napped for forty minutes. Steinitt dressed him, using one of the black satin dining ties from the Rudolf Valentino Collection which Bitsy had given him for

Navy Day three years before. When he was dressed Steinitt sprayed the air four feet away from him with Essence of Zapote and the Captain settled into thirty minutes of concentration at the naval war games board which occupied a twelve by six foot area in his large bedroom. He kept a duplicate of the board in Yvonne Bonnette's bedroom in Charles Street. For seven years he had spent not less than an hour a day at one of the boards refighting Pacific naval battles against his board adversary in Tokyo, Commander Ito Fujikawa, Imperial Japanese Navy (ret.). The conduct of this war by daily air post was an important part of their lives.

He ate the dinner he had ordered.

As he left the dining room he discovered that tension had drenched him in perspiration. With great self-control, he went upstairs, removed the damp clothing, took a stingingly cold shower, then stretched out on the massage table to have Steinitt powder him. They redressed him in a fresh dining suit, chose a black silk butterfly tie from the General Kitchener Collection (which had started his own and Bitsy's combined interest in assembling historic sets of dining ties). He put on a white scarf, a gibus hat, and a black evening coat with moire lapels, and went out to the waiting car. He drove himself in the 1935 chocolate-colored Rolls sports sedan to the Denbigh Club in Debo Terrace, his hands sticky on the leather steering wheel.

The moment the Inside Man saw Captain Huntington through the peephole, he sounded the buzzer and the Shift Boss appeared at the front door as the Captain came in. He walked with the Captain, subduing eagerness, to the high stakes roulette table, saying how pleased everyone was to see him so soon again.

"I should think so," the Captain said.

The dealer nodded to a waiter who scudded away to bring a chilled half-bottle of Pommery '53 to the Captain, just as McCarry appeared. It was almost physically painful for the Captain to take himself away from his concentration to listen

3

to the casino manager. To his amazement he detected from his speech that McCarry had been born north of the river in Dublin and that the plummy U diction he used so carefully must have been acquired from Gramophone records.

"Shall I post a limit?" McCarry asked.

"What is my credit line tonight?"

"As ever. Unlimited, sir."

"No limit then."

"Enjoy yourself, sir." McCarry nodded to the dealer.

Captain Huntington wrote a check for £10,000 and tossed it to the dealer with a wintry smile. A tall stack of French blue ivory counters were moved across the table to him. The Captain played at the Denbigh, not only because it had once been the residence of the beautiful Weldon ladies, mother and daughter (both of them having won the Thousand Guineas at Ascot on the same horse, Fred Foalie), but because the counters were ivory, not Belgian plastic.

He settled down to play the "Skip Transversal System," developed in the summer of 1904 by a young Scotsman, Winchester Paterson. Captain Huntington had bought the system (and the story which went with it) from a dreadfully old, former croupier in Nice who claimed to have been witness when Paterson broke the bank at Monte Carlo with it; the sort of warranty which only a compulsive gambler would accept.

Black six turned up on the first spin. He wagered £100 on the *transversale* which was 4, 5, and 6. Number 4 turned up on the second spin. He won £1000, less his two bets on 5 and 6. He skipped a spin to get a new number; 16 came up. He bet £100 on the *transversale:* 16, 17, and 18. He lost, then he lost again. He became bored with system play. He did not think gambling was meant to be pure drudgery, as much as he needed to win back the £37,000. System play was tiresome.

He bet £500 on Number 13 because October 13 was Yvonne's birthday, then placed £100 on each corner of 13 which gave him bets on 10, 11, 14, 16, and 17 as well. He put a £1000 on black, £500 on the *transversale* of 13, bringing in

13, 14, and 15, then nodded absently to the croupier. The wheel turned. Number 13 hit. So much for system play, he thought with pride in his own judgment, as the croupier pushed the mountain of counters toward him.

He was moving well. Real luck had come back. He decided to rely entirely on extrasensory perception. He felt strongly that people who didn't have proven ESP abilities should not make ESP proposition bets—but he had that gift. It had won him many a low house advantage. If he concentrated, using ESP to choose the right wheel patterns, and if he used correct betting progressions, he had to win. He settled himself to receiving the psychic signals, ready to test for expanding ESP capability.

At 1:35 AM he had finished the half-bottle of wine and, counting the losses of the previous night, had lost £287,000, all in, in round numbers. He passed a £100 counter to the Head Croupier who slotted it, bowing. He gave a £10 counter to the waiter. Equably, even amiably, he bade good night to all and strolled to the men's toilet where he vomited excessively. In a cold sweat, a sick-smelling, damp sweat, his hands and upper arms trembling, his legs like water, he went to the manager's office.

"Ah, Captain," McCarry said. "This has been a thoroughly bad night."

The poor man must be very tired, the Captain thought. Fatigued, he could not control his TH sounds and the words had come out, "Dis has been a t'oroughly bad night."

"I wanted to tell you, McCarry," the Captain said with bogus cheerfulness, "that, at the moment, there is not enough in the bank to cover the checks I wrote tonight." He felt a humiliating flush flood his face but he decided that it was correct that he should be shamed and to look ashen would have been much worse.

"Not to worry, sir," McCarry said. "I have the broadest authority to make credit decisions according to the individual characteristics of a particular situation. Your credit is A-1 here,

5

Captain Huntington." The plummy speech had returned.

"How kind."

"A frequent customer—and that you are, sir—will lose so much money to a casino that he will—inevitably—write a check he cannot cover, you see. When we issue credit to a repeat customer we are only giving him back part of his previous losses. But if our cage issues such credit to a new customer it is giving him part of our bankroll."

"Delicate difference there."

"Oh, yes," McCarry said. "Central Credit World-Wide assures us that you have the very highest credit line from Aruba to Divonne-les-Bains, from Vegas to Macao. Your In-Transit reports are impeccable. The Telex tonight from Nevada proves that. I mean to say, sir, we are not far from the day when Central Credit will be completely computerized with television monitors in every casino cage—and possibly in the pits. We are on the verge of an instantaneous exchange of credit information, sir."

"No doubt," the Captain answered.

"Central Credit does have a Bad Rack, of course."

"Of course."

"It is more important, you see, to have a record of bad customers who have unpaid casino debts than to know the value of good customers. Their Bad Rack holds the name of every player who has faulted with any major casino in the world. And they are emphatic about requiring us to report all bad debts, sir. I must say I feel real pity for the high roller who does not honor his casino gambling debts, because he is a man who will have no place left in the world to play."

The Captain shuddered. "Good night, McCarry," he said.

He drove back to Farm Street. He parked the car in front of the house. He was feeling better. The staff were asleep. The night watchman was somewhere on the premises. Little Jean, Bitsy's chief maid, was on holiday.

He went to the shoe vault off Bitsy's dressing room and took a piece of paper from the toe of a two-tone pink slipper on which was written the combination to the safe that was sunk into the bottom of Bitsy's bathtub, covered with a blue, non-slip bathmat. He opened the safe and removed the small black book that held the combination and time-lock cut-off formulae for Bitsy's air-conditioned walk-in money vault inside the false boiler in the north cellar. He took the lift to the first cellar level, seemed to enter the boiler itself, and took down a prime selection of Bitsy's opals in diamond and emerald settings. With the jewel boxes in his pockets he drove the 1935 Rolls sports sedan to the Denbigh Club and went directly to McCarry's office.

McCarry was playing Mah-Jongg with a Sicilian-looking fellow who was clearly his superior, because McCarry did not tell the man to leave when the Captain came in. He stared the Sicilian out of the room, showing that the fellow was a decent chap at heart.

He stacked up the jewel cases on the desk. "You will hold these as security against my indebtedness," he said, "until they are redeemed. Keep my checks, of course, but give me receipts for the jewels."

In the car he felt grossly entangled in chains of guilt. He wondered if it were a fear of dying that pressed him to such desperate actions so many times. Everything now depended on whether Bitsy regarded his borrowing the opals as his having stolen them. He hoped she would see at once that in order for him to meet requirements of honor and casino credit, he had had to act as he did. But he feared this was hoping too much. Bitsy was sentimental about jewels, money, stocks, gold, mortgages, call notes, and bonds generally. He wondered for a moment if she would be sentimental enough to make some show of putting him in prison.

2

When she returned, he told Bitsy at once about the opals. She moved out of the house immediately to the family's yacht, the *Perfection*, in Southampton harbor. Six days later she summoned him to appear.

A light wind moved down the Thames between the Chelsea Power Station and the Battersea heliport. It was a sunny Sunday morning, the last in May. Captain Huntington sat in the pilot's seat of a tandem two-seat helicopter, formerly a military aircraft, which had been an Arbor Day present to him from Bitsy the year before. A. Edward Masters sat sleepily in the rear under his Irish bookmaker's black bowler hat.

"Strapped in, Edward?"

"All strapped, thank you, Colin."

The Captain called for take-off clearance, lifted off slowly, hover-taxiing on the pad. He turned the chopper into the wind and into forward flight. The Thames dropped away. One and three-quarter minutes after take-off, over the Fairfax Memorial in Clapham, the tower ordered him to change radio frequency to London on 119.9.

"London?" the Captain said fruitily. "This is helicopter Golf Alpha X-ray Yankee."

"Golf Alpha X-ray Yankee, your clearance is special VFR via H.1 to Southhampton not above one thousand feet on

1011.5, clear of cloud and in sight of the surface. Report leaving lane at Woking."

"Copied."

When the yattering stopped, Masters spoke through the headset, which coped with the awful noise that the machine made. "Are you thinking of your plan, Colin?"

"I was thinking of Tokyo in two days' time, actually," the Captain answered, "and of the awfulness of needing to leave Bitsy and Yvonne behind." He was not a promiscuous man. He held to the notion that two young women were enough for any man. When one was angry the other was, automatically, glad.

"But surely you have a plan for coping with this matter of the jewels?"

"My plan—if one could possibly call it that—is simply to pay back the gambling debt."

"Two hundred and eighty-seven thousand pounds?" the lawyer asked incredulously.

"If that is what I owe them—yes."

"You know damned well that is what you owe them!" Masters said hotly into the headset. "And you also know that Bitsy has chosen to view the circumstances of the debt as a felony unless this entire matter is settled today." From the rear seat he could see the Captain shrug and heard his reply through the headset.

"First, I shall repay the debt and redeem the opals. Then I shall reveal to her that I am going to accept a job, to prove to her that I am still a serious man."

"Colin!" Masters was genuinely moved.

"Oh, come off it, Edward. What did you think my Tokyo trip was all about?"

"Colin, if you please—where are you going to get two hundred and eighty-seven thousand pounds?"

"I have been assured of it."

"How? By whom?"

"There are people who buy one's inheritances."

"Good heavens! Has Glandore died?"

9

"Nonsense!" the Captain shouted into the headset. "Why do people even *think* of Glandore in relation to me? Besides, Glandore will never see any amount like two hundred and eighty-seven thousand pounds in his entire life!"

Captain Huntington's older brother, Lord Glandore, was the sole proprietor of LORD GLANDORE'S BOWLING & BILLIARDS (20 ALLEYS NO WAITING) WEINER CURB SERVICE, in Boise, Idaho, having sold Clearwater, the family seat in Leap, West Cork, Ireland, before the body of their father, the first Baron, was cold. Captain Huntington's snobbery was based upon the awful facts of primogeniture by which the elder brother, not he, had inherited the Glandore title which his father had won for procuring clean young women for King Edward VII.

In 1890, the Challans duck served to the King at the Tour d'Argent in Paris had carried the number to show that it was the 328th duck served by the restaurant. To prove how close his father had been to the King, the Captain had taken the trouble to research the fact that the duck served to his father, then merely Mr. Adrian Huntington, had carried the number 342!

Captain Huntington clung to many such bouquets of achievement concerning his family. He would never forget that on May 20, 1910 his father had been summoned to march in the royal funeral procession directly behind H.R.H. Prince Bovardy of Siam, H.H. Prince Leopold of Coburg, and H.S.H. Prince Wolrad of Woldeck, to become identified throughout written history as Assistant Sub-Vice Chamberlain (though not as a White Stave).

The subsequent Lord Glandore's heinous use of the title at his sordid little sausage bar and skittles slum had shattered the Captain, who had been left an orphan at twelve when the rotter had sold off Clearwater House, deserting him, leaving him destitute *and* a Protestant in the West Cork village. Thanks only to the kindness of his Aunt Evans he had been apprenticed in the wine trade in Bordeaux while his brother prospered first with LORD GLANDORE'S GENUINE CHINCHILLA FARM, in Peru, Indiana, from which he had sent Christmas cards printed on whoopee cushions for four years running, then at his vulgar pool room. Merely the mention of his brother's name was capable of unmanning the Captain with shame and outrage.

"Then—my *God*, Colin—" Masters gasped into the headset. "You don't mean you have mortgaged the *Schute* estate for this?"

"Yes. That is, not quite."

"You will *please* state whether you have mortgaged the Schute estate?"

"I have taken no final step, but I have all the papers with me." He looked down at the dotted green countryside.

"Colin, you must not do this!"

"Edward, really! Everything has been most carefully thought out. There is a firm in the City which sells lives. They sell them to speculators who buy against the odds that the lives will shortly cease to exist. It's all done at a monthly auction in Queen Victoria Street and it's been going on since 1843. Quite Dickensian. The setting, that is. 'Who will start me on Lot One,' the auctioneer cries. 'It is an absolute reversion receivable on the death of an old man, age ninety-one, a very promising investment.' There will be twenty-odd death dealers there, all gentle-seeming fellows. They watch each other carefully and somewhere at the back of the room three or four much younger people stand, wondering how much old Gangrad's estate might bring them. And I do believe there are some very large amounts paid out in Queen Victoria Street. Why—the day I was there a stunning opportunity for a £408,000 reversion on the death of a lady of ninety-seven brought £201,000."

"Oh—my God!"

"It's a low-risk business."

"Are you childish enough to trade an inheritance of five million pounds for a pittance of two hundred and eighty-seven thousand pounds? Great Wellington, Colin! You won't even be selling them a one-hundred-year-old man. Schute is as dead as as man can expect to be."

"Bitsy means more to me than money, Edward. And because of her family training, money means more to Bitsy than I do. That is no reflection on either of us, really."

"But what is your *plan*?"

"I shall have Bitsy's lawyers read these papers in my pocket; then I shall give the Schute estate to Bitsy providing she settles the gambling debt and redeems the jewels."

"Well, at least it is more sensible to give one's wife five million tax-free pounds than to borrow against it at terrible interest rates."

"Just bear one thing in mind, Edward. Bitsy's work is accumulating money, which many wise men say is a mania as bad as any. My work, you might say, is wasting money. It isn't a case of one of us being right. We are both right."

Masters marveled at the energy of guilt. By preparing to confer this ton of gold upon his wife who was already overburdened with the stuff, the Captain was actually transferring it from one convenient locker marked HIS to an equally convenient locker marked HERS. Nothing else would change. He would continue to gamble. When he lost he would be relieved of the guilt of accepting his wife's money when she had to pay his gambling debts because he would have given her the money with which to repay them. But he would be acknowledging his dependence on her nonetheless.

Masters knew the Captain didn't reason these things. He merely wanted Bitsy to be happy. Through gambling, Masters felt the Captain spent the useless part of himself away, allowing him to sleep well and to awaken without screaming. Gambling meant so much to the Captain because for it he had sacrificed what he felt was the meaning of his life—the command of Her Majesty's aircraft carrier, *Henty*—because he was unable to comprehend the laws of consequences.

Captain Huntington sat in his gig, moving from the Henty *to the flagship for the last meeting with Admiral Sir Francis Heller before he would be called before the board. He wore his white tropical uniform and all his decorations including the Victoria Cross. Sir Francis stared at him sadly for an eternity from behind the mask of his white full set, the uncompleted shawl of his needlepoint in his lap. He said, "They don't understand your sickness, Colin. They are not psychiatrists, they are men who have had a navy for nine hundred years and, in the course of that time, they have learned things about their commanders. They learned that when a man must gamble, he is a terrible risk. You are finished in the Navy, my dear boy."*

They were over Southampton water twenty-one minutes after being airborne in London. Bitsy's yacht sprawled out upon the blue water below them.

The *Perfection* had first been registered to Daddy's Ghanaian company in 1964. The Ghanaian company had sold it to Uncle Pete's *société anonyme* based in the Marquesas, which had sold it to Uncle Jim's Labrador corporation, each taking tax benefits on the yacht's depreciation along the way. Uncle Jim sold it to Bitsy who sailed it under a Sikkim registry although most of the Sikkim shares were held by a Liberian trust which she and Daddy controlled out of Lausanne. In every way, including its astounding original acquisition price of $197,000, the *Perfection* was a stupendous and constantly renewing bargain, despite a crew of ninety-one. It was used for business entertaining, the only sort of entertaining the family did, which paid for the yacht's operation in tax deductions.

The *Perfection* was 416 feet long, just a few sweet feet longer than the Queen's own yacht, the *Britannia*, Bitsy was proud to say. It displaced 4815 tons, had a cruising speed of 24.75 knots, and a range of 5700 miles.

Daddy had entered Big Government when it was relatively small, to help out Mr. Roosevelt at RFC. All the men in Bitsy's family served their nation in top jobs without pay. Daddy had soon chosen the State Department as his base, but he had been "on loan" to the executive suite of the Central Intelligence Agency since the early fifties, at the urgings of both Messrs. Dulles. The older men in the family, Daddy, Uncle Jim, and Uncle Pete, had served seven Presidents at $1 a year. To their surprise and delight, by serving their nation in high places, they had found themselves at the center of sound, sounder, soundest investment information.

Perfection, the yacht that is, was a case in point. It demonstrated the sometime windfalls of government service if that service was strategically distributed at pivotal points within upper government. Uncle Pete had been a U.S. Senator when the yacht was commissioned as a naval vessel at the shipyards. He had persuaded the Navy, whose common cause the family had always sponsored with zeal, to reclassify the vessel from destroyer class to that of despatch boat. However, because of modern naval improvements such as telephones, radio, satellite communication, television, and other electronic helpers, BU-SHIPS reluctantly was forced to rule that a despatch boat of that size was anomalous.

The vessel, then called the U.S.S. *Harold Bjørnstadt Matson* (after the hero of Montauk who had scattered the English fleet under Admiral Capole during the War of 1812), was put into suspended service though only two years old. It was used as a training ship where knot tying, rope splicing, sailmaking, and pitch blending would be taught. Meanwhile, at the White House, Uncle Jim explained to the President, who planned an atomic-powered fleet, how the *Matson* affair could snowball into a big liability if the press got hold of it.

The President ordered an investigation that was chaired by Cousin Larry at Treasury and, with the tacit consent of Cousin Gary at the Bureau of the Budget, and Cousin Harry, then at Defense, the investigatory board ruled, and the Navy readily accepted, that the *Matson* must be declared surplus and sold at auction.

An announcement of the auction, limited to classified advertisements placed in Juneau and Guam newspapers, asked for sealed bids. As it happened, when the auction was over, Daddy was fortunate to find himself owner of a 2.7-year-old naval vessel at a cost of only $197,000, although his name was not connected with the sale.

Captain Huntington had become accustomed to living with the peculiarities of his wife's family. It was a rarefied atmosphere. Until he married, he had lived in easy, close quarters among thousands of men on warships. He had friends all over the world. Now, since his marriage, although the population of the world was said to be thickening, he seemed to see all people only from far distances: from the cabins of private jet planes; out of ever-moving limousines; over the high, broad shoulders of bodyguards, or from the decks of yachts. The people the family entertained were not friends (they did not believe in friends just as friends) but other power brokers and heavy people who never made an uncalculated move and whose women were only permitted to talk about shoes.

These were the major reasons why the Captain needed to install a mistress. Not all the reasons; there were several connected with Yvonne's face, figure, psyche, and mind—as well as her appetites. When he was with Yvonne he had Yvonne totally, including her soprano saxophone which consoled her while he was with Bitsy, which was whenever Bitsy could contrive to be at home from her long business trips. He had his war games played with Commander Fujikawa. And he had his gambling as a relief from Daddy, Uncle Jim, Uncle Pete, Cousin Harry, Cousin Larry, and Cousin Gary.

3

The Captain reported his approach to the *Perfection* by radio, got his instructions, switched on the emergency float-landing toggle, did his landing check, and began descent toward the landing pad of the immense yacht. With the right pedal balancing the aircraft, he lowered the lever and eased back on the cyclic stick to maintain altitude and reduce airspeed. The lever controlled the rate of descent; the cyclic stick held the speed; the pedals controlled yaw. His approach was straight in.

While the chopper was made fast, the Captain and A. Edward Masters followed the First Officer through a labyrinthian route of ladders, decks, and companionways to the main saloon.

Everyone was there.

The incredibility of the family's massed presence, the awe which overcame him when he thought of the hundreds of deals they had left behind just to be here, made the Captain think he was hallucinating.

"Good afternoon, Colin," Bitsy said gravely.

"You are looking smashing, Bitsy." He turned to face a florid, white-haired man who was as tall and as slender as himself; the oldest man in the room. "Good afternoon, sir," he said. He felt he could not possibly call this man Daddy and yet, although the man's first and last names were among the world's myths, he could not call him by name either.

Daddy was amiability itself but rather in the manner that a top hitman can be jovial as he stands with his contract and two helpers at the Elizabeth, New Jersey, garbage dump. "Must say you are looking fit, Colin," Daddy answered with a high, reedy voice that rippled and rasped with multi-layers of privilege. He pumped his son-in-law's hand with the tensility of a Tenth Dan. Disengaging somehow, the Captain turned to the first uncle in line. "Good to see you again, Jim," he said. They shook hands primly. Uncle Jim had undertaker-objectivity. He was not smiling. Professionally, Uncle Jim was the most constant smiler in the family, so the Captain sensed it would be this kinsman who would handle the espada at today's fiesta brava. In fact, it was a chilling thing that Uncle Jim was not smiling. "You smile all the time at the White House or you get out," Bitsy had explained. "President Ford wants a jolly, open atmosphere. There are photographers and rumormongers all over the goddam building so everybody better make it look confident."

The Captain shook hands with Uncle Pete. Pete was a big, bluff man whose very manner ordered, "I am lovable and you better believe it." Uncle Pete was currently handling the implementation of the really new, efficient S–1 legislation for both parties, which made it necessary that they move Cousin Harry out as Assistant Secretary of Defense, put Cousin Gary in that job, and have Harry take over for Uncle Pete as the solid bridge between the militaries and the manufacturers of the sorts of items that cost two and three billion dollars. That joint industry had not been having such an easy time since the Vietnam war. Harry had to feel his way at first, but the fact was Uncle Pete had to be freed to pioneer two new fields that Daddy said were going to throw off "an astounding amount of net money for the highest body count," the new binary chemical and germ warfare breakthrough and, secondly, that burgeoning industry so inherent to the system, the industry that had grown into an entire shadow government as more and more functions of the primary government were "contracted out" to consultants who did studies on government problems so that the wholly untrained elected officials of Big Government would be able to find some basis for making the rare decision they did make.

Uncle Pete's greeting to the Captain seemed the same as always: hearty and lovable, just the way Hermann Goering had been with his crowd. The three cousins were smiling and cordial; therefore it was Jim who would play the assassin, the Captain deduced.

A. Edward Masters followed behind the Captain, greeting all with courtly ease. He had been through the ritual before. Hovering in the background were Bitsy's principal American and British lawyers: Dr. Francis A. O'Connell, Jr., and Lord Clogg, respectively. Dr. O'Connell occupied the Hoffa Chair at Cornell. Captain Huntington knew these lawyers as well as a man might have gotten to know his wife's old nannies because, over the years of his marriage, they had always been somewhere close by Bitsy.

Bitsy was an achingly handsome, dark woman in her middle twenties whose perpetual expression since she had met her husband was one of puzzlement. Away from her husband she conveyed about as much puzzlement as had Kemal Ataturk. They all sat facing each other in a wide, oval arrangement with the heinously expensive lawyers lurking in the background.

"I think you, of all people, understand how our family operates, Colin," Uncle Jim began, not smiling.

"Indeed, yes."

"I think you will agree we are a unit—that is, all for one and one for all."

"Indubitably, Jim."

"And you are a part of what we are, and share in everything we own, you see."

"Under a carefully limiting definition of that, I would agree, yes."

"Jim? Please? Let me innarupt here?" Uncle Pete said.

"Colin and me has been good ole buddies so it's my job to break the bad news."

"Bad news?" the Captain said, in a pale voice.

"Our Bitsy wants a dee-vorce." Uncle Pete was a Rhodes scholar who had studied English literature at Oxford but he had become habituated to speech afflictions affected by American politicians.

"Out of the question!"

"I am going to divorce you," Bitsy said and began to sob gently.

"You gone hafta face that, ole buddy."

"I would like to speak as Bitsy's father," Daddy said and intuitively the Captain knew everything was going to be all right, that everything which had happened so far was a half-rehearsed measure of punishment, merely token torture. Daddy had never spoken deferentially in his life, including certain meetings with Winston Churchill, Charles de Gaulle, and John Dean III. All eyes were on him.

"Colin, we are all intelligent people here," he said, using a voice from File 524E, the Kindly Tones drawer, "and we realize that you are not defying Bitsy's happiness with malice when you gamble but that you are the victim of a terrible disease which can smother you."

Cousin Larry shuddered delicately. Cousin Gary looked bleak. Cousin Harry was outraged.

"See here, Colin," Uncle Jim said deliberately. "We've never made it a secret from you that we are fed surveillance reports on you every day including Sundays because we have felt that to be necessary for your own protection."

"If you say so, Jim."

"We have provided you effective, expensive, but wholly invisible U.S. government security people who really know their jobs. You have been given everything, three shifts a day, that a President of the United States gets in the way of personal protection."

"I haven't felt I've really needed that in London, but

nonetheless I appreciate your solicitude."

"We have never objected, for example, to your keeping your little French mistress."

"She is five feet nine, actually."

"That little mistress is your private business. Why—even Bitsy was big enough—uh, that is, uh—*understanding* enough, to acknowledge that all work and no play makes us dull boys. Until now we have never complained about your gambling. But this time it is different. This time, because of your gambling, you stole your wife's jewels to pay gambling debts."

Ice began to form over the Captain's head and posture. He stared chillingly at each member of the family in ever more chilling silence. He seemed to grow taller and more threatening as he sat in utter stillness on the chair. He was done with being conciliatory. He was finished with toleration.

"I shall now require that you restate that sentence in more precise terms," he said. "I did not steal my wife's jewels. They were jewels from a rare opal collection which I built for her in a succession of gifts. Further, let it be clear, I bought this collection with gambling winnings at various parts of the world which, as I recall it, made all of you quite happy at the time."

No one answered. A. Edward Masters beamed at him from across the room.

"You will be careful to remember this: I borrowed my wife's jewels and installed them as collateral. I informed my wife of this within five minutes after her return. If you wish to continue this we will do so after I have had your apology."

"God*dam*. I *do* apologize," Uncle Jim said, leaping to his feet and bouncing across to pump the Captain's flaccidly held hand. Uncle Peter and Cousins Larry and Gary also rushed to his side. Harry and Daddy remained seated but they provided forms of smiles.

Bitsy was overwhelmed with pride and love at the way Colin had disciplined her family. But the past blocked the way. Nausea overcame her as she saw him, in her memory, in the basement of the Central Hotel in Macao where he was a shouting part of a mob of eighty or ninety Chinese coolies, fighting to bet pennies in a fan-tan game after losing ninety-one thousand pounds in the plush gambling rooms of the same hotel three floors above, his white uniform of a Captain of Her Majesty's Navy sweat-stained and ruined.

"I want a divorce, Colin," she said distinctly.

"No."

"There is another way," Daddy said. Everyone listened. "Colin's gambling is a pathological affliction. Therefore, my boy, you must agree with us that, since you cannot stop gambling, you must undertake reeducation which will enable you to gamble and win."

"All we askin' is that you win, ole buddy," Uncle Pete said.

The Captain's face went into shatter-effect. "Enable me to *win*?" he said with loathing, as if they were asking him to rape the family collie. "To learn to *cheat*?"

"I am going to believe I did not hear that," Daddy answered in a way which suggested many, many bodies lying about, quite dead, under various bridges of his life.

"Daddy, no!" Bitsy cried out with fright. "Please tell Colin what you mean!"

Daddy inhaled and regained control of himself. "I put the Rand Corporation and the Hudson Institute—Herman Kahn agreed to think it for me personally—on studies of your problem. Neither of these are family consulting companies. They proved that there are professional gamblers who win eighty-seven percent of the gambling transactions they undertake, that winning at gambling is a matter of improving the emotional thrust of the player while impressing upon him that all gambling is merely the effective management of money."

"I don't understand any of this," the Captain said stiffly.

"You are classified as a compulsive loser. Rand and Kahn want you to be retrained as a compulsive winner. It is as easy as that. Money is merely a convenient means of keeping score among competing players. The objective is to behave constructively enough toward your own attitudes while gambling that you can insure that the score will terminate in your favor."

"What sort of retraining?"

"No brainwashing, no chemical persuaders, or immense bio-feedbacks such as we have developed so successfully at The Company. That course was strongly recommended by me, because I have seen some of the impressive results it has achieved in making people believe they are someone else. We came within a hairsbreadth of convincing Nixon that he was human. We did convince Mr. Ford that he was Harry Truman—" he sighed—"but Bitsy rejects all forms of mind control. Therefore, Rand and Kahn have had to come up with a conditioning system that will teach you to rethink you own reflexes as a gambler in the same way you would learn a new language, by total immersion in it."

"By what conditioning system, sir?"

"You will be exposed to the psychology of a successful professional gambler. We want you to agree to spend most of your waking hours with the man chosen. Rand and Kahn know this will transform you into a winning gambler and save your marriage."

The Captain stared soulfully at Bitsy. "If I agree to undertake this didactic madness," he asked her, as if they were alone in the room, "will you stop this talk about divorce?"

She nodded.

"Then I agree," he said to Daddy. "And I assume this reconditioning can happen wherever I happen to be."

"Of course! And congratulations, my boy," Daddy boomed, reaching out to give the Captain a two-handed handshake.

"Goddam, ain't this the greatest thang that ever happened?" Uncle Pete said.

"I am totally relieved," Uncle Jim said, "now we can sit down and talk about paying off that gambling debt and getting those opals back. We want to lend you the money, Colin, and to make it as easy on you as possible while staying within the bounds of sound business practice. We'll only charge you fourteen and three-quarters percent, providing you will put up the assets of your opal company and your racing stable as collateral."

"I think he should include the balloon," Cousin Harry said, revealing that he coveted the Huntington balloon.

"No," the Captain answered.

"No to the balloon?" Uncle Pete asked.

"No to all of it."

"NO?" six voices yelled.

The Captain tugged at a manila envelope in his pocket. "If you will study these papers with Lord Clogg and Dr. O'Connell, Mr. Masters will explain the fine points."

Daddy rose and led the way to the lawyers, envelope in hand. All the men and their advisers sat at a long conference table at the end of the room. Lord Clogg began to read the papers aloud in a low voice. Captain Huntington looked down tenderly upon his wife.

Bitsy was movingly beautiful, dressed in a black rubber wet suit. The heavy fabric was unable to suppress her developed figure. Her lustrous black hair had been pulled into a round knot on top of her head causing the lines of her lovely face to stand out cleanly. She had dark blue eyes which offered a level, humorless gaze; humor being too frivolous an attribute for anyone as psychologically secure as Bitsy. At just under six feet tall, Bitsy was three inches shorter than her husband.

Also, she had a magnificent behind. Hardly a man alive, possessed of even indifferent health, did not pant to bed her— the impossible dream. Bitsy was madly, which is to say, insanely, in love with her husband.

"I've been waiting to tell you that I have accepted a job," the Captain said emotionally.

"A job?" She was not able to comprehend at first. "A *job*? Oh, Colin!" She wanted to shout the news out across the salon but the men at the table were intently engaged. He looked covertly over her shoulder. He had two hours to get back to London. Bitsy was saying, "What kind of a job?"

"In oil, actually."

"Oil?" The very sound of the word bathed Bitsy in sticky money. "Did Brown, Shipley get it for you?" Brown, Shipley was Edward Heath's old firm, the merchant bank that had such sound sheikh connections.

"No. I did it myself actually. Marine oil. Offshore. That sort of thing."

"You'll be *maaaaarvelous*! What does it pay?"

"A hundred and fifty thousand dollars flat."

"Isn't that nice? And you'll be helping England's balance of payments."

"Japan's balance of payments, actually."

"Oh."

"When they finish their meeting we can go someplace and talk."

"Someplace?"

"Bed."

"You know we don't talk much in bed." She lowered her eyes to conceal the glaze of lust but she could not control her manteling.

The nine men rose from the table as if moving against natural laws. Each returned to his former place in the room like a chess piece. Daddy had to clear his throat to speak, he was so moved.

"Lord Clogg, Dr. O'Connell, and the family are in fullest agreement," he said to Bitsy. "Colin's proposal is indeed acceptable—even immeasurably generous. We have arranged with Mr. Masters for a transfer of funds so that the gambling debt may be discharged and the opals redeemed—without interest charges, I might add. Everything is settled to everyone's total satisfaction."

"Oh!" Bitsy said, springing to her feet, grabbing her husband by the forearm and pulling him out of the chair.

There began upon the large bed, with a fervor matching the level of Olympic finals (the 1980 Olympics would surely include free-style sexual events), impassioned bucking, rolling, sunfishing, and counterpoising, mutually testing arcane physical theorems, the violent locomotions and daring by people of their length, weight, and zest, squared by the time of absence from each other, which moved the vast, heavy bed one-third of the way across the stateroom. Their blood plasma grew milky with droplets of suspended fat squirting reserves of energy into their body systems. Bitsy's frequent outcries were so piercing that they were taken for small craft warnings by fishing vessels as far as a quarter of a mile away from the yacht. The increasing pace and contortionistic apogees of movement and sensation were passed from one to the other like erogenous beanbags until Bitsy ascended to her ninth and (mercifully) ultimate fulfillment and the Captain to his second (and incontrovertibly final) exhaustion. Bitsy was happier than she had been since the last time she had bedded Colin, or even since the time the little bank she had bought in Belgium had merged with the big bank in Düsseldorf.

The Captain was gasping terribly for breath, no more able to speak than a haddock on a mountaintop. Quite some considerable time passed while the world went about its business. The family and their lawyers had departed from the ship. The Captain began reflexive thoughts about Yvonne Bonnette. He was cursed with the compulsion to think about one while he was intimately engaged with the other.

Suddenly he remembered that he had to get back to London. While Bitsy slept, he dressed hurriedly. He left a note beside her that said: "DARLING: TO LONDON. MUST LEAVE FOR TOKYO TUESDAY. ETERNALLY, COLIN."

4

Alone, Yvonne Bonnette lay naked upon her superbed. She was sensating her twenty-fourth year; spectacularly red-blonde; openly, naturally, reflexively sensual in every life-motion she made. Her large, pink, soft, wet mouth had a slackness that could seem bestial to sexual fantasts or merely crazing to straights. Her figure, as it stretched itself out upon the blue silk sheets, resembled a young boy's in no way whatsoever. It was the body of a ripened Nereid every square inch of whose skin was an erogenous zone; every muscle formed to envelop, to tighten, to grip. Yvonne ate food as if she were living hardcore pornography, such as a lipstick commercial or a popsicle commercial. She walked with avidity, as though she were lurching headlong toward a gala picnic of sex. One day, if she reached 109 years, she would probably be too stiffened to copulate. When that day came she was going to devote her life to the poor.

At the far end of the large bedroom stood the Captain's war games board, showing the Pacific Ocean, abutting countries, and emerging islands in bas-relief upon a heavy table with six legs, upon which small replicas of Allied and Imperial navies were arrayed. Yvonne was daydreaming of Captain Huntington while fingering upon and blowing into a long soprano saxophone. She enunciated it with greatest feeling, playing out the mock-sadness of the "new" nineteenth-century music, achieving brilliant bravura passages and massive tongue coloration, using wide overblowing intervals to achieve control as if the straight soprano saxophone were the cavalry bugle of the women's liberation movement. Her play upon the instrument, and no less upon Captain Huntington, was a moving thing. During the hours when they were not at it, or when they were not eating Francohogar's startlingly endowed food, the Captain would stand at the war games board in his floor-length white beaver dressing gown and his old white Royal Navy captain's hat, staring down at the deployment of model ships while Yvonne intensified his concentration with brilliant, if melancholy, soprano saxophone solos.

The Captain pounded up the stairs at the Charles Street house, hoping perfervidly that he was on time to meet his obligation, hearing the saxophone passages of "Come Rain or Come Shine" wailing out of Yvonne's bedroom. He burst into the room and, at the moment he seated himself beside her on the bed, the telephone rang. He picked up instantly.

"Hello?" he said into the telephone. "Commander Fujikawa?"

Yvonne stopped playing. She raised her eyebrows. The Captain put his hand over the receiver. "Tokyo," he explained.

"I say—what a splendid connection! Yes. How are you? Good! First-rate, thank you. Ah, yes, I have the plane ticket, thank you. I should be on the ground at Haneda airport on Wednesday evening. Why—how very kind of you."

Commander Fujikawa was responding to all this with his tri-dimensionally fruity, British royal family accent and, in subsequent sentences, forcing the Captain (the way an expert at tennis or billiards can force the pace of the game) into the most magnanimous sorts of vowels and diphthongs, jumping his vowel pitch entire octaves in mid-sentence in the summit U manner. The Captain fielded and returned each verbal volley with honed skills. Jointly, it was a prodigious feat of elocution; the sort which great English diction champions, such as Princess Margaret or Terry Thomas, produce dazzlingly.

"We have a full training schedule prepared for you here," the Commander said. "The only delay at the moment is the yacht we must have. It has to be a huge, madly posh yacht to perform both as your base and your cover, you see."

"Uh—did you say cover?"

"Yes. We need you, as a non-Oriental, to conduct field explorations off Australia. The cover is entirely legal. Full authorization from the powers-that-be in Brisbane and all of that but, damn it all, the sight of a Japanese face does frighten those people for whatever reason."

"The war probably. Perhaps even that Nanking thing years ago."

"Perhaps. But there is much crude oil at stake here. My father wants it. We must find the right yacht."

"I say," the Captain put in, "my wife's yacht is a good size —slightly larger than the *Britannia* actually—and quite comfortable."

"My dear fellow! Do you mean—you can't mean—the *Perfection*?"

"The very ship."

"How fortunate! Could she be made available for charter?"

"I don't see why not."

"At what cost—all in?"

"In dollars?"

"Please."

"I suppose about a hundred and twenty-five thousand a month."

"Where is she now?"

"Southampton harbor."

"Where may I send my check?"

"I suggest you make it out to the First Mesilla Medical Publications Company of Sikkim, and send it along to my wife in Farm Street."

The Commander mumbled the data into the phone as he

wrote everything down. "Five hundred and sixty-two thousand dollars—First Mesilla Limited—"

"Not Limited actually. It is a *Gesellschaft mit Beschrankter Hafttung.*"

"*G.M.B.H.*" the Commander murmured. "As in *Kabushiki Kaisha.* Very good." Thriftily, the Commander hung up.

"What was that all about?" Yvonne asked.

"I have had to take a job," the Captain said.

"A *job.*"

"Yes."

"But—where?"

"In oil."

"Olive oil?"

"No, no. Fuel oil."

"In London?"

"In Tokyo, then in Australia."

"What is going to happen to me?"

"Well, you *can* run the opal business. It *is* only temporary."

"Oh, yes! Only temporary! *Only!* You have to take this filthy job where you get oil all over your beautiful face to make the monnaie to pay your wonderful wife so she won't send you to prison!"

"Not at all, darling girl. That's all settled."

"I want to go with you."

"How marvelous! Of *course* you must go with me! I couldn't bear to be without you for eighteen weeks."

"Aha! But what about your wonderful wife?"

"I am arranging that. Thinking it all through, as it were."

"I have a sister in Australia."

"How nice."

"In Adelaide."

"A beautiful city."

"She is crooked, like my father. Colin, are you doing the right thing?"

"My dear, the sea is my milieu."

"Perhaps. But not your true milieu. Oh, Colin, my cabbage!

My glory!" She pulled him down upon the bed and began to undress him. She unbuttoned his trousers frantically (after a savage accident they had experienced he no longer wore zippers). She tugged at his shorts, lifting his spare rump with unexpected strength, flinging them behind her. He still had on his Hawks Club tie, his shoes and socks. He was monumentally ithyphallic and she flung herself upon it as earliest rites dancers did at the Maypole.

Much later, Yvonne spoke first, for she was younger. "Tell me the real reason why you have taken this job."

There was a long delay. At last the Captain spoke weakly. "Because I have spent all the faith people had in me."

"No, no! I have faith!"

He had made the full snap turn into lugubriousness, undoubtedly post-coital. "My honor, my dignity—and indeed my reason for existing—is the faith my Queen had in me when she gave me command of the *Henty*."

"Pooh."

"I destroyed that faith." He was utterly sincere. "My wife has lived by her faith in me—"

Yvonne made an excessively aggressive, rude noise with her tongue between her lips, blowing with all the trained force of a virtuoso saxophonist.

". . . and I treated *her* faith and since we have been together the four most important years of *yours* with helpless stasis of my anti-life. And—now—Commander Fujikawa, perhaps the last male comrade I have—"

"Don't snuffle, Colin, please."

". . . has reached out to touch my spirit because he says he needs my help and is willing to pay one hundred and fifty thousand dollars for it."

"Now you are getting to the heart of the matter," Yvonne said.

"I am taking this job to give surest meaning to the three women who have supported me with blind loyalty—"

"Three?"

"You, Bitsy, and the Queen."

"No one has even told the Queen that you are alive," Yvonne said fiercely. "Your wonderful wife would send you to prison if you got dust on her rotten money! Only I love you! Only I would die for you! Not your Queen, not your wonderful wife!"

"Then, by God, Yvonne," the Captain said, rolling over on top of her, "I must accept this job to bring honor to you while returning dignity to me." He grabbed her with intense feeling at her most private place. He covered her hips and, gathering momentum like a ship in a newsreel being launched down the ways, slid into her, feeling far, far more idealistically motivated than he had the time immediately before.

5

The five-story house in Farm Street had once belonged to Captain Huntington. He had deeded it to his wife, as he had most of his other real property, in return for her assumption of other gambling debts. No one ever thought of looking at it in just that way (except Daddy), but Bitsy had accumulated a large (separate) fortune as a result of her husband's weakness.

She and the Captain lunched at Farm Street on the day before his departure.

While he waited for Bitsy to come down, sipping from a thimble of John Jamieson's Irish whiskey, Daddy telephoned him from the American embassy at Kabul. It was the delicate time of the American nominating conventions in the United States and it had become somewhat necessary, for the Republican President to please his far-right crazies, to keep Dr. Kissinger under cover in what was inexactly termed as a "low profile." Professor Kissinger was Daddy's personal charge. Daddy and his team had grabbed the Secretary of State as he came out of a fashionable Washington restaurant and had spirited him away, overseas, in the manner of a short-term Philip Nolan. Daddy had the CIA work out a schedule of meetings and treaties and negotiations to keep the doctor busy but not too noticeable. With just the right amount of activity so as not to frighten the American conservative community. They had just wound up a Kabul session at Mazar-i-Sharif.

"I am calling you from a secure phone," Daddy said. "When did The Outfit sweep your phones last, Colin?"

"This morning, sir. They clear it every morning. They never find anything."

"Good. This is something I couldn't very well bring up at the meeting with Bitsy the other day, but the family has this opportunity to buy into a gambling casino operation—maybe a chain of them if we can clear up some token opposition in New Jersey and New York State legislatures, and I wanted to check with you about general investor yields from propositions like that."

"I should say very good, actually," the Captain answered, appalled. "For example there was an instantaneous twenty-two percent pick-up on the two hundred and seventy thousand I lost the other night."

"But is gambling a *growth* industry?" Daddy asked.

"I should have to answer yes. The industry shows a twelve point three percent annual increase. That's good growth when one considers that this year's increase was up over the previous year by nineteen percent."

"My! That steady."

"Steadier still, sir. You can increase your win by liberalizing credit procedures. I mean, accounts receivable at an active casino in a well-populated area can be sent up as high as fifty million over the Christmas–New Year's period."

"Good. Oh—good!"

"However, you'll find yourself in business with an entirely different set of people."

"Not to worry, Colin," Daddy said. "We've maintained a fine working relationship here at The Company with Mr. Lansky over the years, and one cannot expect them to be more intently different that that."

They hung up. The Captain shivered.

He and Bitsy were well into a bottle of Bonnes-Mares '60, when he told her in detail about his job and, along the way of the narrative, remembered the charter deal he had made for the *Perfection*.

"What is the charter rate for the *Perfection*, Bitsy darling?"

"Eighty thousand a month but I am determined to get it up to a hundred."

"How odd! Then I made a mistake on the telephone to Tokyo and got it up to one hundred and twenty five. Chap leaped at it. With a four and a half month guarantee, all in, out and back to home port."

"How did you ever do that?"

"Has to do with this job. Employer needs the poshest sort of yacht to prospect for oil—a higher grade of oil, one suspects."

"But—Japanese! Daddy knows almost the entire *zaibatsu*. How did they find you?"

"He's the fella I play war games with through the post. His family owns the Inland Sea, or something."

"Bitsy?"

"Yes, dearest?"

"I have had the best idea of a decade. I know you can't take too long away from your work but—well, how about a second honeymoon on the Great Barrier Reef?"

"Colin, how *heavenly*. Let me look!" She dashed to her desk, thumbed a large appointments book, and asked for specific dates excitedly.

"Beginning of August," he said.

She studied the book. "Oh, *damn*. I have to meet Cousin Harry in Provo. Daddy thinks we ought to put the grenade factory there. Then at the end of the week we've been invited to Kykuit by Nelson and Happy."

"Give my best to Nelson. And Happy, too, of course."

"But—look! I've got the whole month of September free! You could cruise down and pick me up at Sydney and we could have an entire *month* to sail all the way home. And—I mean—

it isn't as though I'll be ma*rooned*. The ship *does* have telephones and radio and Daddy's satellite. Oh, Colin! Isn't it *wonder*ful?"

"Dazing. But the separation from June to September is more than I can bear."

"How pleased Daddy will be that you have—single-handedly—lifted our charter rate to one twenty-five. Yesterday, again, Bryson tried to buy the *Perfection* based on a charter rate of eighty-five thousand."

"You mustn't sell it now!" the Captain said with a burst of anxiety. "Old Baron Fujikawa has his heart set on it!"

"I know what," Bitsy squealed. "I'll sell it to *you*, right now, and take a capital gain. Then, with the new charter rate and your bill-of-sale from some dummy company, we will be able to fix a new sale price to Bryson or anyone else."

"Why to me?" the Captain cried with horror. "Besides, there won't be time. I must fly to Tokyo in the morning."

"Because Bryson thinks he's got to have that ship—and our wire taps show he's just made another enormous profit out of one of his massive borrowings. He wants to hold the hundredth birthday party for his old grammar school fraternity— he never made it to high school—on his own yacht, providing that yacht is the biggest in the world."

"But—why?"

"His nickname in grammar school was Shitty."

"But that must be sixty years ago."

Bitsy's voice got hard. "Look, Colin—everyone else in this family has taken a turn at buying the *Perfection* to kick its price higher and higher and to earn tax money. Now its your turn. And it will look better when we ask some crazy price like four million for the ship, because you'll actually be doing business aboard her. I mean—after all—what is it but a lot of transfer papers? They won't *mean* anything. Daddy will still own the yacht."

"Well, if you say so, Bitsy, but—"

"Good. You have just bought the *Perfection*, which cost Daddy one hundred and ninety-seven thousand dollars, for four million dollars. Congratulations!"

She hugged and kissed him. "And if Bart Clogg can't have the papers ready tomorrow morning we'll send them straight on to Tokyo."

The Captain lifted his glass of wine and was alarmed to see that his hand was shaking. He hated even the semblance of owning such valuable things. Now it would look as if he had taken advantage of Commander Fujikawa on the charter price. Damn Bitsy's family anyhow!

6

Captain Huntington relayed two complete kits ahead of himself when he traveled. The first kit, for Japan, had been shipped out five days before by air freight; today an identical kit would be driven to Southampton and unpacked in his set aboard the *Perfection*. When he left Japan for Australia, the Fujikawa people would return his first kit to Farm Street. In this way he avoided having to scramble for porters. It was simply a more dignified method and it saved on tips.

He and Steinitt went over the second kit early on the evening before his departure to check that the brass grommets (on the shoes which *had* brass grommets) had been polished; that the soles of his shoes were shined so that, were he to wish to put his feet up, he wouldn't offend others with messy footwear. They checked that his socks had been neatly pressed and filed unfolded. The matching wallets for each suit were checked to be certain that they contained emergency currency in Japanese yen and Australian dollars worth £10 with a £3 equivalent of local silver set into the change pockets of each of the thirty suits for local tipping. The suits were checked for their credit card inventories, and duplicate copies of essential address and telephone listings. He interrupted their inspection to ask Steinitt to telephone Miss Bonnette for such data on her sister in Adelaide. Steinitt typed this information on a magnetized card that caused the address to be typed thirty times for gummed insertion into the thirty address books. Although Bitsy had not yet been able to get him thirty copies of his passport, even after asking Daddy to ask Dr. Kissinger to exercise pressure upon the Foreign Office, she had run copies of it off on her color Xerox machine and they had been installed in the left breast pocket of each suit.

They checked that night check books were in the pocket of each set of pajamas. They packed black dining ties from the Cecil B. De Mille and the Salmon P. Chase Collections. Against any misfortune arising from chance impulsiveness they packed vials of oral contraceptives and 7,500,000 units of penicillin. "Avoid the very young if you can, sir," Steinitt said. "Clap and herpes infections are endemic among them."

They checked off: fishing gloves, handball gloves, golfing gloves, ski and archery gloves, and Bar-B-Q gloves. It might be a little late for skiing in Australia, but Bitsy might like to try Perisher Valley or Crackenback.

For thirty-two hours, Steinitt had kept the Captain's deep-blue homburg lowered into a bucket of iced water at the end of an encircling nylon rope to insure that the brim roll of the hat would be properly high when it was dried under the forced air jets that Bitsy had had built into the Captain's hat cupboard. The night before, Steinitt had ironed £1000 worth of equivalent currencies and had stacked them on an electric jigger to make neat blocks of paper money that were then bound into flat pads from which the bills could be easily torn off as needed, reducing unsightly clothing bulges.

Yvonne laid her head across the Captain's thighs on the broad bed. He had been reading aloud to her. When he finished a chapter, he put the book aside with reluctance, and hid the glasses.

"Tomorrow we fly away together," said Yvonne. "Then after the wonderful days we will have, you will be with your wonderful wife and she will bring you home to me."

"Unexpected things happen."

"No."

"It is always best when I stay away from the world. That business about your father's death and Gash Schute's. Who could have foreseen such things?"

"I know it seems more pleasant," she said dreamily, "to live away from the world with one's cook, one's lover, one's war games, and one's wonderful wife—but it isn't that way with you. You gamble wherever you are. That is what changes everything."

"Not this time."

"Oh, well."

"There will be neither time nor opportunity to gamble. We will be away from everything on the high seas where I have always been safe."

"Then why are you afraid you will be changed and stained?"

"Because I so much don't want to be. I want to be the way we are, without change. There has been enough change. When change comes it always stays as stain upon me."

"Because you gamble, your wonderful wife's family thinks you are a weak man. But I know you are not weak. You are a man, Colin. A good man. That is enough for me. That is even enough for your wonderful wife."

On the morning of departure for Tokyo, the Captain and Steinitt were ready for the tense moment of the neckties, which took utter attention. The Captain stood in socks, shorts, undervest, and shirt before a full-length mirror. Steinitt stood beside him with a dozen identically patterned ties draped over his left arm. He handed the first of these to the Captain, who hung it around his neck and then, in a series of rapid, seemingly careless moves, tied a four-in-hand knot.

"Missed, sir," Steinitt observed.

The Captain grunted, discarded the tie into a bin to be pressed and started again. He made a flawless knot with the fourth tie. Had he tried to retie the failures they either would have been rumpled or would have given the impression that he was a man who took a great deal of trouble about tying his ties. The object was effortless perfection ineffably arrived at. One did not face one's friends in a peaked cravat.

Steinitt held the Captain's trousers.

The Captain then slipped into a waistcoat and an essentials-loaded jacket. "Splendid, sir," Steinitt said. "We are ready for breakfast with Madam."

Bitsy was achingly beautiful in a filmy green peignoir which floated around her like the lacunae of a Portuguese man of war. They confirmed the reunion date: Thursday, September 1, when Bitsy would be waiting for him on the main pier at the Royal Yacht Club in Sydney. The Captain high on the flying bridge of the *Perfection* would come steaming through the Heads to swoop her up and take her off on a romantic sweep from Bali, where the family had a dry cell battery factory, across the South China Sea to Manila where they operated the largest foundation garment manufacturing and export business in southeast Asia *("With Us Your Cups Are Always Running Over")*, then north to Japan where the family operated extensively in guitar picks, barber chairs, ecclesiastical garments, and canned fish. Daddy expected to be "somewhere near Khabarovsky Kray" with Dr. Kissinger for secret meetings with the Dalai Lama and the Prime Minister of Ireland in September and it would be necessary for Bitsy to cut away from their main thrust for five days or so to report to Daddy on the various factory quotas' progress along the way.

"Give my best to Henry if that happens," the Captain said.

After that they would just laze and loaf across the blue Pacific, visiting the immense deep-sea mining barge the family had in operation. Bitsy apologized in advance. "You'll have to remain aboard the yacht when I make the barge inspection, darling," she explained. "You don't have the kind of security equipment for this one. But we'll be off to Panama in no time for some grand duty-free shopping and then I'll have to sneak off alone for an on-the-spot inspection of the shrimp farms Daddy had me buy off Balboa."

"I suppose I am cleared for the duty-free shopping," the Captain said jokingly.

"Of course you are, sweetheart! What a trip! Not only will I be able to improve operations wherever we stop and jack up the quotas, but this whole second honeymoon will offset income from the charter as a tax deduction. Isn't that marvie?"

"Utterly romantic," the Captain said. "I shall bring my *Moonlight In Kahlua* record."

"I have a *wonderful* idea," Bitsy exclaimed. "Let's ship the balloon to Australia ahead of us."

"Yes. Oh, yes! The outback must be splendid ballooning country."

"Where is the balloon?"

"Venice, I think. We raced it over the Alps from Rapperswill —then I think your people stored it."

"I'll check the office," Bitsy said. "Where should they ship it?"

"Alice Springs. Dead center in Australia."

"I'll ask Uëli Münger to go out with it," Bitsy said making a note. Münger was Bitsy's chief ski instructor, European hotel booker, and ballooning professional. He also coached her in cooking and the high jump.

"Excellent! Ask him to have the balloon there by September first; then we can decide what we want to do. And if you prefer to ski at Crackenback instead, we will have Uëli in any case."

At 9:20, shortly before the time to leave for the airport, the contracts for the sale and transfer of the *Perfection* arrived at Farm Street from the Clogg office. Their signatures were witnessed by a young woman solicitor, Lady Jane Montant, who had witnessed the transfer of the five million pounds from Colin to Bitsy the day before. The impact of the husband and wife gifts of five million pounds and four million dollars happened so closely that it left the young lawyer badly dazed. She tried to strike the Captain with her heavy brief case but Winikus, the West Cork butler, easily overcame her. She was sedated with stout, then driven back to her firm's chambers with no one the wiser.

All at once Bitsy asked if he would go down to the computer rooms with her. They dropped six floors from street level in the locked lift. Six people were working in blue smocks in the area. Their security clearance, Bitsy said, was higher than that of the Director of the FBI. Appalled, the Captain realized that he must have been assigned the same astral clearance to be allowed into the chamber, yet she had just said he did not have enough clearance to board the family's deep-sea mining barge or to enter their Panama shrimp farm. He decided he never wanted to know what they were doing on the barge or at the farm.

It was a spacious, well-lighted area enclosing a large on-line computer installation. They stood before a scheduling, communications, retrieval computer which was linked with the computers in the base transportation of members of the family, to the family's three geosynchronous satellites, to Air Force One, to the Office of the Director of Central Intelligence, to Dr. Kissinger's huge blue-and-white Boeing, to the President's private office tape machines, and to *Gourmet* magazine (for Juan Francohogar). Two U.S. Marines, armed with carbines, in dress uniforms, guarded the machines.

"Daddy's message is intact on that table just as it came in two hours ago," Bitsy said simply. "He wanted you to know, from the heart, how happy he is that you are his son-in-law. Read it, darling."

The Captain stepped forward and took up the output sheet. It said: AFFIRMATIVE TO SPECIAL LINKAGE, DADDY.

"What does it mean?" Colin asked anxiously.

"The box, please, Gunnie," she said to the Marine Corps sergeant, who opened a wall safe smartly and produced a walnut box, ten inches long, six inches wide, and five inches deep.

It was highly polished. The gunnery sergeant extended the box to Bitsy. She took it and placed it on the message table. The heavy carpeting, the depth below the city, the immobility of the Marine produced an awesome silence. Bitsy nodded gently to the sergeant. He did an abrupt about-face and strode to another part of the great room.

"I have a little going-away present for you," Bitsy said softly. "It's so we can never again be really far apart. It took all of the power of Daddy, and Uncle Jim, Uncle Pete, Cousin Larry, Cousin Harry, and Cousin Gary to arrange it."

"Arrange what, dearest?"

"You know about Daddy's geosynchronous satellites which are gravity-balanced at twenty-two thousand, three hundred miles in space, moving with the Earth at six miles a second?"

"Well, in a vague way—"

"They can receive messages from any point on earth and transmit them back to earth again."

"Oh, yes."

"Well, The Company—you know—has worked out a system whereby very special indivi*d*ual field telephones can talk to other special satellite telephones, anywhere in the world."

"I say!"

"Ooh, yes."

"How ingenious."

"The space program has meant *so* much to our security and intelligence operations. I mean it *cost* eighty billion. And they had to fake the people out with all that balls about moon rocks and is there life on Mars and all that crap, but let me tell you, it really has paid off for The Company."

"But—and really, I mean just roughly—how does it work? The telephone, that is."

"Oh, it has the usual computerized circuit gates like everything else powered by the sun. Pick up the phone—go ahead." She reached over and opened the walnut box to reveal two matched instruments in ivory and gold. "I know you'll want to thank Daddy. Well, Daddy is in Lesotho right now, I think.

Anyway he's somewhere in Africa and Africa is handled by the Satellite Two exchange. So—we pick up our phone and we dial the cipher O-O-TWO, which is Africa. Then Daddy's number which is ONE-O-O, then the Satellite which serves Africa which is TWO-TWO-TWO, then we code in your telephone which is SEVEN-SEVEN-ONE. You see. It's just as simple as can be. Hello, Daddy? Yes. Just a minute, Colin wants to speak to you." She handed the phone to the Captain.

"Hello—uh—sir? Yes. Oh, my word, yes! Why, it's just as though you were in the next room. I must thank you for this overwhelming honor. The weather here? Uh—overcast a bit today, I'm afraid. Rather dull. Rain this morning. Oh, is it? That hot there? Still, I suppose that can be very pleasant. Give my best to Dr. Kissinger, won't you, sir? Yes. She's just fine. By all means. Thank you." He hung up.

"Terribly warm in Africa," he told Bitsy.

"Isn't that the neatest telephone," Bitsy said, leading him back to the lift, the walnut case tucked under his arm. They entered the lift and pressed for the second upper floor above street level. "The President has one, of course. The Director has one. The Chairman of the Joint Chiefs has one—and Dr. Kissinger, and that's all except Daddy and Daddy had his copied and now each member of the family has one. You can't imagine what it saves in phone bills. Oh, darling! No matter where you are—in Japan or on the high seas—we'll be able to talk to each other in seconds."

"I—I hope I can learn all those dialing codes," he said weakly.

"Of course you can! They're all pasted right inside the lid. But try not to call the President. It scares him. He gets it mixed up with the Hot Line."

As they came out of the lift into the living room, Winikus, the West Cork butler, was waiting for them. "The president of the Union Bank of Switzerland is calling, Moddom," he said. "The call is waiting in the secure booth."

"Oh. I forgot!" Bitsy exclaimed, dashing away. "Sumatra!"

"Give Frank my best!" Colin called out after her, reflexively.

The Captain hastened off with the walnut case to Francoho-gar's office off the kitchens. "I haven't much time, Juan," he said. He opened the walnut case and handed the cook one of the two matched telephone sets. "Please ask your brother to make me an exact copy of this. When you have it please bring it and the original to me in Japan. Tell them never, never to dial any number below number seven. That is vital. Thank you." He rushed out of the room, back to the lift, and up to the living room.

"I say, Bitsy," the Captain said as she returned ten minutes later. "What about this gambling fellow of Daddy's? Am I not supposed to be spending my waking hours with him?"

"I'm awfully vague about the specifics of that, dear," she answered, "but if Daddy promises anything we can be sure that it is going to happen."

Steinitt was seated demurely behind the wheel of the choco-late-colored 1935 Rolls-Royce sports sedan that the Captain had had built at a hidden engineering works deep inside Dor-set. He had bought the chassis of a sturdy Silver Cloud of the early 1960s, which had fortunately been used only by a suicide club and had had only thirteen miles on it, then had placed upon it the body of the most memorably beautiful automobile, the unutterably clean-lined, long, fleet 1935 sports sedan by Barker, creating a Rolls-Royce unique in the world. True, the completed car had cost £2263.12 more than a Camargue, count-ing Value Added Tax, but it was a motor car of enduring beauty and effectiveness, so superb that Daddy had bought the tiny Church Green Engineering, in Semley, which had created it.

Bitsy gloated as she kissed her husband good-bye, thinking of the eighteen cheerless weeks ahead for his little French mistress. She wasn't jealous; jealousy required a belief in rejec-tion, something Bitsy had never experienced. She and Daddy,

Uncle Jim, Uncle Pete, Cousins Harry, Larry, and Gary, all felt that a man of Colin's ineffable style should have a French mistress. It was better than having him sit in some drafty club in St. James's all day. And she would not like to think that he might visit one of those unsanitary massage parlors while she had to be away on business. Nonetheless, she could not *help* grinning to herself as she thought of the plans the little mistress must have had for a big holiday in Tokyo with another woman's husband.

Daddy wasn't Executive Suite at the CIA for nothing. Modern medical science, an engineer's usage of air-conditioning ducts plus certain viruses introduced thereby into the nasal passages of a young woman while she slept—when organized as only Daddy and The Outfit could organize—were capable of working miracles of interference with the travel plans of little French mistresses.

"Good-bye, darling," Bitsy cooed. "Don't be too lonely. Remember we will both be heinously busy—time will speed by like arrows." She did not mention gambling. Her dignity and her health would not allow her ever to speak directly of gambling to him.

He got into the chocolate-colored Rolls, which rolled off fueled with petrol from U.S. government agencies that were beholden to Uncle Jim at the White House, glided down Chesterfield Hill, across Hill Street to Charles Street where it stopped in front of Yvonne's house.

"Sound the horn, please, Steinitt," the Captain asked. The klaxon blew. There was no response from within the house. "It is damned difficult traveling with women," the Captain snarled, slamming out of the car. He romped up the few steps to the main door and sounded the bell with vigor. The door was opened almost immediately by an unknown man, short but unbearably distinguished, affecting white hair and looking somber.

"Captain Huntington?" he asked.

"Yes. Where is Miss Bonnette, please?"

"I am Lord Weiler."

The Captain started with alarm. "Harley Street? *That* Lord Weiler?"

"Yes."

"Are you here for Miss Bonnette?"

"Yes."

"Well, dammit, Weiler! What the devil is happening here?" He moved to go around the man, but the physician barred his way. "That would not be wise," he said. "I very much regret to inform you that Miss Bonnette has contracted mumps."

"*MUMPS?*" Involuntarily, the Captain's hand went to his crotch. "But we were to leave for Tokyo this morning—now."

"Out of the question, I'm afraid. It is a severe seizure. Maître Francohogar, from whom I take the occasional cooking lesson, telephoned me three hours ago—at seven this morning. The glands are severely swollen on both sides. It is, perhaps, the most classical case of mumps I have observed in thirty-two years of medical practice."

"I must see her."

"Have you ever had mumps?"

"No."

"You are male. Mumps could have a disturbing effect on your—on the essence of your maleness."

"Oh, *God*! Then I must speak to her on the house phone."

"She cannot speak. She suffers. She wrote this note with the greatest difficulty before I dosed her. She is sleeping." Lord Weiler handed the Captain a blue envelope piped with scarlet, with the aplomb which comes of having been a titled physician to royalty since the Regency. His great-great-great-grandfather, in a long line of royal physicians, had attended Princess Caroline, the Regent's consort, during her only official accouchement.

The Captain tore open the envelope. He read: "BON VOYAGE, DEAREST, WRITE TO ME. I WILL TELEPHONE WHEN I AM ABLE. FOREVER YOURS, YVONNE."

"How very brave!"

"Oh, yes."

"When will she be able to speak?"

"At least three weeks."

"What a terrible disappointment for her."

"Oh, yes."

"Will she be able to play her saxophone?"

"No."

"Is there nothing I can do?"

"Nothing."

The Captain thanked Lord Weiler, descended the steps, and entered the car. "Please tell her I am desolated," he said from the open window of the super-Rolls. "Get moving, man!" he barked to Steinitt.

As the car moved away from the house, he took up the microphone of the fitted Dictaphone. "My darling Yvonne colon," he said into it, "I cannot believe that you will not be at my side five miles above the Earth as I leave pitiable space between us at such headlong speed. To have to leave you farther, then farther still behind me while you are in pain is more than life has the right to deal me. I shall remain alive by pretending that you are in my arms. Oh, *Gaaad*! How I miss you and we have not yet reached even Knightsbridge. Eternally, Woofie." He then dictated instructions for Francohogar to deliver the duplicate telephone to Miss Bonnette before he sailed for Japan on the *Perfection*.

7

As Captain Huntington came down the ramp at Haneda airport, he was aware that it had been eleven years since he had been in the world's most crowded city. He had always thought that Tokyo could be a wonderfully pleasing place to those with a hankering for Purgatory. Mainly, it was hideous; the most chaotic city on the planet.

In about A.D. 1600 the Shogun Tokugawa had designed the city in such a complicated manner as to insure that strangers could immediately be noticed, wandering about, confused and lost. Natives were confused by it, in most parts of it. Tokyo was still without street names and, to the greatest extent, without building numbers. To find a building one had to know the ward, the precinct, then block area, then to find the local policeman. A house was numbered depending upon when it was built, with no relation whatever to its location. Often three or more houses on the same block were known by the same number, but those numbers were seldom marked on the houses. Night and day, buildings were being ripped down to erect something taller; roads were constantly being sunk or elevated; subways were being dug across historically vindictive earthquake faults; expressways were flung across rooftops.

There were more than 15.2 million people in the city; 38,000 taxis; nearly 100 newspapers. It was the largest collection of organized confusion in any single place in the history of Earth; a terrible distinction compounded by all the automobiles, carts, motorbikes, trams, and prams. In the downtown Ginza area, Tokyo land prices were the highest in the world. Fujikawa & Company owned a skyscraper there. Daddy owned three. Bitsy was proud that Daddy had led the family's capital into Japan, twenty minutes behind General MacArthur, all that long time ago. Daddy liberated the best of the investments after the war, when the prices were right.

Commander Fujikawa awaited Captain Huntington's descent from the plane, standing on the tarmac slightly in advance of a group of seven other Japanese. One man held an open umbrella over him to keep off the steady rain. The Commander moved smilingly forward. The two former naval persons reunited with much mutual happiness. He moved the Captain toward the group, in position to pass in review along the smiling line.

Where Western companies have a basic structure of directors, managers, foremen, and workers, Japanese companies have about fourteen levels of operation. Many positions, since their parallels do not exist outside Japan, cannot be translated.

"This is our Executive Floor *bucho*, Mr. Sachi," the Commander said. The two men shook hands and exchanged two-sided business cards.

"Here is our Electronics *kacho* in geology, Mr. Marayama. Mr. Okinora, the *kansayuku* of our Catering Department, who will stock your beautiful yacht."

The Captain very nearly staggered backward a step as he came to the end of the line and saw Miss Expediter. She was the most beautiful woman he had ever seen. "This is Miss Expediter," Commander Fujikawa said with a special pride. "She is also Chief Geologist for your expedition to Australia." The Captain felt an erection forming but he willed it to subside by visionary flashes of the gardens at Kew; by memories of Arctic beech trees (*Notofagus*) and a sloping bank of *Hypernicum* at Rossenarra. "Perhaps you brought photographs of the *Perfection*?" the Commander was saying. "If not, no matter."

"Indeed, yes." Still staring at Miss Expediter the Captain handed over a manila envelope. She hurried off with it.

The group removed to the air terminal building escalator, which descended to the monorail station below. In fourteen minutes they were at the Hamamatsucho depot in central Tokyo where Miss Expeditor was waiting with an extraordinarily elongated version of a Rolls-Royce Silver Ghost. "What is it?" the Captain asked with awe.

The Commander was greatly pleased. "Our family motor cars are the longest and most elegant in the world. We stretch them ourselves at a special factory in the south. This limousine is thirty-one percent longer than any other Rolls ever made. The trade-in value is so enormous that the cars themselves cost us virtually nothing." The Captain made a mental note to tell Daddy and Church Green Engineering in Semley, Dorset.

As they drove to the hotel, the traffic pattern moved to the left, the special feat of Sir Rutherford Alcock, Queen Victoria's Minister Plenipotentiary to the Court of the Tycoon in 1859.

"How weary you must be from that awful flight."

"I am wilted."

"Dr. Wei-Lah, our Chinese medical specialist, is waiting at your hotel. He will examine you and, no contraindications being present, will arrange to put you into a dreamless sleep for twenty-four hours. Then I will come for you at seven tomorrow night when we will dine together." Commander Fujikawa's English speech was so magnificently achieved as to make Prince Philip's seem like that of a Cockney street arab.

"I say, Fujikawa, I missed the name and title of that last chap in line because of the dramatic beauty of Miss Expediter."

"Ah, so? That was Mr. Ikeda."

"What does he do?"

"He is our *torishimariyaka* of all security. He is *ichiban;* utterly tops in his work."

"Rather a sinister-looking chap, if I may say so."

"Oh yes, Mr. Ikeda is a *very* sinister man," Commander Fujikawa said.

The Captain was settled into an apartment at the Hotel Okura which looked out over the Kuminigaseki: government ministries, the financial center, embassies, the Diet, and the Imperial Palace itself. The apartment had an immense living room, a dining room, two bedrooms, and three bathrooms (each equipped with a brand-name toilet paper called WELL DONE), an arboreum, and many Hiroshige prints. From his bed the Captain would be able to see the hazy loveliness of Fujiyama through the dense smog and from a distance too far away to see the banana skins, cigarette butts, and other litter that scarred its slopes.

Dr. Wei-Lah, an elderly Chinese with a wispy white goatee, examined the Captain with a stethoscope, then triangulated each of the Captain's elbows with three gold acupuncture needles. "What is he doing?" the Captain yawned.

"He is sedating you. He has decided against chemicals. You will sleep until five o'clock tomorrow afternoon."

The doctor's eyebrows shot up. Quickly, he reached out and plucked one needle out of the left elbow, muttering.

"He apologizes. By mistake he dosed you to sleep until nine-twenty tomorrow night. Do you wish Miss Expediter to bathe you before you sleep?"

But the Captain was already sleeping. The two men caught him as he dropped and carried his snoring figure off to the huge bed.

8

The day before the Captain had left London, Bitsy had darted across the Mount Street Gardens and Grosvenor Square to see the Japanese Chargé d'Affaires to check protocol. She learned about the Japanese mania for exchanging presents and the rituals for doing this properly.

First there was the color of the string; it had to be red and white—black and white string was used only for condolences. Another vital part of it all was that, whatever the gift, it must be nonchalantly accepted, put immediately to one side, and opened later, privately. Her husband had to be ready to have his gift received with just such total indifference and the further custom was that the giver must apologize profusely for the poverty of the present—to such an extreme that the recipient would not think of embarrassing the giver by opening the gift in his presence.

When Commander Fujikawa arrived at the Captain's set at the Okura the next evening, his *temiyage* wrapped in a *furoshiki* was offered to the Captain with a deep bow and a wry smile. Ritually, the Captain cast the *temiyage* from him as if it carried a typhoid infection. He then rushed to a cupboard, returned with an oddly shaped package, and extended it to the Commander, bowing and bobbing, mumbling that he was humiliated by the gift's worthlessness.

The Commander opened it instantly. "What the deuce is it?" he asked. He ripped away sheets of silvered paper. "I can tell from the shape and the weight that it must be something terribly important." He stared down at something green from which protruded an aluminum socket. "What an ugly thing! What is it?"

"Looks like a collapsible golf putter with a jade head. If it is, you're in luck. Perfect weight and balance. Takes strokes off your game."

"How supah! Untelescope the handle, please." He tested the golf stick. "Oh, I say! We must get one of these for my father."

Dinner was served by Miss Expediter wearing a pale-green kimono with a wide pink sash.

"These are salted trouts' guts," the Commander said. "How do you like them?"

"Delicious."

"I know you are a renowned European gourmet and—although it is a national policy to deprecate everything we offer to a guest, I must say I am simply wild about salted trouts' guts. You can't get them outside Japan, you know."

"Really?"

Miss Expediter refilled their tiny cups with turtle-blood-and-sake cocktails.

"Here—please," the Commander said. "You must try this sliced pig's ovary with mushroom. And a little of the vinegared sparrows of Wakayama."

"Ah! Oh! These ovaries are fan*tas*tic."

"Wait till you taste this. Crimpled snake meat with pickled cherry blossoms." They ate with chopsticks. Like the Greeks, the Japanese were indifferent about serving food hot. What was not lukewarm, was quite cold. Thick, whipped, foamy tea was poured quickly between courses to clear their palates for the next new taste. Most decidedly, including the fish-eye soup, the food was all suggestive, tranquil, beautiful, and understated, positioned on exquisite plates with a perfection that balanced colors, shapes, and proportions.

As they finished eating the sweet and sour sexual organs of an ox and moved on to the great raw fish dishes, the Commander asked the Captain to give him an example of what he considered to be the most satisfying dish in all French cuisine.

The Captain deliberated with himself. He spoke carefully. "I will quote to you from the culinary novel of Marcel Rouff which is called *La view et la passion de Dodin-Bouffant, gourmet.*"

"To be able to quote from a novel. How accomplished!"

The Captain cleared his throat. Miss Expediter stood off to one side, listening carefully. The Commander concentrated tightly. "This is rather important to me," he said. "My father was once the most famous eater in all Japan."

"The boiled beef," the Captain began, "itself rubbed lightly with saltpeter and sprinkled with salt, was cut in slices and its flesh was so delicate that one's mouth felt it in advance, and guessed it to be deliciously fragmentable and tender. The aroma that emanated from it came not only from beef juices steaming like incense, but from several, not many, cubes of lard, transparent and immaculate, with which it was pierced. The slices, which were fairly thick and whose texture one could anticipate, rested gently against a cushion of a large circle of sausage whose meat, freshly chopped, was pork mixed with the most delicate veal, seasoned with herbs, chopped chervil and thyme. But these delicacies, cooked in the same bouillon as the beef, were themselves supported by generous cuts of the white meat—breast and wing—of a fat capon simmered in its own juices with a veal knuckle, and rubbed with mint and wild thyme." The Captain's voice trembled as if with song.

"And to prop up this magnificent superimposition, the rich and robust buttress of a comfortable layer of fresh goose liver —cooked simply in Chambertin—had audaciously been slipped behind the white meat of the fowl which had been fed only on bread soaked in milk." The Captain sighed heavily. His eyes had glazed slightly.

"If you will permit me to say so," the Commander stated simply, "I think any honest Japanese would tell you that that sort of food is not only barbaric, but utterly disgusting."

To ease the tension as the Captain glared across the table, Miss Expediter said quickly, "Has Captain Huntington opened his *temiyage*?"

"Oh!" Commander Fujikawa yelped, totally diverted. "You must see this!" He ran out of the dining room to bring back his present. As the Captain unwrapped it, he provided a running commentary. "It is our war games board, you see, done by one of our electronics companies. It is pocket-sized, and the board has a memory. After you complete your positioning of the battle lines at the end of the day, you strike the M key, then punch out the full date. The system will hold 365 days of naval maneuvers and you can see the position of the entire fleets on the miniature viewing board."

"It is mag*nif*icent!"

"There are no post boxes on the high seas where you are going, but we'll be able to keep up the play, nonetheless."

They moved into the living room, which overlooked night-time Tokyo, and Commander Fujikawa got down to business. "Last year we imported two thousand million barrels of oil into this country," he said. "Each year it becomes more difficult. We have a larger oil requirement than the United Kingdom and West Germany. We will catch up with the United States in 1980. Coal cannot begin to meet the requirement, although we have now processed liquid coal. Dry weather reduces hydroelectric production. Nuclear power is hopeless. But the bill for oil, which was four and a half billion dollars in 1972, was sixteen billion in seventy-four, then twenty-eight billion in seventy-six. It is essential that Japan produce and own the oil we use. Our capital made the Khafji oil field possible. We operate in the Kuwait neutral zone and with the Indonesian State Oil Corporation in Sumatra. We have acquired leases to explore in Alaska, Sabah, New Guinea, Canada, Kalimantan, and Qatar. By 1985 we should be exploring or producing in about forty-five countries of the world.

"Recently, my father has become enormously excited—*I* say unnecessarily so—by the chance of bringing in important crude oil from the Great Barrier Reef of Australia."

"One of the most beautiful places in the world," the Captain murmured.

"Exactly! And for that very reason I have respectfully opposed my father's plan in this. It is something we both feel strongly about and he insists upon drilling on the reef. I am opposed because—although we have all the legal options to explore there—the world is filled with people who still think a pretty view is more important than progress."

"Pretty views don't come into it, dear fellow. The reef represents one of the most vital ecological chains in the world and is a direct link to the survival of all of us, who are made of carbons, and who need the oxygen which the life forms and chains on the reef produce."

"Nonetheless, my father wants the oil for Japan; therefore we need you."

"But—why me?"

"Because you are aristocratically English, Royal Navy, a model pommy gentleman, a fine tennis player, a yachtsman, a golfer, a skier—all the things Australians most admire."

The Captain winced within himself. He was the son of a dishonest farmer who had turned full-time procurer. He had not played tennis in six years. His famous yacht belonged to Daddy. He had been cashiered from the Royal Navy. His wife and her family had been willing to concede that he had criminal tendencies.

"Your meanings are still somewhat obscure to me," he said.

"You see, a main point is that you are not Japanese. We have a peculiar relationship with the Australians. They admire us because we bring them so much money. They are lazy people. But they fear us because we are Asiatics and they think they are not. Do you know what a drilling ship is?"

"No."

"They are almost as rare as one-legged ballerinas because they are so frightfully expensive. We have just built one in our own shipyards at a cost equivalent to sixty million dollars. It can drill for oil in a sea bottom six thousand feet below the surface, then to twenty thousand feet below the seabed. Its drilling sites are located by satellite twenty-two thousand, three hundred miles out in space."

"But how does the *Perfection* come into this?"

The Commander grinned. "My father's plan is to mothball the *Perfection* as soon as it arrives, for the duration of the charter. Our drilling ship, which no one knows we have, will be transformed to look *exactly* like the *Perfection*. The ship will masquerade as a luxury yacht which takes you to a grand holiday on the Great Barrier Reef. While you snorkel and water ski, the ship will be testing and drilling to confirm where the largest oil fields exist on the reef."

"I see. Very cunning."

"When the oil is confirmed, you will take Australian cash to Brisbane, accompanied by our Australian lawyers, and secure the actual operating leases. Where is the *Perfection* now?"

"Heading down the African coast and if my wife's family knew that they would probably want to engage her in a little slave running."

"How far out from the Inland Sea would you say she is?"

"About eighteen days."

"I say—you were joking about your wife's family running slaves, weren't you?"

"I *think* so."

"I know a Bolivian who did very well out of running slaves last year. It could be the coming thing."

The Captain saw the Commander to the lift. When he returned, Miss Expediter was sitting at a window in the main room staring out over the city and he was nearly transfixed by her beauty.

"Tell me about yourself," he asked.

She faced him serenely. "I was born a geisha. I was *shikoni* when I was six years old. I became *maiko,* an apprentice geisha, when I was fourteen. Baron Fujikawa found me. He bought my freedom and he sent me to the Colorado School of Mines."

"But—how old are you now? Nineteen?"

"I am twenty-nine years old."

He filled two glasses with wine and gave one to her. He lifted his glass. "To your beauty," he said.

She clinked her glass into his. "To your courage."

"Courage?"

"If beauty is the woman, courage is the man."

"What is your name?"

"I am Kimiko. I am called Kimiko Shunga."

It was an astounding night. He thanked Providence for his intensive training with Bitsy and Yvonne. More than once, by some physical illusion, Kimiko spun him into the air like a tumbling Indian club to land, face down, directly *en point,* as they achieved boxes within boxes, as she appeared, not infrequently, to be standing sideways on a part of him, like a circus performer on the center pole of the center ring. It crashed into his mind that this girl had to have taken degrees beyond a doctorate at the Geisha Academy, studying over, under, and all around a legendary Oriental contortionist. Never had he been used so gloriously. For most of an entire hour, while she suspended him in mid-ejaculation, he considered taking out Japanese citizenship or, perhaps, having all his bones removed as Kimiko obviously had done. When he fainted with exhaustion, she brought him around with draughts of what she called mushroom tea which he secretly vowed never to do without for the rest of his life. After drinking it, huge appetites would return and they would go at it again. And again. And again. At last something threw an enormous black softness over him. He knew nothing until he felt a soft prodding at his shoulder. He opened his eyes. Sunshine filled the room. Mount Fuji was swanning it across the horizon. Kimiko was dressed. "Captain

Pappadakis is on the line," she said, handing him the telephone.

"Hullo? Pappadakis?" he said dazedly into the telephone. "Am I calling you? Ah! Yes. Where are you?" Carefully he explained the plan of Fujikawa & Company to publicize the yacht as it moved from fueling port to fueling port to Japan. He explained that at each port a Fujikawa PR man would come aboard and tell him what to say to the press about the glorious holiday the yacht was bound for on the Great Barrier Reef. As soon as he hung up, he persuaded Kimiko to get out of all that clothing and get back into bed. The mushroom tea held him together like a bonding agent. She descended upon him like coal roaring down a chute.

Later, as he gulped mushroom tea, Daddy's satellite phone began to buzz. There was a frantic search requiring that they get themselves unknotted from each other first. Kimiko found the walnut box in the closet and rushed it to him as it buzzed relentlessly. He opened the box and took up the phone. "Hello?" he said weakly.

"Colin? Are you all right?"

"Fine. The old jet lag."

"Oh, how awful. The checks for the charter arrived. It seems so odd because Daddy has an interest in Fujikawa and Company so, in a sense, he is paying for the use of his own yacht."

"Oh, my God."

"I had a sweet note from Glandore. He has added a huge, new bingo parlor to the bowling alleys and the et cetera and has invited us to attend the opening. What shall I say?"

"Say? WHAT SHALL YOU SAY?" he roared into the telephone so savagely that Kimiko, recoiling, fell off the bed and Bitsy dropped the phone in London. The Captain leaped out of bed in an insane rage and began to jump up and down like a maddened baboon. "What shall you tell him?" he squeaked shrilly. "You will not so much as reply to the bounder, that is what you shall tell him. Is that clear, Bitsy?"

"Yes, dear," Bitsy said contritely, fully intending to reply to

Lord Glandore because she adored to correspond with peers and she most certainly was not going to offend a peer of the realm who was her brother-in-law. She had also made some pleasant small money when she had invested in Glandore's chicken-sexing company. She intended to be at the gala opening of the bingo parlor which she could make easily when she and Harry went to Provo to set up the grenades factory. She was determined to meet her brother-in-law.

The Captain slammed the phone down and strode naked into the bathroom and took a cold shower. When he emerged Kimiko flopped him upon the massage table and kneaded him deeply, causing him to need her deeply. As she leaned over him he chewed thoughtfully on a nipple. This sent her into a new massage series. Handed down by the senior mistresses of the most powerful founders of the Japanese establishment, beginning with the experiments made by those gallant women upon the male body as far back as A.D. 917, the series had been improved indescribably, century by century.

Daddy's satellite telephone rang again. The Captain picked up, stone nude. It was a heavily accented German voice. "This is Dr. Kissinger," the voice said. "Who is this?"

"I am afraid you have a wrong number," the Captain said and hung up. Almost at once, the phone buzzed again. Pathetically weakened by so much sex and rage, looking perhaps as his father had looked as he marched in the funeral procession of Edward VII, stricken as was no one else that day, the Captain spoke hollowly into the special telephone again.

"Hullo?"

"Captain Huntington?" a high-pitched voice chirped at him, higher in tone than an Abercrombie & Fitch dog whistle. "This is Sister Joyce, Miss Yvonne Bonnette's nurse in London. Not to fret! We are fine, just fine. But we cannot speak. However, we can write little notes and I am going to read these notes to you. Ready?"

He croaked affirmatively.

"Note Number One: I love you. Miss Bonnette is making

that statement, not I. We have never met."

"Thank Miss Bonnette for me, please. Convey my identical sentiments to her."

"Will do. Am writing that down. Second note: How is Tokyo?"

"Fine."

"Got it. Next note: Have you been laid yet?"

"What?"

"Miss Bonnette wished me to ask you—in the vernacular—if you had had sexual intercourse in Tokyo yet, Captain Huntington."

"Most certainly not!"

"Very good reading there. Will convey tone as well as text. Now, a simple request from a sick girl: Please telephone Miss Bonnette's twin sister when you reach Australia but do not—repeat not—have sex with her due to probable infection. Do you have any counter-messages for Miss Bonnette? Nothing too personal, please. I am British."

"Please tell Miss Bonnette that I am about to leave for the Inland Sea and that I will write her a long letter forthwith. When will she be able to speak?"

"It will be at least three weeks, sir. It is a terrible case of mumps."

"Thank you, Sister Joyce," he hung up.

"Was that your sister?" Kimiko asked.

"Hardly."

She helped him to totter into the dressing room where she sat him in a barber's chair and shaved him and combed his hair. She dressed him. She took him down to a waiting Cobra two-seater and drove him to the Fujikawa skyscraper in the Ksumigaseki district. On the forty-fourth floor, she removed his shoes, put slippers on him, and they waited together in a room whose only furniture was two Western chairs. "You will be received by Baron Fujikawa," she said. "It is an extraordinary honor."

In seventy-nine seconds the double doors at the far side of

the room opened, revealing Commander Fujikawa in a wine-colored kimono and trousers. He bowed deeply to the Captain. The Captain returned the bow. Fujikawa beckoned him to follow. They walked across a rose-colored room having blue pottery and low tables. Kimiko remained in the waiting room. They continued forward through three more exquisite, sparsely furnished rooms. The Commander opened a set of high, bronze double doors into an enormous room where a very, very old, grim, and tiny man in a scarlet kimono was seated on a mat in front of a low table, staring fiercely at the Captain. The old eyes held him in silence for forty-five seconds, then the old man spoke like a pistol shot.

"Get the oil!" he shrilled.

9

That afternoon they flew to Shiumuzu, the Fujikawa industrial complex on the shores of the Inland Sea. There were four passengers aboard the Fujikawa-built Sikorsky S–62A helicopter: the Commander, the Captain, Kimiko, and Mr. Ikeda, the security chief. The cabin of the flagship, normally for ten passengers, had been redesigned to seat five. They were on the ground at Shiumuzu one hour and four minutes later, after overflying Kyoto, Osaka, and Kobe.

As the aircraft approached the Fujikawa industrial city, the Captain looked down upon the complex that had resulted from Japan's "New Comprehensive National Development Plan" which, beginning in 1969, called for one-sixth of the country's agricultural land to be converted to industrial use by 1985. Even in 1969 Japan had been dangerously short of farm land and heavily dependent on increasingly expensive agricultural imports. As new Fujikawa industries were installed on the newly recruited farm lands, the demands for further imports of raw materials rose while the factories contributed a high level of pollution to the surrounding area, which was, not so slowly, becoming the entire country; a frantic explosion of an orchestrated effort to manufacture gadgets.

Upriver, in an enclosed and guarded pier, they inspected the oil-drilling ship *Gyo*. The pier was on the perimeter of a combined industrial conglomerate that included shipyards, a steel works, aerospace manufacturing, heavy machinery fabrication, a brewery, a shoe factory, and a building materials factory. The landscape was dotted with Fujikawa high-rise buildings which housed insurance companies, central banks, and the sales executive of Fujikawa electronics, automobile, pharmaceutical, and piano companies. Fujikawa distilleries, textile plants, and oil refineries worked without stop. The Fujikawa industries occupied part of a 64-square-mile area that also held employee housing, roads, electricity and water supply, police and fire departments, and dense entertainment facilities; the city of Shiumuzu, considerably automated, but still employing 1,609,052 workers.

The *Gyo* was a miracle of Fujikawa technology. The ship existed around a framework of a 35-foot, 90-ton blow-out preventer stack. When it began drilling operations, the ship's bottom slid away and the stack went down through the hull, through the "moonpool" at the middle of the ship. With the ship revolving around it, the oil drill remained stationary no matter which way the wind was blowing. For every thrust of wind or heavy slam of wave, eleven push-propellers and six hydropones, lowered through the hull in retractable turrets which were spread along the length of the ship's bottom, and fixed at right angles to the hull, provided counterthrust, moving the ship sideways or swinging it on its axis.

As the ship was holding, a space satellite twenty-two thousand miles overhead would recheck the ship's position over the oil deposited under the seabed, six thousand feet below the waterline of the drilling ship. When oil was struck, every wellhead would be piped far beneath the ocean, running the oil to 450-foot-tall vertical spars that floated four-fifths submerged in the sea, each capable of holding 300,000 gallons of crude oil. Later, the oil would be pumped out of the spars into Fujikawa tankers moored to the spars hundreds of miles out to sea.

The *Gyo* was only seven feet longer than the *Perfection*. The camouflage experts were at work transforming her exterior into a replica of the luxury yacht.

10

Captain Huntington opened the door to the owner's cabin aboard the *Perfection,* and found himself staring into the amiable face of a stocky, darkly moustached man of about thirty-eight. "Where ya been?" the man said. "I hate to hang anywheres alone."

"Who are you?" the Captain asked icily.

"I'm Keifetz. I got in this morning on a flight outta LA whence I got in from Vegas."

"Ah. The gambling instructor."

"The Winner Engineer."

"You must be shattered by the time lag."

"I am beat, baby. I just wanted to check in witchew, then maybe you can find me a bed someplace."

Mr. Ikeda questioned the Captain about Keifetz the next morning. "Why is this man on this ship?" he asked abruptly.

"Visiting me."

"That will not do. I must know all about him. I must know why you dared to bring him into this intensive security area."

"Then I suggest that you ask Baron Fujikawa. Surely, it would take at least orders from Baron Fujikawa to get a stranger into this pier?" He decided Mr. Ikeda had an especially evil face. He was too tall, too heavy, and too heavy-handed. Mr. Ikeda walked away rapidly.

Within twenty minutes Kimiko came to the stateroom. "Please, Colin. It is very bad to defy Mr. Ikeda."

"Perhaps so. But that doesn't concern me."

"He feels his responsibility so deeply. He is Baron Fujikawa's fiercest dog. Baron Fujikawa has told him nothing about this man. If you will only tell Mr. Ikeda all about him, Mr. Ikeda will be your friend."

"I don't want to be his friend. In fact, I don't care for him at all."

"Please, dearest Colin! Mr. Ikeda is a dangerous man. Please help him."

"My darling girl, the fact is, Mr. Ikeda has no need to know."

Captain Huntington was shaken to think of explaining to Kimiko, to Mr. Ikeda, or to anyone else, that Keifetz had been sent 15,000 miles across the world to teach him how to win at gambling because his father-in-law preferred it that way.

Keifetz was on deck at 8:45 AM. He found Captain Huntington breakfasting on the sheltered fantail of the ship, which was enclosed by the sealed pier. He was chewing daintily from an enormous *saucisse de veau* cooked with shallots in butter, sipping tea, and reading Volume H–K of *Groves Dictionary of Music*. Steinitt had packed the Captain's favorite dictionaries; his Beerbohm, his Firbank, and his Neiman-Marcus catalogue, knowing well that anyone might tire of sex, but never of the masters.

"I just had a funny breakfast," Keifetz said. "It was a little like white lox and a little like Rice Soggies. You ready to work out with me?"

"Sit down, please. Tell me about yourself first."

Keifetz sat down. "I'm a Brooklyn boy. I used to take the occasional contract in Brownsville. No mob stuff. Just to help out friends and to make a living without working." He accepted a cup of tea.

"You killed people?"

"Yeah. But—you know—pretty rotten people. Then my wife inherited a *Shopping News* from her Uncle Marek in Vegas. She is a natural editor. So we moved to Vegas. I been sitting in a poker game downtown for about nine years. We have two kids and a bulldog. I never take anything stronger than whiskey and I don't smoke. Also, no contracts since we left Brooklyn."

"A nice life."

"We got it good. We own the house. We got a pool and two '76 Cutlasses. My wife is also a helluva cook who can, like, blow a wall out of a kitchen. And if you like sun you can keep going in Vegas for a hunnert years."

"How did my father-in-law find you?"

Keifetz didn't mind questions. The Captain was forming an opinion that nothing bothered Keifetz. "There was a fella used to work for Hughes. He also used to be with the CIA and Meyer Lansky and around Nixon and he knows me. One morning after the count-up we bite a copple bagels. He asks me if I want to make a hunnert and fifty dollars. I say—it couldn't hoit—how?"

"A hundred and fifty dollars?" The Captain was incredulous.

"That's the way they say it in Vegas. It means a hunnert and fifty thousand but they don't want to overexcite the tourists. He says it also pays expenses and he tells me a certain person put a proposition to him. This certain person, you know who, was the one who set my friend with Hughes so he wants to do him a big favor."

"And they want me to take gambling lessons."

"They want your whole perna view overhauled, gaming wise."

"It cannot be done."

"You always lose, right?" Keifetz asked.

"Not at all. I lose when I get carried away by some emotion."

"Yeah. I know all about it and I don't need no Bell Adjustment Inventory or MMPI profiles or mean, estimated WAIS or any Shipley-Hartford because this is my field. Guys like you have been a helluva living for me."

"But—what is there to know?"

"You got an antisocial personality, right? You never learn anything from experience and you just happen to have no personal or group loyalties."

"I was a captain in the Royal Navy," the Captain answered stiffly.

"So? Are you still a captain with them?"

He refused to get angry. He would react to this man as if he were a physician. It was all for his own good, probably. So he said nothing.

"Also, you have lousy judgment. You got big gaps in your responsibility and you can rationalize and justify anything. So don't resist me. I am twenty-three years knowing you guys. All of you hand over maybe fifty billion dollars a year to people like me. There are about six million of you in the States alone, so don't get the idea that it's anything special."

"If you please, there is no need to speak so loudly. I realize that this is a part of your therapy but why should Mr. Ikeda have that sort of information about me as well?"

"You are a hunnert percent right. I always talk too loud," Keifetz said, whispering in a conspiratorial tone. "Okay. I'll control that. You got chronic marital difficulties. I ain't reading your palm. We both know that. Your wife is a martyr like all compulsive gamblers' wives. But you got a strong marriage. It works and it lasts no matter what you do to ruin it. But you always owe a lotta money. If you got brothers and sisters, you don't get along with them. They wanna get along with you but you can't stand it if they look like they might be making a dollar. You get depressed. You get moody."

"How can you know all these things?" He began to feel that concentrated talks with Bitsy must have been arranged for this man, or that Daddy's surveillance had been made available.

"It's my work, baby. I wanna win. So I gotta know the people I'm playing with."

"You are certain that my wife or my father-in-law and his invisible institutional teams of psychiatrists haven't helped you along?"

"I never seen your father-in-law or your wife. He never sent me any files or any tips and neither did she. I wouldn't go near a psychiatrist because my wife is scared the neighbors would talk. Anyway—whatsa difference? I'm on your side. I wanted to show you that I understand you so you'll know I'll be able to understand your problems. Just trust me and we'll put you together again a winner."

"Do you really think that is possible?" The Captain's voice held aching appeal.

"Absolutely. Like gorronteed. Now—you said before you lose only when you get carried away? That figures. Lose your head and you lose your shirt. Believe me, smart is better than lucky. You just got to be rerouted to the smarts, that's all."

"But how?"

"Look—life is a pretty simple proposition. Either you win or you lose. Nothing else. No other way. You can't fold, you gotta play because when you are breathing, you are playing. Nobody ever broke even with life. You take a for instance, a monk. He sits in a cell. He don't talk. He plays it safe because he wants to break even. So what happens. He wears sandals and they give him athlete's foot, has to be rushed to a hospital where he meets a gorgeous nurse and she gets him talking. He talks too much and he's back in the game again. If you could break even with life, there wouldn't be enough trouble and stress to hold the whole thing together."

"That may be correct theoretically," the Captain answered indecisively. "But nothing can make it function that way."

"*Evvey*body makes it function that way, baby. You don't need rules to tell you how to flip heads or tails. To get us started it might be a good idea if I told you what a loser isn't. Okay?

I am talking about players who are compulsive winners, you know? Take me. That's my thing. I win. I don't lose because I don't believe in it. If everybody believed in crime, there couldn't be enough prisons. Crime is losing. The people who don't believe in crime don't believe in that kind of losing. I don't believe in any kind of losing—except sometimes having to eat my wife's cooking—and I am very big with believing in winning."

"For heaven's sake, Keifetz! This sounds like some crackpot faith cure. I thought my father-in-law was more subtle than that."

"Call it anything. What's the difference? Just don't lose. I play maybe nine hours of poker a night, all night. Against the best. And I am talking about the best who also don't believe in losing. I pick up maybe three hunnert and fifty dollars a year and I suppose you have noticed that I don't have a wrinkle in my face."

"Why should a man of your age have wrinkles?"

"I don't have a wrinkle because I eat only fish and liver. I lay off meat. I lay off eggs. Also no bread. I never touch pasta. My wife dug up this diet for her column in the *Shopping News*. So, I have no wrinkles."

The Captain stared at him levelly. "I don't eat much fish," he said. "I detest liver, love pasta. I'm at least ten years older than you but I don't have wrinkles."

"Wait till you're seventy, eighty," Keifetz said with equanimity. "Look, I don't wanna give you too much onna first day. The main thing is that you gotta think 'win' all the time."

"Mr. Keifetz, I am not sure I do want to win all the time. Risk is what makes gambling an interesting pastime."

"Look—Captain—losers do not believe in risk—I swear to you. They are not people who would gamble on anything solely dependent on chance. They want money. They need it more than other people. That's why they gamble. It's not a pastime. They got a terrible fear of losing, so they lose. It's the money laying out there on the tables that kills them."

"I cannot agree."

"Please! Agree! Think of your father-in-law!"

"Perhaps you have a system for teaching how to win half the time?"

"Impossible. Like I told you—to try to break even is a waste of time, mental and emotional resources, money, and energy. I'm telling you! Life is not a break-even proposition. You win or you lose. No halfway."

"You give me a lot to think about, Mr. Keifetz."

Keifetz got up. "We got a great start today, baby."

11

Captain Pappadakis brought the *Perfection* into port at Shiumuzu to the cheers of the waiting Australian and Japanese press and television. As owner, Captain Huntington took them all on a tour of the ship. French champagne flowed. After the press reception, the *Perfection* was moved upstream into the enclosed, guarded pier with the *Gyo*. Captain Pappadakis was amazed at the reproduction of his ship, but when he went aboard the *Gyo*, there was no interior resemblance—everything was grimly functional.

"We should get hardship money," Pappadakis said.

"Double pay for you and your officers," Commander Fujikawa told him. "The rest of the crew will wait ashore in Osaka until the time comes to rejoin the *Perfection.*"

"What about Francohogar?" Pappadakis asked.

"Who is he?"

"My cook," Captain Huntington said.

"He is more than just a cook," Pappadakis said. "He is the best there is."

"Then you must invite me to dinner," the Commander answered. "Tonight will be my last chance to taste his food."

The Owner's Dinner for Commander Fujikawa was also attended by Captain Pappadakis, Keifetz, and Mr. Ikeda. Francohogar prepared Japanese food with interpretations of his own. Mr. Ikeda was enthralled by it. Commander Fujikawa's appreciation exceeded all bounds.

"Oh! My dear friends! You *must* have such a cook sail with you! How does he do it? What could he possibly do to salted trouts' guts to make them even more heavenly than I ever remember tasting them?"

"Salted trouts' guts?" Keifetz said with dismay.

"Less wrinkles for you," the Captain reassured him.

"I mean to say," Fujikawa went on, "I have spent a *life*time adoring salted trouts' guts. My father has brought in cooks from all over Japan, some of our greatest cooks, to make salted trouts' guts for me on various birthdays, but I could just as well have been eating a copy of the *Nihon Keizai Shimbun* compared with those your cook has prepared tonight."

"Good of you to say so," the Captain replied, "but this is merely the beginning."

As course succeeded course, the more Fujikawa and Ikeda tasted, the more insatiable they became. "This becomes a matter of some urgency," Fujikawa said feverishly. "You must allow me to borrow this cook to prepare just one last perfect meal for my father. I know—I know that will represent a hardship for you, but my father is an old, old man. He helped to rebuild Japan. He is the pinnacle of our house and once the greatest eater in Japan. He deserves that I ask for this to bring him so much final pleasure. You must, Captain Huntington. You cannot say no to this!"

"But, I—"

"Four days at the most!"

"But we sail tonight."

"We will fly this great cook to wherever your navigator says you are. Don't you see, my old friend? You will bring honor to our house."

"He is yours, Commander. With all joy that I can do this small service, I thank you for valuing his art so highly."

"Thank you. Will you send for this artist so that I may thank him for his genius?"

The waiter was sent. The stately cook entered, enormous under his tall, white hat. Commander Fujikawa stood solemnly. The others got to their feet. "I wanted you to know that I have never tasted salted trouts' guts which could remotely match the towering flavors which you brought out in those guts tonight."

Francohogar smiled. "A *tourne du main,*" he said.

"Are you able to break down the ingredients of a dish merely by taste?" the Commander asked.

The great cook nodded.

"Our company has just secured the rights to a most successful American convenience food, called Farm Girl Foods. It is a taste sensation which has swept the United States and it is our intention to manufacture it here on the original American formula for distribution throughout Asia and Africa. Will you honor me by tasting our Farm Girl Old Fashioned Chicken Fricassee Gravy?"

Francohogar looked at Captain Huntington blankly. The Captain nodded. The cook agreed to taste. Commander Fujikawa clapped his hands. A Japanese attendant entered bearing a steaming bowl, which was set down on the table. Carefully, the Commander ladled out the hot gravy into a small bowl and extended it to Francohogar. The cook sniffed the rising fumes and made a stricken face.

"Yes, taste, please!" the Commander cried.

Francohogar lifted a spoonful of the brew to his lips and tasted. He gagged. He recovered himself. "Can you fathom what are the ingredients which make up our delicious Farm Girl Old Fashioned Chicken Fricassee Gravy?" Fujikawa asked with excitement.

Francohogar took a drink of water gratefully, then he said, "It contains chicken fat, wheat flour, a partly hydrogenated vegetable oil base, corn syrup solids, soy protein isolate, dipotassium phosphate, sodium silico aluminate, tricalcium phosphate, about three-quarters of a percent of BHA antioxidant, modified food starch, lipolyzed butter fat, monosodium glutamate, hydrolized plant protein, polysorbate eighty, turmeric extractive, and disodium insonate." He belched horribly.

"Marvelous! You have revealed the exact recipe!" the Commander said. "What a feat of gourmandise!"

After the emotional dinner, Commander Fujikawa asked Captain Huntington for a private meeting before he left for Tokyo.

In the Captain's quarters, Fujikawa went directly to a hanging wall chart of the northeast coast of Australia. The chart had a concealed hinge and hid a wall safe. He gave the Captain the written combination. He dialed the lock, opened the round door, reached in and removed two manila envelopes. He took them to the round table under the hanging light. "Envelope Number One is so marked. It contains one half of your fee of one hundred and fifty thousand American dollars. The balance of the fee will be made when the assignment has been completed."

"Excellent," the Captain said.

"The envelope marked Number Two contains three hundred and fifty thousand Australian dollars. This is the down payment to acquire the oil leases in Brisbane which will secure the oil fields on the Great Barrier Reef. When Miss Expediter's computers confirm that sufficient oil exists you will go ashore to meet our Australian lawyers, as described fully in the envelope. Mr. Ikeda will accompany you, at my father's orders, and the final contracts will be signed at a designated Queensland government office."

"Quite clear."

"The Australian press and television will be on hand to give the transaction the best possible face."

"That is very little to do to earn such a fee."

"You won't have a lot of motions to go through, no. But your contribution is the most important part of the undertaking. Your own, highly publicized glamor aboard the largest private yacht in the world will keep off the horde of wild-eyed conservationists who would interfere if we were just a normal appearing oil-drilling ship, proving what it was sent out to prove. It is vital work you will do."

"Just one other thing. When do I get the *Perfection* back?"

"When Miss Expediter's data is checked in Tokyo, and the agreement on the presence of sufficient oil made unanimous, the *Perfection* will leave Shiumuzu by night with your crew and all officers except Pappadakis aboard. The yacht will rendezvous with the drilling ship on the reef, where you will board her."

"First-rate."

"I say farewell. I shall be leaving within the hour. Will your cook be ready to travel with me?"

"He will be ready." They shook hands warmly. The Commander left. Captain Huntington passed the word to have Francohogar sent to him.

Francohogar took the news of his departure for Tokyo stolidly.

"I am curious to see such a huge city," he said, "but what are you going to eat, sir?"

"I shall fast, actually. Must lose a kilo."

"When they say four days, I know it means a week. If I am able to please the Baron he will want more and more."

"He is so old, Juan, that a small biscuit inside him would be like a mule inside a python."

"You don't know the great feeders, sir. Age makes no difference. The great feeders are different from the rest of us. They eat like vacuum cleaners."

The Captain wandered out on the deck to sit at the taffrail within the enclosed pier, to smoke a fine Cuban cigar, and to listen to the activity of preparations for a voyage. He made himself face the disconcerting but undeniable fact that Kimiko was now deeply in love with him. He had assumed from the very start that she had been planted upon him at the old Baron's orders to insure complete information. Despite that he knew he loved her. He loved her differently from the way he loved Bitsy, more differently still from the way he loved Yvonne, and he was also keenly aware of time between them. He knew, at age forty-seven, that to love two splendidly healthy young women was sufficient unto the day and night.

He had refused to show in any way how dear Kimiko had become to him because, when this cruise was over, it had to be the end. She belonged to a brilliant future as a geologist and manager in Japan. He belonged to two women in London, to his tailor, his chocolate-colored 1935 Rolls-Royce sports sedan, and to the genius of Francohogar.

12

The camouflaged drilling ship moved out into the Inland Sea at 2:14 AM heading toward Korea, to move southward past Okinawa, then into the Philippine Sea. Days succeeded days of perfect sailing weather as they plowed southward. Kimiko worked fifteen-hour shifts drilling tool pushers, riggers, computer operators, geologists; studying the dynamic positioning system in relation to the satellite; lowering and raising the hydropones and coordinating the preventer stack and hull mechanism. Meanwhile, the Captain took his how-to-win lessons under the awning of the ship's fantail.

His life became as a message in a sealed bottle which bobs across a landless sea. The past was dimming; light withdrew from it until memory could hardly see its way. Bitsy began to exist as a voice on Daddy's satellite telephone. He would sip champagne, and listen to Bitsy tell about the weather in London, staring at Kimiko who sat on the deck at his feet.

Fujikawa Industries flew Francohogar by jet from Tokyo to Manila, then by seaplane to join the drilling ship. He was more somber than usual when he reported to Captain Huntington.

"It was very sad, sir," the cook said. "Baron Fujikawa became too enthusiastic about the food and had to be taken away to hospital after two days and nights of eating. He is an amazing feeder and, if he had not collapsed, I would not be here. I was locked into kitchen and quarters. I reminded Commander Fujikawa that this was hardly the compliment which was meant to be paid to himself and his father and—it was pitiable —he wept! He said there was nothing he could do, that no one had ever foreseen how his father would react to my food because the Baron had not eaten much more than a few wisps of seaweed and tiny amounts of raw fish for the past fifteen years. The Commander blames himself for everything. He is a good man."

"But—did the Baron recover?"

"He is recovering. He has such a strong heart. Ah, but what a feeder! That old man ate more than some of the great gluttons of Belgian history. And it was all that light Japanese food. My God! Think if I had started him off with the *Pâté de Banquier Henri Emmet!*"

As they entered the Coral Sea the ocean water was so transparent in the bright sunlight that Captain Huntington could watch the beginning of their passage over the Great Barrier Reef, the largest structure in all history built by living creatures. It was 600 to 1000 feet deep and covered 80,000 square miles of ocean floor, an area equal to the combined space of England, Ireland, and Wales. The stupendous structure of the reef was greater and taller than the assembled skylines of all the cities of the world. The reef extended from the mouth of the Fly River in western Papua to Breaksea Spit east of Gladstone, Queensland, a distance of 1250 miles. It was the largest coral reef in the world; a living mass of coral polyps, sheltering thousands of varieties of fish and marine life and symbiotic parasites who lived because the reef manufactured oxygen—all in colors that were riotously spectacular. Scattered among these jewels was casual, instant death: textile cones, which killed in thirty seconds; sea wasps; stone fish; butterfly cod; sea snakes; Portuguese men of war, and sharks—all deadly. The reef teemed with death because there was so much life in it.

The greater part of the reef was at all times submerged, but large areas of crest were often exposed at low water, depending on the tides, to a depth of two to five feet. The reef was studded with innumerable cays and continental islands, the larger of which supported dense vegetation. South of Cairns, in Queensland, opposite the area where the drilling ship would engage in its most deliberate explorations, the submarine slope of the coral flattened and thrust eastward as far as 200 miles to sea. Three hundred and forty varieties of coral combined to build the great reef, which was the feeding grounds of giant clams, red emperor fish, beche-de-mer, and green sea turtles, of dugong and a congress of seabirds, sustaining casuarina trees and pisonias, pandamus and coconut palms, tournefortia and mangrove.

As the drilling ship moved 160 miles east of Thursday Island in the Torres Strait, the reef beneath it was like a Pucci scarf in colors from acorn to zinc-orange, from opera pink to fluorite violet, and Captain Huntington's separation from reality became more total as he stood hunched over the railing of the flying bridge for hours at a time in the bright sun, dreaming about his time on the *Henty*, staring downward into the spectacularly colored, transparent ocean as all the ships of his life seemed to move across the landscape of his mind: a grotesquely painted, kaleidoscopic void which had slipped awareness of consequence, trouble, or time.

13

Keifetz wore the trousers of one of the two-pair-of-pants blue serge suits which his cousin manufactured, but he was barefoot and stripped to the waist. To lend just a soupçon of Maugham, Conrad, or the Bowery, he had stopped shaving from the night they left Japan.

"You look like the outcast of the islands," the Captain told him.

"No flattery. I happen to look like a native South Seas cantor."

"You're getting a million dollar tan."

"If I still lived in Brooklyn and it was winter, it could be a million dollar tan. But I live in Vegas so it isn't worth four dollars. Even the tourists get to look like this. How are your attitudes today?"

"Firming up, I hope."

"There is only one thing you gotta understand," Keifetz said, sitting down. "To win you gotta have confidence. It's what you know about yourself that gives you the edge over the other guy. You can't fake confidence. Look at Nixon. You have to know you got it because guessers are losers. Smart is better than lucky. And luck is the line. One side of the line is right. The other is wrong. You gotta have confidence."

"You say it like a mantra."

"What's that?"

"It's something people are afraid they will forget. They believe if they say something over and over again it will somehow find its way inside them. They can no longer trust truth from the outside because they think that is other people's truth."

"Bet your ass on that. You got to believe—not just do something like other people do it. You also got to count how many hours you put in at a roulette table, then you got to demand compensation from that wheel for so much an hour. Are you worth ten bucks an hour? If you spent two thousand hours playing roulette you should be ahead twenty thousand dollars. How much are you ahead?"

"I am behind about two million, eight hundred thousand dollars, a few buildings, a wine business, the lives of a few friends, and a part of my own sanity."

"Don't revel in being a schmuck. So now you know what you are worth at a roulette table—say three thousand dollars an hour. So cut off all the negative thoughts. Just refuse to think negative. Get your confidence together. If you bet all the time—and I bet almost all the time—then everything is just a bet. You don't think about money. You set up your propositions and money is just the way you keep score."

"I wish it were the only way of keeping score."

"Forget about that! You are a hooked gambler. To you gambling means risk and success or risk and failure. You get rewarded or you're punished. The fear of money gets you drunk on gambling."

"How?"

"You are afraid to lose the money you need to win so the money rules you, not the gamble, and that kind of thinking ruins your confidence."

The Captain smiled ruefully. "In all other religions," he said, "it is man's nature which decides whether he will be saved or damned."

"What are you asking me?"

"I ask you how I can gain the confidence if it is my nature to want to lose the money."

"That's it! You got it! We are changing your deepest nature so that, instead of wanting to lose, you only want to win."

The Captain stared at him bleakly. "I am afraid that was settled when I was a small boy, when my father died and my brother went away to America and didn't take me with him."

14

Daddy's satellite telephone buzzed. Captain Huntington picked up. It was Yvonne; in London.

"Your voice is back!"

"Back? I just dialed something wrong and spent two minutes talking to Dr. Kissinger."

"Oh, my God!"

"It's all right!"

"What happened?"

"He said good-bye as if he thought it was someone else."

"But it is wonderful that you have recovered."

"Medically. But I cannot live without you."

"It is very hard for me, as well."

"You are you. Colin! When?"

"October."

"*NO!* No, no, no, no! But your wonderful wife will have you."

"But, darling, you knew that. We just didn't know about those mumps."

"I have my own ideas about those mumps. Colin! Tell me now. When?"

"Well, I—"

"I shall fly to Australia tomorrow. Tell me where to go."

"It just can't be done. Australia takes forever with visas—

things like that." He had been able to think of Kimiko, Yvonne, and Bitsy in high-walled, widely separated castles. It would be conceivable that Yvonne could meet Bitsy because they respected each other's status. But if she boarded the *Perfection* where Kimiko, despite fifteen hours of work a day, spent every other hour with him, he did not see how he could make Yvonne understand why that was now his life. Oh, damn the bloody mumps!

"You can begin to accept what is going to be, Colin. My Australian visa has been stamped into my passport since before the mumps."

He tried to think. This caused a pause. The pause reacted upon Yvonne. "Colin! Either I go to Australia tomorrow or I go back to France forever."

"Yvonne, darling! Yvonne, in a sense I am violating a confidence when I tell you this, but I am not aboard the *Perfection*. I am on a—" Mr. Ikeda's hand pressed down on the telephone and broke the connection. In a rage of frustration, the Captain put a karate lock on Mr. Ikeda's arm and threw him down upon the deck. Mr. Ikeda got to his feet with dignity. The men glared at each other with dislike.

"What kind of a telephone is that?" Mr. Ikeda asked.

"None of your business. If you ever do again what you just did, I shall throw you over the side."

"You are an agent for a British oil company?"

"I am no one's agent but that telephone call was so personal that, by breaking it, you have made me your enemy, Mr. Ikeda."

"It would be worse for you if I became your enemy."

Daddy's satellite telephone buzzed.

Watching Mr. Ikeda ten feet away from him on the deck, the Captain picked up the receiver.

"Hello?"

"Colin?"

"Yvonne, this is what I want you to do. Fly to Hong Kong and rest for at least forty-eight hours at the Peninsula. Then fly to Sydney and have the travel agent transfer you to the flight to Cairns—that's C-A-I-R-N-S—in Queensland. Check into the Great Northern Hotel in Cairns. We can have three days and nights together."

"We will pull down the shades and they will all run together."

"Call me when you get to that hotel."

"Why? Why can't I be with you?"

"Because I am working with an army of oil people and there just isn't any place for you out here."

"All right. Anyway, I can see my sister."

The Captain hung up. "Satisfied, Mr. Ikeda?" he said.

Mr. Ikeda grunted and strode away along the starboard deck.

Four days later he left a note for Kimiko. It said: "FAMILY BUSINESS ASHORE. WILL RETURN IN THREE DAYS' TIME. ALL LOVE. COLIN." He went aft to the helicopter pad, climbed into the chopper, and flew it off in the direction of Cairns.

Yvonne was waiting, naked against large pillows which she had enclosed in ice-blue pillow slips from London, playing "A Cat Don't Know" on the soprano saxophone, tonguing with the supreme mastery he was thrilled to remember.

Mr. Ikeda faced Kimiko Shunga. She handed him the Captain's note. Mr. Ikeda said, "He is with his mistress from London in a hotel in Cairns."

"If he could not pay honor to his friend who had to see him then that would dishonor him—and me—as well."

"They are under electronic surveillance. If she is the mistress from London who is in my dossiers on him then I don't care what they do. But if it is not that woman—and I have her photographs—then it is the agent for a foreign oil company and I will have to deal with him."

15

On August 22, more than two months after Colin had left for Tokyo, nine days before her own departure to join him in Sydney, Bitsy sat in her Farm Street living room and listened to Daddy read a report from a man named Keifetz to a man in Las Vegas. "Before I start reading this," Daddy said, "I want you to know that it is simply a *marvel*ous progress report. This gambling expert seems to have achieved every goal we set out for him."

"Daddy! Isn't that wonderful!"

"The Vegas contact sent the report along intact and, I must say, the prognosis is spectacular."

"Daddy, you really are a genius."

Dear Pal: Well, we did it. The man is cured; completely turned around. He is a guaranteed winner. I can absolutely certify that to you. He may not win seven days a week—who can? But he will not lose much. This is why, baby: If he does not feel confidence, self-respect, and a total understanding of whatever proposition he is going to bet, then he will simply walk away from that proposition. I try him out all the time, I offer him different propositions which are the kind like we can bet by radio. At first, eight weeks ago, he would bet on anything available. He bet fifteen hundred with me on the Siamese elections. I trapped him into that. I know he don't know

89

anything about Siamese elections so I says to him, "Is this a correct proposition for you?" He says to me: "I got confidence." I says to him, "Then you don't yet understand confidence. How can you have confidence in a Siamese election which is happening, not even nationally but in some little hick town in the north." Immediately he sees my point but he wants to bet it just the same. He asks me what price I'll lay. I says I'll get a price from Jimmy the Greek. No, he says, you lay the price. I say, okay, the price is five to one you are wrong on whoever you pick. He pretends he is being robbed, which he is, but he wants to bet. He gets clobbered. We talk about it. We analyze. We say, was that a good proposition to bet? When all the reasons are in he sees that he should not have had confidence in that situation. The next day I ask him if he wants to play a little gin. He says, look out, Keifetz, I know a little more about gin than I knew about Siamese elections. I says to him—did you ever play gin six hours an afternoon for nine years against professionals so your kids could ride around in two Cutlasses? He looks at me like I am a schmuck. He says: Get the cards. He says: How much a point? I says: Name it, you got it. He says a hundred a point—square dollars. He goes to a safe in the wall and comes back with twenty-five which I win off him. We talk about it. We analyze. We say: Was gin a good proposition against a full-time professional card player who ain't a dummy and who don't do nothing else? He says he sees the point. When all the reasons are in he sees he should not have had confidence in a proposition like that, that he was only pretending confidence, like Nixon.

In the next four weeks I win a total of seventy-five off him at different games from matches to quoits. He takes it exactly right because he is a real gent and because the actual breakthrough is happening to him. He now KNOWS. He has been changed from a loser into a winner.

I test him all the time. Now he won't make a move no matter what proposition I throw at him. I says, what kind of golf do you play. I got a one handicap, he says. Okay, I says, let's go ashore and play a little golf, say fifty dollars a hole, Vegas counting. What's your handicap, he says. I tell you what I'm gonna do, I says. You play with a full bag of sticks. You get tees. You get a caddy and a golf cart if they have them. I will play you with only a rake for a club. We'll go nine holes. What do you say? One thing: He don't look at me like I'm a schmuck anymore. With a rake? he says. What kind of a rake? Any kind of rake, I says. A garden rake. You pick the rake. What you say? He looks me right in the nose and he turns the proposition down. No, he says. I don't have no confidence in that proposition.

Next day I try him out on Mah Jongg, counting fish off the right side of the ship, klob, and high dice. He says he doesn't have the confidence. I says: Are you tapped out? Is that it? If you got no more cash I'll take your marker. No, I am okay on the money end, he says. I just don't have the confidence.

Now comes the part. We are plotzing one night and I bring out a whole miniature roulette layout. I says, this is more your game than my game. You can be the house or you can be the player. Let's go. He just gets pale. He says, I feel sick and disgusted if I even look at a roulette layout he says.

"Oh, Daddy!" Bitsy cried out in delight. "You've done it! You've done it!" Daddy grinned, then continued reading Keifetz's letter aloud.

So I wait. We go ashore when we hear about bush racing. This I gotta see. How do you race a bush? You got any confidence in that, I says. He thinks. He says he has to see a form sheet before he answers, so we have a horrible lunch in town then we hire a car and we go out to race a bush. They should know what a bush is in Brooklyn. A Flatbush.

Ready? He didn't even bet. He studied the form and he looked at the beetles, he actually introduces me to two bookmakers and they almost cry with gratitude when they see him, but he don't bet. I got no confidence to bet horses I never saw with form sheets I don't know, he says. We spend the rest of the day drinking a little icy beer and watching.

This guy is completely turned around from a loser into a winner.

I'll go further than that. If he ever sits in my poker game I am gonna play a more than usual conservative-type game. Inside a year, this guy will be winning at golf with a rake.

Hang loose,
N. Keifetz

"Oh, Daddy," Bitsy yelled, "have you ever *heard* such good news?"

16

Captain Huntington felt safe with himself for the first time since he had begun to gamble. He gave the credit for the escape from himself to Daddy and to Keifetz. He thought he would have resented losing such a complexity of pleasure and pain. He would have resisted the loss had he known that it would surely be taken from him, but he had accepted Keifetz without believing in his ability to make it happen. Now that the pain and the sick despair had been stripped away, he never wanted to go back again. He thought of the man who had had a blocking operation to stop high blood pressure and got a duodenal ulcer, cured that and developed diabetes, worked that out and ended up with a face tic. He wondered what fetid horror he would next visit upon himself. The chill of its promise burrowed into his bones: What other punishment would take the place of gambling and losing? He felt doomed that his symptoms would change like seasonal clothing but the causes of his despair would remain neatly stacked up in the arsenals of calamity. What if he began to put ketchup on everything he ate? What if he took to wearing his shirts unbuttoned to the navel to show his dugs and heavy gold symbols on chains? What if he suddenly took up reading analyses of the work of D. H. Lawrence?

Kimiko was waiting at the rail as the launch brought them

back to the ship from the race course. She separated him from the others and led him aft to the fantail where there were two bottles of Blagny chilling in silver tubs. She was wearing the beautiful green kimono with the wide pink sash. Her soft, black, amygdalid eyes under epicanthic folds gave him the attention of her soul. "We have found the oil field," she said. "It is immense, bigger than anyone—even Baron Fujikawa— had dreamed. Tokyo has confirmed all my data and the *Perfection* is already under weigh to the rendezvous."

They could not speak. She was smiling. It was a gallant performance.

"You will sail north to Tokyo," he said. "I must go south."

She stopped smiling and nodded.

"We must not tell ourselves that it is over," he lied. Here it came, with the rush and weight of a train; worse pain, more despair than any caused by gambling. This was dying slowly, locked inside a junked refrigerator under heaped debris of loss upon a city dump.

"It is over," Kimiko said. "But we will always have it. It is very bad now, but I would rather feel what I have felt since Tokyo confirmed the strike than never to have known you, never to have held you, or never to have touched you."

"I am not that brave," he said.

"Man is courage. Woman is only beauty," she said.

"I won't go back. That part of my life is over. So many things finished themselves since I left London that I have entered a new life anyway, and I won't go back."

"And make two women wish they were dead—instead of one? You won't escape anything if you stay with me because they will always be with you. And I was educated by Baron Fujikawa to serve Japan. You belong in England."

Daddy's satellite telephone buzzed. Kimiko and the Captain were locked, staring beyond each other's eyes into the far-off past of twenty hours before. The telephone buzzed. Kimiko nodded. She crossed to him. She kissed him softly, then drew back to lift the phone from its cradle. She handed it to him, then turned and hurried away.

"Huntington here," the Captain said into the phone.

"Huntington *here*," Bitsy's happy voice answered. "I'm so excited. Six more days and I'll be waving to you from that Yacht Club pier in Sydney. I just can't wait!"

"How many years has it been?" the Captain asked.

Captain Pappadakis, Francohogar, and Keifetz came aft to invite the Captain to a farewell picnic on Dunk Island the next day. They told him Kimiko had already accepted. The Captain accepted.

Mr. Ikeda was last to appear. "Commander Fujikawa has instructed me to tell you that your appointment with Mr. Stanley Ivory, his Brisbane attorney, and the meeting with the Queensland government has been confirmed for ten o'clock on the morning of the day after tomorrow. Your yacht will be alongside this ship in two mornings' time. Finally, I have given my approval for the farewell picnic ceremonies for Shunga-san at Dunk Island tomorrow."

"That is how everything ends for me, Mr. Ikeda. With a picnic. Please signal Mr. Stanley Ivory that I will join him one half hour previously."

Kimiko and the captain clung to each other desperately all through the night.

17

Keifetz, Kimiko, and the Captain sat on a primeval beach and stared at the pavonine sea whose waters were as transparent as the air. Francohogar and Mr. Ikeda, his diligent disciple, were building a wood fire thirty yards away. The picnic was being assembled on the west side of Dunk Island, a place of fine palms and exquisite offshore coral gardens, where hundreds of sea turtles came ashore in season to lay millions of eggs. Captain Cook had named the island after Montague Dunk, Earl of Halifax, a nineteenth-century peer who breakfasted on doughnuts and coffee.

"I think I'll go back and watch the magician cook," Keifetz said. "My wife could learn something."

The Captain rolled up his trousers and kicked off his espadrilles. He got up and pulled Kimiko to her feet. Holding hands, they ran out into the sea.

Keifetz sauntered up to the fire. "What's cooking?" he asked.

"We will have sautéed bamboo shoots," Francohogar said, "beche de mer, and shark's fins in creamstock. Then some jellyfish which I will prepare with sesame oil and soy sauce with a little sugar."

"Jellyfish!" Mr. Ikeda snorted ecstatically.

"Then spiced tangerine chicken with steamed cucumbers."

"The chicken sounds great, Juan," Keifetz said, "but maybe

you could find me a hard-boiled egg to start?"

"I brought you a ham sandwich and a hard-boiled egg as your hors d'oeuvres."

"What is a ham sandwich?" Mr. Ikeda asked.

They heard a piercing scream. They turned to track it. The Captain was shouting harshly and grappling with Kimiko's limp form. He was shouting noises not words. The three men sprinted into the sea. The Captain and Kimiko were over forty yards out in the sea, on the reef. The three panicked men churned through the water, yelling, questioning; confused and frightened. When they reached the Captain his face was bloodless with fear. He held Kimiko close to himself and made no further sound.

"What happened here?" Mr. Ikeda took charge.

"She saw something under the water," the captain said, tortured. "She pushed me away from it and the impetus carried her forward. She stepped on whatever she was saving me from. My God!"

"Lift her! Everyone lift her and get her into the launch," Mr. Ikeda shouted. All four men took a part of the limp figure and moved it as quickly as they could through the water toward the shore, on a diagonal toward the launch. On the shore they laid the body down while Keifetz and Mr. Ikeda prepared the boat. The Captain took up one of Kimiko's feet, then another. The underside of her left foot had turned into all of the extraordinary colors of the reef and the foot had swollen to three times its normal size. He opened a clasp knife and slashed deeply into the foot where it was most swollen. She did not react. He began to try to suck the poison from her foot.

"Get her aboard!" Mr. Ikeda yelled. They put the body into the launch and pushed the boat out into deep water. They climbed into it, the engine turning over. The launch set out on the four-mile course to the drilling ship, Kimiko's beautiful face asleep upon the Captain's chest. "She is dead," he wept. "She is gone."

"Dead?" Keifetz asked blankly.

"How could she be dead?" Francohogar asked dully.

The four men sat like boulders until the launch reached the ship's side. The ship's surgeon was waiting. He knelt beside her. He examined her with tortuous deliberation, studying the left foot.

"Speak, man!" Mr. Ikeda cried. "This girl is Baron Fujikawa's ward!"

The doctor shone a bright light into Kimiko's eyes. At last he stood up slowly. "She is dead," he said. "She was probably killed by a tiny textile cone." He ordered the body below to be prepared for burial.

"There will be no burial at sea," Mr. Ikeda said. "She must be taken to Japan. She must be returned to Baron Fujikawa. Please come with me, Captain Huntington."

They went to the radio shack. Mr. Ikeda told the radio officer to place a call to Commander Fujikawa and to leave them when it was secured. When the man left, Mr. Ikeda said, "I will fly out with her body tonight. There will be many mourners. Under the circumstances, while I am making the arrangements for the return to Tokyo, I ask you to call the lawyer, Mr. Stanley Ivory, in Brisbane and ask him to postpone the government meeting and the press conference about the leases until I can return."

The Captain nodded numbly.

"Ask for a three-day postponement."

Dazed, the Captain went to his quarters. He lowered himself like a bucket into a deep well of pain, into the knowledge of Kimiko's death. He was in shock and unable to find the release of grief. He called Stan Ivory. He explained that they had suffered a tragic accident and asked for the postponement.

"That would be a disastrous course, Captain Huntington," the lawyer said. "I don't want to sound unfeeling about any problems you have had aboard, but there are new developments in Brisbane. American and Dutch oil companies are aware that your ship has been intensely active on the reef. If we do not take up those options for leases tomorrow morning, those leases will surely go to someone else."

"Expect me in Brisbane as scheduled," the Captain said.

Mechanically, he reported the developments to Mr. Ikeda. The security man shrugged. "Oil companies have best security. We know what they are doing and they know what we are doing. Very well. I am to take Shunga-san to the Brisbane airport by ship's helicopter. Our plane from Tokyo will land there at seven o'clock tonight. Please do not fail to telephone Commander Fujikawa when the leases have been secured."

18

He had gone over the side of a launch in this same Coral Sea twelve years before when the shark had taken Gash Schute's arm off. He had cut deeply into the underside of the shark with enough knife to keep it away from Schute, who was bleeding all over the sea and would attract other sharks. Both of them had been pulled to safety over the side. He should have died there that day and been saved the shame of losing the *Henty*, other disgraces, and the shattering pain of the loss of Kimiko, but he was intact and, as a direct result, Gash Schute had left him five million pounds. It did not matter how much the Captain explained to Gash that what he had done had been an utterly reflexive act. Gash did not want to understand that. Gash wanted to understand that the Captain had risked his own life to save him.

And now—he had become Gash. He would never be able to sleep again because he could not stop thinking about what Kimiko had done for him. He was able to demonstrate to himself, out of the same Coral Sea with his own past, that she had not deliberately given her life to save his. But he knew she had been far more valuable than he was; she had saved him because she loved him. If she had loved him less, he would be dead and she would be alive, which was how it should be. A revulsion overcame him. His physical memory had him feeling that she had shoved him with all her weight, so he knew she could not have been pulled forward by any impetus; she would have rebounded backward. It became too starkly clear to him: To make certain forever that he would never leave her, that she would never leave his mind—to make him her prisoner with an illusion of having died only to save him—she had stepped forward upon the textile cone. She had died.

He became revolted by the thought of her. His hate was so strong that it had him clapping his hand over his mouth and reeling into the bathroom to vomit. He could have loved her for all of life left to him, but she had taken that away from him with selfish brutality.

He lay on the bed, breathing heavily; eyes like glass beads. Claws of terrible logic began to clutch at him like the eagle's tearing beak upon the liver of Prometheus. He understood her now, too late. He did not want to understand her. He wanted to despise her and reject her but he saw what she had done. She had known, with the power of her love, that he would reject her for seeming to die on the day they were leaving each other to move off to contrasting and distant parts of the world. She had loved him. She had made herself die to make him hate her, to be able to forget her. Could this be how her death had happened? Could this really be what had been meant or was he going mad?

He forced himself to his feet. He poured a tumbler of Irish whiskey and lighted a cigar. He sat facing the wall, facing another wall, again; empty and despairing. If he was going to remain alive and sane, there was only one way he knew that could make him nearly whole again.

The ship's telephone rang. He went to the wall and answered it. It was Commander Fujikawa calling from Tokyo.

"I have been unable to call you until now," he said. "I loved her and I was proud of her. But, as much as she meant to me, she was everything to my father, so it has been very hard to tell him what has happened."

"She passed away like a flash fire. She said, 'Live!' and she died."

The Commander disconnected. The Captain removed Envelope Number Two from the safe in his stateroom. He called for the ship's launch to take him across to the *Perfection*, which had arrived two hours before. He was greeted by Captain Pappadakis at the *Perfection*'s ladder. "I'm going ashore in the chopper in a few hours," he said. "And I must be in Brisbane tomorrow morning to finalize this oil business."

"Yes, sir."

"Be ready to sail to Sydney tomorrow evening. We will pick up Mrs. Huntington at the Royal Yacht Club in Sydney harbor on Sunday morning."

"Aye, aye, sir."

"Keifetz is asleep in the drilling ship. After I've gone, signal to have him and Juan transferred to us when he awakens. Keifetz will sail with us to Sydney, then fly out to America from there."

The Captain sat in the enormous stateroom drinking Jamieson's Irish whiskey slowly. His life had become a circle. He was approaching the same starting point again. His face had lost all the invisible mooring pins which had held its angular features together in a serene design. It was disjointed and haunted. He ordered the helicopter made ready for noon. He climbed into the cockpit clutching the large envelope. The chopper hovered on the pad, then lifted straight up, turning to make course dead ahead for the mainland.

19

Tokyo began to try to reach Captain Huntington at 7:20 that
night. Captain Pappadakis suggested that Tokyo try the Captain at Lennon's Hotel in Brisbane. Tokyo was back on the line
in twenty minutes. Captain Pappadakis took the call from
Commander Fujikawa in his quarters. "We have tried him at
Lennon's, the Belle Vue, and three other hotels. The lawyer
has not heard from him. This is most irregular."

"He may only have gone as far as Townsville or Mackay for
the night. He could have put down for fuel and then decided
to stay over and go on to Brisbane in the early morning."

"When did the *Gyo* voyage north?"

"At noon, sir."

"Dammit, Pappadakis. Please put your radio officer to con-
tacting every hotel between Townsville and Mackay."

"Yes, sir. Shouldn't be hard. The Captain always chooses the
best."

"Call me in two hours."

They could not find the Captain. Francohogar and Keifetz
sat with Captain Pappadakis waiting for a positive report.

"He looked terrible, I can tell you that," Pappadakis said.
"You really know him, Juan. Would he do anything crazy?"

Francohogar shrugged. "Why not? We all went crazy yesterday."

"You mean—like kill himself?"

"Never."

"Why not?"

"He wants to inherit his brother's title. He loves his wife. He loves his mistress. He wants to live. In that order."

"You could be wrong."

"Well, he's not wrong," Keifetz said. "Jesus, if that's all you know about Huntington, I'd love to get you alone with a pack of cards. He's a compulsive gambler. He can only get relief if he gambles. Wherever they're gambling that's where he is."

"But—where?"

"My hunch is that he went up to those bush races behind Cairns. He's gonna bet and bet until he's all right again."

"We must stop him!" Pappadakis said.

"We have to stop him," Francohogar said.

"The races were over hours ago," Keifetz answered. "Whatever he was gonna do, he's done."

"I've got to report this to Commander Fujikawa when I call him."

"No!" Francohogar yelled.

"Captain, lissena me," Keifetz said in a soft voice. "You don't work for Fujikawa. You work for Huntington. You want to get him killed?"

"*Killed?*"

"If he bet that oil option money and he lost it, then he can't pick up the leases in Brisbane. If there are no leases, the Fujikawas lose a copple billion. What would you do to a guy who lost you a copple billion?"

"I see what you mean, Keifetz," Captain Pappadakis said.

"We gotta support our man. You gotta tell Fujikawa that you found him in Townsville and that he's set to go into the meeting tomorrow."

The tropical city of Cairns, about as far south of the equator as Acapulco is to the north of it, is the gateway to a lush hinterland at 1043 miles north of Brisbane and its August, winter, weather, is dry and sunny. North and south of it are the great sugar plantations and at Cape York to the north, the enormous cattle ranches. Nearby and due west is the high Atherton Tableland with its waterfalls, tranquil crater lakes, deep ravines, and rugged, fern-filled valleys.

Captain Huntington secured the ship's helicopter at the small Cairns airfield and telephoned for a taxi to take him out to the last day of bush racing. They drove across the Mareeba tobacco field, past Tinaroo Falls and the Barron Gorge, and when they reached where they were going, the Captain gave the driver ten dollars to wait for him until the races were over. He walked into the crowd just as the second race was finishing. He found his friend, the bookmaker Dickie Adler. "Hey! Great. This is tremendous!" Adler said. "We thought we'd lost you."

"What do they like in the third while I study the form for the fourth?"

Adler was a huge, stout man who had once been as thin as a rail and who had used hypnosis to gain weight because he had been told all fat men are good dancers and he loved dancing. "The favorite, London Lady, a Garrity horse, could be an accident about to happen in the third," he said. "That's where the smart money is going."

"Can you handle twenty thousand to win on the Garrity horse?" The Captain opened his brown envelope. His hands were trembling. His eyes were as gritty as dead coals.

"Well, this ain't Aintree, and I ain't Ladbroke's, but I'll take it."

"Can you find a runner to take a bet to Bobby Musel?"

"Sure."

"Twenty more. On Fiona Bear. The nose. Send me the betting slips in the bar."

The Captain stood where the cold, cold beer was sold and sipped it slowly. The horses ran partly in the open and partly under splendid arches of great trees. Potomac Avenue won the third race.

The Captain found a chair. He concentrated on the form for

the fourth race and finally saw the winner clearly and with the same celerity picked the horse which would run second. The price on the first horse was 11–1; on the second, 4–1. He bet fifty thousand dollars on each horse. Adler and Musel shared the bets. They had closed down their stands for the day to concentrate on the Captain's business. They agreed to take the hundred thousand if they could lay it off by telephone to Sydney and Melbourne. That turned out to be quite possible but there was no need for it. Both horses ran out of the money.

He was down $140,000. By the end of the last race, out of the $350,000 he was going to need to hold down the leases in Brisbane the next morning, he had lost all but $90,000 and would have lost that if the lay-off bookmaker in Sydney hadn't balked. The Captain was stuck with the $90,000 so he said to Adler and Musel, "Do you fellows ever play poker?"

"I like poker," Musel said.

"Seven card stud is the beauty game," Dickie Adler told him.

"Can we round up a few more players?"

"Why not?" Musel said.

"I'll get my two brothers-in-law," Adler said, "the Wilson boys."

At 10:15 the next morning, in a parlor in the Great Northern Hotel in Abbott Street, Cairns, the Captain decided to keep his last hundred dollars for room service tips and gasoline for the helicopter. He was aware that the meeting with the lawyer, the press, and the Queensland government was supposed to start in eighteen minutes in Brisbane, 1043 miles away. He had lost $349,900 but he was released, he had gotten out, he was sane again, and able to accept her death. He had mourned Kimiko in the only way he could understand.

He shook hands amiably with Dickie Adler and Bobby Musel, giving them his home address in London because they insisted on sending him Christmas cards. It was not until he had lifted the helicopter out over the Coral Sea that he remembered Baron Fujikawa's expression when he spoke about the oil and thought of Mr. Ikeda's total fealty to the Baron. He knew he could hardly expect anything less than that which the Fujikawas would plan for him. It was their turn at bat. Although he was resigned to expecting to escape from them, for the first time in his life he was able to peek from behind the curtain of his egocentricity to see the shape of future events forming under what A. Edward Masters had called "the laws of consequence." He had passed himself from day to day as if he had been an idle fire bucket with nothing to extinguish or, more aptly, an empty fire bucket discovered at a conflagration.

He had lost their money. The oil leases had been cast adrift. Kimiko had told him that Mr. Ikeda was a killer. But Mr. Ikeda was only the Baron's instrument. If he could checkmate the Baron, Mr. Ikeda would be stopped. The Captain tried to think about his problem as objectively as he could. The loss of money was serious but the loss of the oil leases was irreparable. He could replace the money; he had done that before when he had gambled money away. But he could not replace the oil that Baron Fujikawa and Japan wanted so badly, so Baron Fujikawa would decide to have him killed. He needed to go where they could not find him, if there were such a place, while he puzzled out a way to neutralize the Baron and the loss of the oil. Within the Captain's odd mental reflexes, all of it had become just another gambling game.

When he touched down on the flight pad of the *Perfection*, Captain Pappadakis and Keifetz were waiting for him.

"How soon can we be under weigh?" the Captain asked in greeting.

"Twenty minutes, sir."

"We go due south by southwest under radio silence and with extremely evasive action in case there is an air search."

"Aye, aye, sir."

"Have Tytell listen for incoming traffic but acknowledge nothing. Our target port is Adelaide in South Australia. I must put through one call to Pittsburgh and that will be the last use of radio equipment."

"Yes, sir. Did you say Adelaide meaning Sydney?"

"I meant Adelaide. Steer clear of Sydney. On the double, please." Captain Pappadakis streaked toward the bridge.

"You look a lot better," Keifetz said.

"Thank you."

"How much did you lose?"

"Everything."

He went to the owner's cabin. He locked the door and went to his desk. He opened the large address book to B and ran his finger along the listings until he came to BRYSON, JOHN: AMERICAN DEBTORS' BANK OF PITTSBURGH. Bryson had developed borrowing into not only a huge business, but a science. He placed the call. He began to make tiny, careful notes on how much money he was going to need to get himself out of the present jeopardy. He would need $1,455,000. "Amen," he said aloud. The call came in.

"Mr. Bryson, please," he said.

"This is me, you ole sumbitch." Bryson's diction made Gabby Hayes seem like Fred Astaire. "Jeez Crast, whut you doong Down Under?"

"Cruising. A little holiday."

Bryson had actually been run out of Amarillo, Texas, for his diction. "Croozin'?" he said.

"John, I am telephoning you from the largest single owner's cabin in the history of world yachting. I'm aboard the *Perfection*."

"Hah cum yew tuck her tew allah way out tew down thar?"

"She was chartered in the Great Barrier Reef for five months for a hundred and twenty-five thousand a month."

"Hunnert twenna fah? Say—Bitzy says you was onee gittin' aydee."

"It's in the ship's log for anyone to see. Anyway I just talked to Bitsy in London and she told me you had a class reunion coming up so I thought you and I might talk charter."

"Hell, Colin, I doan *charter* nothin'. I own ever'thang. I'll buy her from you."

"But I just bought the ship from Bitsy myself. I figured to have a big charter business going."

"You'll sell if the price is right. Whut's yer price, Colin?"

The Captain took up the slip of paper with all the figures on it, took a deep breath and said, steadily, "Five million five, with a million four fifty-five down on delivery in Adelaide outer harbor four days from now."

"Then by Jezzuzz, yew gotcherself a deal!" Bryson was exultant. He could now, at last, make the nine surviving classmates of his grammar school class eat shit. "Ah'm callin' a correspondent banker in Adelaide right now—feller name of Harvey Zendt—to meet you on that ship and bring all the money and the papers."

"John?"

"Whut?"

"To avoid misunderstandings—that is a million four fifty-five Australian. Not American."

"Jeezcry! Yew addin' a preemyun!"

"John, face it. As you said yourself, you're one lucky sumbitch to get the yacht."

Bryson roared with laughter because he knew he could hold back any further payment for the *Perfection* in endless court battles run by lawyers he kept on salary. Where money was involved it was a point of honor for Bryson to screw everybody.

The Captain hung up, drenched with sweat. He had just committed the impossible sin; he had crossed Daddy. Daddy's reactions to being crossed were capable of making Baron Fujikawa's seem like a romp with the kids at Disneyland.

The ship was moving.

Captain Pappadakis knocked. The Captain unlocked the stateroom door and poured Pappadakis a John Jamieson after he had asked him to sit down, then sat facing him.

"I have just sold the *Perfection.*" he said.

"My God!

"The new owner's representative will take delivery in Adelaide."

"Will Mrs. Huntington meet us in Adelaide?"

Captain Huntington wiped his face with a large, white handkerchief. "To be frank, Pappadakis, Mrs. Huntington will most likely take it particularly hard when she learns I have sold this yacht without consulting her or her family. However, Mrs. Huntington will be waiting in Sydney and the explicit reason why we must race to Adelaide, avoiding Sydney, is that there was a Japanese security officer aboard the drilling ship who monitored all radio and telephone traffic. He knows we are supposed to arrive at the Royal Yacht Club, Sydney harbor, Sunday morning. And he very much wants to—uh—talk to me."

"I heard about it."

"Therefore Sunday morning should find us in Bass Stair, somewhere between Melbourne and Tasmania, heading for the Roaring Forties."

"But why Adelaide? Why not Capetown?"

"Adelaide is an opal center. I know everything will turn out much, much better if I can make a handsome addition to my wife's opal collection."

Captain Pappadakis knocked back his drink and stood up abruptly. "Please, sir," he said. "You may be telling me more than I need to know."

"Ask Mr. Keifetz if he will come in please."

"Did you give it to those two bookies?" Keifetz asked as he came in.

"Yes."

"You tried to lose—right?"

"I didn't think about anything."

"Oh, you tried to lose all right. That's the story of your life. Things get bad and you shed the trouble by losing everything you don't have so you'll be able to punish yourself for whatever happened, then so you can think again how to get it back somehow to pay off what you lost—but you lose the troubles just the same."

"Yes."

"What happened with the oil leases?"

"Lost."

"Holy shit! Does Ikeda know that?"

"By now he does."

"About how much money in the oil?"

"Kimiko estimated between two and three billion dollars."

"Then the old guy is gonna have you hit, right? And Ikeda gets the contract."

"Exactly what I thought."

"So—you feel great. You got the euphoria because this is the kind of gambling you been looking for all your life. I know it. You look younger. You got great color. So—how you gonna play it so Ikeda gets called off?"

"I wanted to discuss that with you actually."

"Tell me. It's gotta be a bitch of an idea. Three billion dollars!"

"First, I'm going to repay the three hundred and fifty thousand I owe for the oil lease money which I gambled away."

"You got that kind of loot?"

"I am getting it in Adelaide. Second, I shall repay the seventy-five thousand in salary which they paid me in advance."

"What then?"

"I need your help."

"You got it."

"Thank you. In Adelaide, I will give you seven hundred and fifty thousand dollars to take—with a plan—to the Australian Conservation Society in Sydney. I ask you to offer them this money as a gift which has a single condition."

"What's the condition?"

"That beginning immediately, they undertake an intensive campaign in the press, radio, television, petitions, direct-mail, street demonstrations, labor union and pulpit action to preserve the Great Barrier Reef, their nation's single greatest natural resource and heritage."

"Preserve the Great Barrier Reef? I don't get it."

"You'll get it. In fact I am counting on you to get it first. The objective is to keep whoever bought those leases in Brisbane from ever taking one drop of oil out of that reef."

"Aaaaaaaahhhhh. I *got* it! Mogg-niff-i-cent! You screwed the Japanese outta the erl on the reef *except they didn't actually get screwed outta it*—they didn't lose anything because nobody, not anybody, will be able to get that erl."

"That's the plan. I am asking you to run that campaign for me. And I am asking you to accept a fee of fifty thousand dollars for doing it."

"I arreddy made three twenty-five outta you and your father-in-law."

"Different work entirely. This is a separate fee for separate work."

"I am in."

When Keifetz left, the Captain telephoned the bridge and asked it to send him Von Tytell, the radio officer.

Martin von Tytell had been Von Kluge's *Nachrichtenfuehrer* at Wehrmacht headquarters in St. Germain where Von Kluge was Commander of the Armies of the West. Tytell had survived the war, as well as Hitler's determination to murder any officer suspected of being a part of the assassination attempt in Rastenburg because every survivor vouched for him. They had marveled over his technical feats with all communications between Paris and Rastenburg during the sixty hours before Hitler escaped the bomb. When the signal had come in that his opposite number among the plotters at Rastenburg had failed to cut off Hitler's headquarters from the outside world and that Goebbels had sent in the *Wachbattalion Grossdeutschland* to capture the Army conspirators' headquarters at the Bendlerstrasse in Berlin, General von Tytell had merely driven due west through the Allied lines in Von Kluge's staff Mercedes and had surrendered himself.

He was sixty-eight years old aboard the *Perfection;* quite plump, with a white moustache, and a white hospital orderly's knee-length coat. He was not capable of being impressed by anything, having been under discipline since he had entered the German Army's schools when he was nine years old. Other boys intended for the Army were educated at normal grammar schools, but Von Seeckt had advised Von Tytell's father, a colonel-general, that the *Kadettenanstalt* background would be ever so much more old school tie and productive of more rapid promotion.

Von Tytell greeted the Captain amiably. The two men sat down. The Captain offered him a glass, a bottle of schnapps, and a box of cigars. Tytell returned the glass and said he would take the rest along with him for when he was ashore.

"What do you know about communications from and to geosynchronous satellites, General Von Tytell?" the Captain asked.

"Communications are total from geosynchronous satellites, sir. It is both a heroic and a fearful thing—mostly fearful. It can spread education by great teachers upon television screens throughout every area of the world where education might never have penetrated. We are told. Unfortunately, like television, it probably will not be asked to do so. But, if it is, that same education will be supervised by governments which will use it for total surveillance of all people, so it is hard to say whether geosynchronous satellites are what you might call a cultural advance. The last modern communications implement ever to be shared freely with the people was the typewriter, so I continue to make a study of that."

"Are you saying they can deliver surveillance from twenty-two thousand miles in space?"

Tytell shrugged his massive shoulders. "They can do high-resolution photography from there, sir. The state of the art is progressing further every day. Photoanalysis is the fastest growing division of the entire world intelligence community. It accounts for more than thirty-one percent of this year's staff increases in the National Security Agency alone."

"One will have to remain indoors."

"So far. But not for much longer. Soon no one will escape those lenses unless they live in a submarine that has burrowed a few miles under the Marianas Trench and keep their hats on."

"Have you heard anything about messages from individual telephones on Earth being transmitted by satellite to other individual telephones?"

"Of course."

"When?"

"When? Now. Why not? If someone has the money, such as the security arm of a government that has great technology— the sort that got the satellites up there in the first place—it must be done already and already be used for top secret communication. Perhaps they would need boosters at the beginning, but no cables or lines."

"How?"

"There are passive reflectors and active repeaters. Forget the reflectors. The repeaters can store messages indefinitely, or send messages back to Earth repeatedly and to as many widely separated boosters as are required to disseminate the messages to different parts of the world. They also amplify the strength of the signals, which may be weak when they reach the satellite. The satellites amplify from measurements of one billion hertz."

"What is a hertz?"

"What do you care? All you have to know is that the signal arrives at the satellite with almost no power but with waves at frequencies of up to six and a half billion hertz each second which allows the satellite to carry a gigantic volume of simultaneous traffic."

"But how does the satellite know which messages are going to be carried at what frequencies?"

"Each user will have a number. The number is an assigned frequency as far as the satellite knows. That is how commercial radio works. It is an extremely beautiful system, Captain. It carries the human voice, or any of the computers' forms of address, or television images all programmed with operational instructions by telemetry. The Earth signal is received in a repeater module, which is filled with diplexers, multipliers, filters, limiters, amplifiers, and mixers. It also holds decoders and encoders for telemetry instructions."

"Where does the power come from?"

"The solar cells. They are in panels that extend from the satellite's body. They collect energy from the sun and the energy is converted into electrical power. Then, just as its power is fading away, the booster on Earth sends it off again at full power to the individual special telephone. By now, the Earthside booster stations are already obsolete. I would bet on that. Nimbus 3 and several other new military satellites carry their own nuclear energy systems with half-lives of 8000 years. I would say Nimbus 3 is what has made your special individual satellite telephone a reality, not just a theory."

"Then if a man is in trouble with a highest government agency—is there no place to hide?"

"As of now there is no place to hide. No matter where you attempt to go, the eye in the sky will find you. But, of course, you may be sure eleven governments and some of the very wealthy organized international crime organizations are working on systems to block the power of such satellites." He grinned.

20

Commander Fujikawa looked biliously across the expanse of his immense, bare desk at Mr. Ikeda who was standing, not quite at military attention, on the carpet directly in front of him. Commander Fujikawa had gotten little sleep since he had been told that his old friend, his own choice to execute his father's master plan, had absconded, failed, betrayed, and cheated. He was having difficulty matching the jagged pieces of the puzzle his friend had become, still unable to believe that the man whose interests he had proven to have been his own interests could have done such things to him and his family.

His father was in deepest mourning for Shunga-san, but each day brought his return nearer. Each hour gone meant that very much sooner he was going to have to face his father with the irreparable loss of an immense oil field with estimated yields of more than three billion dollars which should, right now, have been the property of Fujikawa Industries and Japan but which, because of a son's bad judgment, a foreigner had been permitted to throw away.

Mr. Ikeda had requested this interview. The Commander knew what he was about to hear and yet could find no honorable way to deflect Mr. Ikeda from his purpose.

Mr. Ikeda was about to tell him that he had come, most respectfully, to report that, because of his loyalty to the

Fujikawa family, he was about to commit suicide. But the Commander knew that Mr. Ikeda must be deflected. No one else possessed his incentive to run the betrayer to the ground and to exact payment for what he had done. He looked up slowly at Mr. Ikeda, took a deep breath, and nodded that Mr. Ikeda might speak.

"Tonight I shall perform *seppuku*," Mr. Ikeda stated with dignity. "My white *kendo* costume has come back from the laundry. Everything will be done in the manner of *Chushingura*, except that I have devised an exceptional self-humiliation to add to the ceremony. A foreigner, my Australian assistant, Bergquist, will decapitate me after I have incised my abdomen to signify that I had betrayed your family to another foreigner by not protecting them from him. The *hara-kiri* will be entirely correct. A large *kakemono* will be displayed on the wall directly behind and above me containing one word, *SINCERITY*, in very large *kanji*."

"I certainly do not dispute your right to kill yourself, Mr. Ikeda," the Commander said grimly. "Please understand that I am entirely in favor of the whole idea. However, so many of your responsibilities still hang like swords over our heads and our honor. I know these would be my father's thoughts."

"I have failed in all of my responsibilities to your family."

"What of the family's responsibilities to our country? To prevent even more shame to our house your must accept eagerly the ancient, feudal requirements due to my father. He will be isolated in mourning for yet more time by his own wish. I do not intend to tell him what has happened—what has been done to us by the betrayer—until he returns. In the time we have, as a most faithful servant of my father's, you can achieve the execution of this *gaijin*. I say to you that your duty is clear: First, you must bring the head of this foreign dog to my father. After that, of course, you may kill yourself."

"I am grateful that you have shown me my responsibility. I will remember your kindness."

"How will you proceed?"

"My Australian visa is in order. Bergquist waits in Sydney. I will fly there within the hour. On Sunday, the betrayer's wife will be waiting for him in Sydney harbor. When he comes for her, we will take him."

"Will you need Van Hooch and Susski?"

"No."

"All right. Now—I have a very sturdy leather hatbox which I picked up for only eight pounds sterling—used, of course—at Mossbros in London. Did you know that the whipmakers to the Queen wanted *ninety-five* pounds for a new leather hatbox and that Lock, merely the best hatter, didn't sell leather hatboxes at all?"

"I have never been to London, my Lord."

"Of course you haven't. But don't you think it was rather enterprising of me to poke around the city until I found this perfectly serviceable, sturdy, used leather hatbox?"

"Indeed, yes, my Lord."

"Well! At any rate, I want you to bring the foreign dog's head back to my father in that hatbox. Best to telephone or cable your arrival so that we may have the right, cooperative customs man on duty to inspect your luggage at the airport when you return."

"I know just the man."

"Then our position is clear? You do know that I appreciate your willingness to commit *seppuku* and, when you bring back the betrayer's head, I will show that appreciation by offering to undertake your ritual decapitation myself, if only to advance the best principles of *Bunbu-Ryodo*. I mean, we do have the need to ritualize the warrior and cultural arts, don't we? But I put it to you that, if you return with the traitor's head, perhaps my father will not expect you to kill yourself. Do you see the line I've taken?"

"Apologies, my Lord, but I have been your father's servant since before you were born. I will only irritate him if he has to *order* my suicide. He respects me. He knows that I deplore what has happened almost as much as he will deplore it and he will expect me to know my duty. I appreciate your tact, but we both know there can be no other way. Two duties remain to me: to bring back the foreign dog's head, then *seppuku.*"

"Good show," the Commander said, rising. "Have a safe journey."

Mr. Ikeda bowed.

Commander Fujikawa bowed.

Mr. Ikeda bowed.

Commander Fukikawa bowed.

Mr. Ikeda bowed.

"Edge toward the door, dammit!" the Commander snarled, bowing.

The Commander had expected himself to be hurt and outraged when told of Captain Huntington's perfidy, but he was astonished that his reactions were so mixed when he learned that the enormous oil leases had been grabbed by an independent American oil operator named John Jackson. He had undergone reflexive motions of having his Brisbane attorneys seek injunctions against Jackson but, more than ever, he was haunted by the same nagging hunch he had held to throughout disputes of the matter with his father, that no one, not in his lifetime at least, would ever take oil out of the Great Barrier Reef. He was astounded to find that, all of a sudden, because of this John Jackson, his conviction was that Fujikawa & Company had not lost three billion dollars: No one, no matter who, would ever be able to get at that oil.

Not that he did not want vengeance upon Huntington. He wanted it bitterly, but not in his father's way. He considered himself to be more subtle than his father's breed. He would not kill because of the loss of face or fortune. But he intended to take away everything that Huntington possessed this side of death. He was going to sue, hound, and shame Huntington through every known process and means. He was going to alienate the betrayer from his wife, her family, his mistress, his cook, and his gambling until they could no longer so much as look upon him or he upon them. He would hound this foreign dog until he became his own executioner.

He felt certain that Mr. Ikeda would not be able to find Huntington before Baron Fujikawa emerged from mourning to demand an accounting. His father would still command that Huntington's head be brought to him. His father would see it as dishonor if his son were to resort to such foreign things as courts, public relations counsels, private detectives, fixers, trackers, and suborners in employing the subtle modern methods of cruelly efficient industrialized disgrace as it had been developed to such exquisitely fine points by the complex agencies of Western government where the most effective terrorists were always inside the establishments. His father's way was the kind, old-fashioned way, but Huntington did not deserve his father's compassion.

However, as long as his father lived, the Commander would have to wait for his revenge, just as he had waited so long and so patiently to become the head of the House of Fujikawa. It was even possible, he thought, that his father could not live forever. He was ninety-six years old now, so he could not have more than fifteen years of active service left in him. Despite his enormous strength time would take its toll and his father would retire from the company. But then, as soon as he assumed power, the Commander would set the resources of the vast underworld of the industrial mind into the interstices of the lives of Huntington and everyone dear to him. Until they had all been ground into dust, Commander Fujikawa could not rest.

If, by some unlikely chance, Mr. Ikeda did bring back the betrayer's head, he would wait for his father's death, *then* he would carry out his vengeance upon Huntington's wife and her family, Huntington's mistress, and his cook. His name had been tainted. He would extract justice from those inscrutable Occidentals.

21

Two days after Colin left her at the Great Northern Hotel, when she had rested enough to find strength to pack her saxophone and still aching with the enormous pleasure he had given her, Yvonne Bonnette moved about the hotel bedroom in slow motion, daydreaming about the only man in the world. She wanted nothing more than what she had. She knew, in wondrous ecstasy, that she had more than anyone else and certainly more than that rich bitch he had married. How she *detested* overrich insensitive women! It was acceptable anywhere to be rich up to a point, as she was, but two million dollars should be enough for anyone. And she was certain Colin loved her all the more because she believed that.

When she finished packing, moving at the speed of a leaf floating across a tranquil pond on a windless day, she rummaged an address book out of her handbag and telephoned her twin sister in Adelaide.

They had once been identical twins. At sixteen, Claire had reigned over the Band Wagram at the Etoile as Queen of the Bidets, but she had gone on to hard drugs, petty crime, harder crime, then into rather vicious sorts of women. She left France ahead of the police. She lived hard in Cairo, Bombay, and in Penang until now, at twenty-four, she was sad, sagging, and changed. The sisters had come to resemble each other in the way the past resembles the present; vaguely, impatiently, and with no true registration. Claire was used. Men who preferred chippies and hard women and cruel women, and who therefore hated women, liked to look at her. Claire was a colonial power operating inside her own mind and body; resident there to exploit both; determined to drain the best from herself for the most fleeting profit until, at last, with greatest relief she could be done with it.

Yvonne loved her sister with fierce loyalty. As with everything else, whatever was hers she felt was worth cherishing. Claire loved Yvonne in an abstract but pleasant way. Sometimes, when they were apart, she felt sexual urgings toward Yvonne in the manner that politicians feel an enormous sexual pull toward mirrors. Mostly Claire thought about herself and what the world was doing to her. Her emotions marched across her skin. She was sick, hooked, and alone. When she answered the telephone, she was elated to hear Yvonne's voice.

"Yvonne! My darling! Where are you? How is it that you are calling me? Oh!! How delicious! How it jumps me out of myself into bliss just to hear you. Is something wrong? Are you in trouble? Why do you call me from across the world in London?"

"I am in Australia, Claire."

"Oh! Where? Why did you come to Australia? Do you mean you came all the way to Australia to see me? My God! Are you in Adelaide?"

"I am in Cairns, Claire. Cairns is in Queensland."

"So far away! You might as well be in London!"

"No, no! There are many planes, and I will fly to see you."

Claire began to weep. "You must come, but you must not look at me. I have been so ill. I have had so much trouble. I need you, Yvonne. I need you to make me well again. My wife—" she began to sob desperately. "My wife died nine days ago." As Claire wept, Yvonne began to weep, and she told her sister to restore herself to calmness, that she would be there very soon.

22

Bitsy arrived at the Royal Yacht Club on Sydney's great harbor at 9:15 Sunday morning with twenty-three pieces of luggage, which were piled up on the pier as her totem to greet the arrival of the *Perfection* as she steamed through the Heads, which separated the harbor from the South Pacific. At 9:50 she asked for a chair. At 10:12 she decided the sun was altogether too hot. She went into the clubhouse and sat upon a sheltered balcony where she could watch the sea. At 1:23 PM she had lunch at that table. At 3:02 a tall, blond, powerfully-built male wearing seaman's clothes approached her, touching his forelock to insure correctitude.

"Ma'am? I am Sven Bergquist? From the *Perfection?*"

She went white. "What has happened? Has anything happened to my husband? Has there been an accident?"

"Nothing bad, ma'am. Ship hit a reef? Captain broke his leg?"

"Oh, my *God!*"

"It's just a broken leg, ma'am? But he can't be moved?"

"But where's the *Perfection?*"

"It hit a reef? We took the Captain off? He's in a house about eighteen miles up the coast right now?"

"Take me to him at once!"

Bitsy was on her feet, striding to an exit. Bergquist followed close beside her. "Mr. Ikeda, the Fujikawa company director, is waiting in his car? To take you to Captain Huntington?"

"How very nice of him."

They walked rapidly to a large black limousine. Bergquist introduced her to Mr. Ikeda who was courtly about assisting her into the interior of the car. Bergquist drove.

"You are not to worry, Mrs. Huntington," Mr. Ikeda said reassuringly as the car bowled along. "It is only a snapped ankle bone. We have flown in the best ski surgeon in Australia to look at that ankle and to set it painlessly and properly. We are going to skirt the harbor out to Bondi beach, then head north along the coast to the Captain."

"I cannot tell you how much I appreciate this, Mr. Ikeda. And how much my father will state that he appreciates it when he speaks with Baron Fujikawa."

They drove through the maritime landscape until it showed fewer and fewer dwellings. After fifty minutes of driving they turned away from the ocean road into a dirt lane which the car followed for a mile to a small blurred-looking brown farm house. Mr. Ikeda helped Bitsy out of the car. Bergquist followed them into the house, Bitsy striding forward with anxiety. Inside the house Bergquist locked the door.

"Where is he?" Bitsy asked.

"That is why you are here, Mrs. Huntington. Either you will tell us where he is hiding or, when we announce that you are being held for ransom and threatened with violent death, he will appear from wherever he is and we will take him."

"*Take* him? Violent *death*?" She was confused for a moment at the storm of unexpected words. "Do you mean my husband is not here? Are you saying I am *kid*napped? Are you out of your wily Oriental mind, Mr. Ikeda? Do you know who my father, my uncles, and my cousins are? For one thing we are very nearly co-owners of Fujikawa & Company. For another you'll be totaled by every American executive agency there is —from the White House to the Pentagon to the CIA—if you either touch me or attempt to detain me. Explain this outrage and be quick about it! You have undoubtedly caused me to miss my husband at Sydney and caused him every sort of unnecessary alarm. Speak up, damn you!"

Bergquist had the very good sense to be frightened blue. Mr. Ikeda was imperturbable. "Your husband has disappeared with your yacht, with our three hundred and fifty thousand Australian dollars, and he has utterly betrayed the trust of Baron Fujikawa by deliberately and maliciously losing and forfeiting for Fujikawa Industries and for Japan, three billion dollars' worth of oil."

"How could anyone lose three billion dollars' worth of oil?" Bitsy asked disdainfully. "Who won it from him?"

"He lost it by failing to appear at Brisbane—the only job he was employed to do—to take up options on oil leases."

"Well! That's the way the oil business is, isn't it, Mr. Ikeda? My family and I were *close* friends of Faisal's and really intimate *family* friends of the Shah's but they went right ahead and nationalized our oil just the same, as if good faith didn't exist. Oh, they paid us for what they took, but it isn't the same thing, is it?"

"Mrs. Huntington! Where is your husband!"

"I would say that he is waiting for me at the Royal Yacht Club in Sydney."

"My people are watching the Royal Yacht Club. We have a telephone in the car. There are telephones in this house."

"Then there is nothing I can do to help you."

"You will help us! We have good reason to believe that your husband acted as agent for this independent oil operator, John Jackson."

"Oh, nonsense. We have shot ducks and geese with John Jackson in south Texas, but I'll bet you we haven't done as much as two million dollars' worth of business with him."

"Very well. You leave me no choice. I must now apply very unpleasant devices to force you to tell me what I must know."

"My God, Mr. Ikeda! You aren't threatening me, are you?"

Bergquist was smoking a bent pipe at her elbow, and a

smelly pipe it was. His back was to her as he looked out the window, preoccupied with worry. Daddy had insisted that she carry a lead-weighted purse ever since she had been a schoolgirl, but she had never had cause to use it. It had been designed as a weapon by CIA operations people so she smashed it into the back of Bergquist's head then kicked Mr. Ikeda in the balls with enormous authority. When he was down screaming, to ease the pain she whacked him on the back of the head with the purse, took the car keys and the house keys from Bergquist's pocket, stepped over the bodies and went out to the car, locking the house door behind her.

"Oh, you rotten son-of-a-bitch, Colin!" she yelled toward the blue sky. "You despicable shit of shits! Oh, you miserable cur! WHERE ARE YOU?" she screamed.

She drove the limousine back to Sydney, then abandoned it in front of the Wentworth. She stamped upstairs and called James D. Marxuach, CIA Chief of Base, Sydney, and told him to get her luggage back from the pier at the yacht club and to hire bodyguards to be with her around the clock while she was in Australia. Then she called Daddy on the satellite phone. He was with Dr. Kissinger in Oslo. She held her stomach with her forearms and rocked back and forth, her face contorted with rage. How *could* Colin have set John Jackson up for such a killing when he *knew* how Daddy felt about deals of that size?

She had to reroute the call through the geosynchronous satellite twenty-two thousand, three hundred miles over the Seychelles, then she reached Daddy aboard Dr. Kissinger's big, blue Boeing en route to Kenya. She held nothing back about what Colin had done. And what Colin had done unmanned Daddy much more than the news that she had been kidnapped and threatened with torture by Orientals. "But—but—" This was *Daddy* trying to speak. He was actually unable to form thoughts or words because of the catastrophe. She could not remember anything even remotely like it happening to him before.

Suddenly she became terribly frightened for her husband.

Daddy was ranting and not making any sense. "John Jackson?" he yelled into the phone. "John Jackson is not only a *youth* but he is an *independent*! John Jackson doesn't have ten million dollars to his name! This is unforgivable, Bitsy. He could have brought the deal to me yet he gave it to John Jackson! We cannot recognize anyone who would do that to the family. You must divorce him without a day's delay."

"Listen, Daddy," Bitsy said with chilled steel in her voice, "I didn't call you to get any goddam advice about a goddam divorce. I want to nail this son-of-a-bitch and turn him over to the Japanese."

"The Japanese? What Japanese?"

"Fujikawa and Company."

"*Whaaaaaaaat?* Do you mean the company he screwed out of three billion dollars' worth of oil is Fujikawa? I have owned forty-seven percent of Fujikawa since the day I followed MacArthur into Tokyo Bay. Why—oh, my God!—this is awful, I tell you this is hor*ren*dous! Well! Ho, ho! Well, I see! Now we really do have to *deal* with that Limey bastard!"

"You keep out of this, Daddy! You sound to me like you'll do something we'll all regret. Colin is mine. This is my personal business. You just authorize James D. Marxuach at the Sydney base to flush Colin out for me and I'll take it from there."

23

After days of evasive action which the Captain knew would
have no meaning if the satellites had been programmed to find
him, it was a clear, cool, spring morning as the *Perfection* sailed
through the west side of Bass Strait for Adelaide. The Captain,
under the awning at the taffrail, told Francohogar he was ready
for what might be the last superlative meal of his life.

"Please, sir. Don't joke."

"It's not inevitable, but I am in rather desperate trouble."

"Gambling, sir?"

"Yes. And in order to defend myself, it was necessary that
I sell this yacht. It is hard to imagine how things could be
worse. But there is one way you can keep me alive and out of
prison."

"Command me, sir."

"Tomorrow—in Adelaide—I will give you twenty-five thousand dollars. That will provide an air ticket to Tokyo and pay
your expenses."

"Tokyo?"

"The rest of the money will get you back to France when the
time comes. And—if anything horrid happens to me—I have
made arrangements for you to be paid a hundred and fifty
thousand dollars so that you may open a restaurant if you
should choose to do that."

"How can I help you, sir?"

"You see, I have rather badly offended the Fujikawa family. So, to survive, I must have steady information about the plans they may have for me. Did your brother make you a copy of that special telephone of Madame's?"

"Yes. And I thank you. And it has brought much pleasure and comfort to my mother. I call her every Sunday night and, the first time I called her—this seems almost impossible—I talked to Dr. Kissinger and he kept insisting that I was Monsieur Chaban-Delmas."

"Pack that telephone. Go to Commander Fujikawa and offer your services to his father. Tell him I stranded you in Australia and convince him of your bitterness against me."

"I will convince him."

"As you overhear any information about me—using your copy of Madame's special telephone—please call Keifetz at eleven o'clock every night. His number is 888. He will be in Sydney and he will pass the information on to me when it is safe for me to call him."

24

It took Daddy almost two days to get through to James D. Marxuach, Chief of Base, Sydney. He had to use the ordinary Signal Corps telephone system and he was with Dr. Kissinger somewhere in the Mekong Delta in Laos. When he had Marxuach on the phone, he made sure that it was a safe phone by having Marxuach have his telephone lines swept then and there. Daddy represented more rank to James Marxuach than he had ever imagined might breathe down upon him. Marxuach stood at attention as he took the call, a blocky man whose body resembled the joined coffins of two short, wide, consenting adults.

"Entirely safe, sir," Marxuach said.

"I want you to use every facility to find a man and I don't want the Chief of Station, Canberra, to know anything about it. MacLeish is queasy about killing."

"Killing, sir?"

"I want this man—when you find him—to be eliminated with extreme prejudice."

"What does that mean, sir?"

"Dammit, Marxuach! Look it up in your phrase book."

"Acknowledged, sir."

"Has my daughter called you?"

"Yes, sir."

"This is a sealed operation, Marxuach. She is not to know anything about it."

"No, sir." As they spoke he leafed through *Fogelson's Complete CIA Phrase Book* and found the meaning of "to eliminate with extreme prejudice." He felt sick to his stomach. Since his first six weeks of training, thirteen years before, he had never handled a weapon.

"This is the name," the voice in the telephone continued. "Captain Colin Huntington, Royal Navy, retired. My daughter will have a picture of him."

"Your daughter? Mrs. Colin Huntington, sir?"

"That's your man."

Marxuach shuddered. "I will nail him, sir," he said weakly. Daddy hung up. Marxuach left his private office. "I'll be with a Mrs. Huntington at the Wentworth, Miss Neill," he said as he went out the door. "Then I'm going to take a haircut."

He got one photograph of Captain Huntington from his wife. The picture showed the Captain as of nine years before, dressed in a tropical white naval uniform, wearing many rows of decorations, with scrambled eggs across the visor of his hat. Mrs. Huntington said her husband had absconded with her yacht and that she would offer a five-thousand-dollar reward for his capture. She demanded that the photograph and an official police announcement of the charges and the reward be plastered across every paper published in Australia and throughout all other media. "What kind of people are these?" Marxuach asked himself as he half-ran, half-walked down the hotel corridor to the elevator. "The wife wants him thrown into prison. The father-in-law wants him killed. After thirteen easy, peaceful years in this business, why did I finally have to run into people like these?"

Shortly after dawn, ninety minutes before John Bryson's banker was to arrive aboard the *Perfection,* where it rode at anchor in the outer harbor before the Royal Yacht Squadron, the Captain sent for General von Tytell.

"General, I realize I've asked you all this before but I can't

quite grasp it and I want to go over it again, if I may," he said.
"Can they *really* do high-resolution photography from geosynchronous satellites?"

"They can take pictures of goldfish in a bowl. If you can
open your mouth wide enough they can show whether you
need dental fillings. Or one person embedded in a dense crowd.
The infrared sensors are so fine that the cameras will follow
him by the heat generated by his own body. Oh, yes, my dear
sir! The tactical command decisions will be made from easy
chairs thousands of miles from land and sea battles while they
happen over hundreds of square miles of battle sectors. The
cameras hang up there in space, watching us, and it proves one
thing to me."

"What?"

"It proves everyone will soon be paranoiac."

The banker's launch drew up at the *Perfection*'s starboard
ladder. It was 9:01 AM. Banking hours had begun. The banker,
Harvey Zendt, came aboard under a large, floppy Panama hat
which had flapping black ribbons like a bishop's infulae.

The transfer papers were duly signed and witnessed. Mr.
Zendt handed over a cashier's check in the amount of Australian $1,455,000. The Captain asked if he and his two com-
panions might ride ashore with Mr. Zendt so that the check
might be cashed at Mr. Zendt's bank. He bade Captain Pappadakis and the ship's officers farewell and descended to the
launch with one steel-reinforced brief case chained and locked
to his wrist, and the walnut case containing the two satellite
phones in his other hand. Ashore, they transferred to Zendt's
Holden Statesman Caprice and rode the twelve miles into
downtown Adelaide, the Captain chatting pleasantly and easily about his fond memories of Australia.

Downtown Adelaide was laid out as a square grid with four
tree-filled plazas placed equidistantly within the grid, all of the
area surrounded by 1700 acres of parkland to serve a population of 950,000. As the car parked in front of the bank in King
William Street, the Captain, as he stepped out of it, was con-

vinced the police would take them all under arrest. He sweated lightly. Keifetz trembled so badly that Francohogar had to take his suitcase. It took forty minutes for Mr. Zendt to get the cash together. The Captain decided that his picture could not have appeared in the morning newspapers. The money was distributed without comment or explanation across Zendt's desk. Twenty-five thousand dollars went to Francohogar with an envelope containing a cashier's check for $425,000 made out to Ito Fujikawa to repay both the advance on the Captain's salary and the money intended for the oil leases. Keifetz took $800,000 in cash, which went into his steel reinforced briefcase, which was manacled to his wrist. Captain Huntington packed $255,-000 into his case. They all shook hands briskly with the dazed Mr. Zendt and left the bank.

Captain Huntington led them to Paxton's, inside Ayers House, so that he could savor the melancholy of so many shades of purple while they sat on steamer chairs and enjoyed the restaurant's version of oysters Mornay with glasses of Roland Flat Spaetlese Frontingnan. "This is a very chic introduction to Australia," Francohogar said. "This wine is splendid."

From Paxton's they went to the very formal, very elegant, and very expensive restaurant within Ayers House, decorated in red from floor to ceiling, which lifted the Captain's spirits; the tables were set with beautiful crystal and china. They ate a lunch prepared with assured pyrotechnics while Captain Huntington explained what had to be done.

"I am greatly surprised," he said, "that neither my wife nor the Japanese have not already notified the Australian police and the press that I am missing—with the *Perfection*—but I cannot have more than one or two hours of grace. Juan, you will be out of the country in a few hours and, since no one is looking for you, will you find some truck rental agency in a telephone directory and hire us a panel truck? I have to have a place to sleep until I can organize my retreat. They will certainly soon be in full hue and cry."

Francohogar left. The Captain asked Keifetz to buy for him

two sets of coveralls, a can of axle grease, a razor, scissors, an aerosol can of foam, socks and underwear, a comb, toothbrush and toothpaste, and the cheapest sort of cardboard suitcase he could find. Then the Captain went to find a telephone. He dialed, waited, and spoke. "Miss Claire Bonnette, please," he said in French.

"I am Bonnette." It was a dulled voice.

"This is Colin Huntington. I am a friend of your sister's from London."

"Ah, yes. How is my sister?"

"Quite well. She said I might call you about some opal business I have in mind."

"I am ill."

"It could be very profitable."

"I want to help you if you are my sister's friend. Please call me again in one hour. I will do my best to feel better."

25

Captain Colin Huntington's photograph ran across four columns of the front pages of the early afternoon editions of major Australian newspapers under the banner headline: HAVE YOU SEEN THIS MAN? The identical picture was flashed across television screens at fifteen-minute intervals. Within twenty minutes, a bank secretary, two tellers, and a bootblack had rushed copies of the newspaper to Mr. Zendt's desk in the Adelaide bank, each claiming the reward. Mr. Zendt immediately telephoned the police, revealing that Captain Huntington had sold his yacht to an anonymous client of the bank for $5,500,000. He refused to reveal the name of the buyer, explaining that he had been specifically enjoined from so doing under the terms of the transaction as outlined by the buyer. The police insistence and what he considered their extreme rudeness so offended his sense of citizen cooperation that he deliberately did not mention the other bank transactions which he had undertaken for Captain Huntington that morning. He clung tenaciously to that position until he read in the evening newspaper that Fujikawa & Company had posted an additional reward of $25,000 and had charged Captain Huntington with embezzlement and fraud. With such a good shot at getting some of the Fujikawa business to his bank as well as buying perhaps a fur coat for his wife, Little Rita, he rushed in with all information to claim the total reward of' $30,000.

The police announced that Captain Huntington had been definitely placed within the Greater Adelaide area. This was confirmed through the police by James D. Marxuach, of the Central Intelligence Agency of the United States of America, at the iron insistence of Mrs. Huntington.

Yvonne Bonnette read the front page of *The Advertiser* which a previous passenger had left on the seat of the taxi she hailed at the Adelaide airport. She became greatly alarmed. She was distraught when she entered her sister's small house in Stanley Street, about a mile and a half northeast of the center of town. She was alarmed about Colin but she gasped with fright when she saw her sister.

Claire didn't look like her twin anymore. She looked like her ghost. "I know," Claire said humbly. "I am dying."

"How do you know that?" Yvonne said sharply. "I don't want any medical opinions from you, I want them from a doctor in a hospital."

Claire threw herself into Yvonne's arms, sobbing. "Don't be cross with me, Yvonne, darling, please. Don't make me go to a hospital. It would kill me. That would really kill me." Yvonne half-carried her into the bedroom and propped her up on the large bed. There was a huge cabinet photograph of a nondescript-looking black woman beside the bed. Its frame was covered with black crepe.

"Heroin is killing you," Yvonne said. The air in the room was as fetid as if a flock of birds had flown down the chimney to die. The smell of death and doom made her think of Colin again. The sisters sat on the edge of the bed, clinging to each other damply.

"I only look this way for the moment," Claire said. "It doesn't mean anything. I will take something now and I am always careful not to overdose." To lose that subject quickly she said, "Your friend called. The man from London."

Yvonne gripped her fiercely. "What did he say?"

"He wants to come here."

"Why?"

"To talk opal."

"What did you tell him?"

"To call back. I will take my medicine and I will feel better and I will be able to talk to him."

"Claire, hear me. This man is the most important thing in my life. Eh?"

"I understand."

"He needs help because he is on the run. It is in the newspapers."

"It isn't good to get mixed up with people like that, believe me."

"Are you going to help us?"

Claire looked as if she were not capable of helping the most sure-footed Boy Scout across a street. She fell back upon the pillow, haggard.

"If I try to help him he will refuse," Yvonne said. "He will explain gently that it would be a waste to have two babes in the woods running ahead of the police instead of one. He will not allow me near danger."

"You can be me," Claire said hollowly. "He knows I am your twin sister?"

"Yes, but—"

"All right. Tell him to come here when he calls again." It was hard for Claire to talk. "Let him ask you, thinking you are me, all the questions he can think of about the *milieu*, then tell him you have to think about it. You tell him you are me and he will believe it."

"Oh, thank you, Claire."

"Hide him in my cellar. You can get it ready for him with books and food and a record player. Then you tell me what he has asked and I will tell you how to run it. You will be me. *C'est bizarre ça, hein?*" A bad stomach cramp hit her and she vomited feebly on the carpet beside the bed.

Francohogar drove the rented panel truck away from Ayers House with an Adelaide street map on the seat beside him. The Captain and Keifetz sat on the floor of the back of the truck. "I will be heading north by nightfall," he told them. "As soon as you drop me in front of the house in Stanley Street, find separate taxis and get out to the airport. Keifetz—be sure you check into the Menzies Hotel in Sydney. My wife stays at the Wentworth and with the way my luck is running she could be in the room next to yours if you go to that hotel." He put them through a drill three times on how to operate Daddy's satellite telephone, giving one half of his matched pair, and the case, to Keifetz.

"Just don't lose any time," he told Keifetz. "Tomorrow morning camp on the doorstep of the Australian Conservation Society until they come to work. You've got to get a deafening campaign going. Concentrate on getting not less than a million signatures on that petition. I'll call you every third night, when I can. In two days, Juan will be in position in Tokyo."

"I got it."

"Hire a detective agency and see if you can frame Mr. Ikeda. If you find him, turn him in to the Immigration authorities instantly for white slavery. Read every newspaper you can find and remember what they are reporting about me."

"Where are you going?" Francohogar asked anxiously over his shoulder.

"Best you don't know."

"Always remember," Keifetz said, "you got to have confidence. You are gonna win, I can feel it. But smart is better than lucky and you got some pretty lousy odds against you."

The panel truck stopped in front of Claire Bonnette's house.

26

Bitsy met Lord Clogg and Dr. Francis A. O'Connell, Jr., as they came down the ramp of the flight from London to Melbourne. Inside the air terminal they were joined by a tall figure who was as formidably bewhiskered as Harry Flashman. He carried three attaché cases. He greeted Lord Clogg.

"Mrs. Huntington, may I present your Australian solicitor, Mr. Harold Harris?"

"I am Lord Harris now."

"Lord Harris is also the head of the Australian Bar Association."

Lord Harris beckoned to a round, mysterious-looking man in the background. "This is Professor Perman, so recently one of our most valued High Court justices." Justice Perman swanned forward. Bitsy cut the greetings short.

"I have chartered a jet from Ansett," she said, taking charge. "We will fly directly to Adelaide. Follow me." She strode ahead of them, flanked by two burly bodyguards whom James D. Marxuach had assembled. Lord Clogg trotted up to reach her side. "I say, Dr. O'Connell is altogether warped by the horrendous jet lag. It would be good if he could get some rest."

"What does it matter?" Bitsy snarled. "He never speaks anyway. How did a man who has never been heard to speak get such a legal reputation?"

"You see, he doesn't speak because he is always so terribly warped from the constant jet travel he does. He has such an inter*national* law practice. Did you know he represented General Amin in that last divorce? I mean to say, around the world thrice a month is nothing for Dr. O'Connell. Hence he is too exhausted to speak."

"Oh, shit! Let him nap on the flight to Adelaide."

"What will our strategy be?"

"We are here to lynch Colin Huntington and you will all be expected to convince the Premier of South Australia just how vitally important that is."

The gleaming white government limousines arranged by Lord Harris dislodged them at the State Administration Building in Victoria Square, Adelaide. Both Lord Harris and Lord Clogg during the last few miles of the flight had at last been able to get Dr. O'Connell awake. They were all passed through two security guards, sent across the carpeted foyer to express elevators that took them to the eleventh floor, Bitsy at the center of a cortege of six men. Dr. O'Connell made the mental notes that he would soon jot down and pass to Lord Clogg, mainly: "Where is the men's facility?" and other suggestions. For thirty years he had refused to speak recklessly because speaking reduced the range of his options. Speech was dangerous. It was said that his greetings to his family each morning took the form of a written brief. "Torts are forts," he said to his wife on their wedding night forty-one years ago, after which he lapsed into silence.

The procession flowed like an expensive river into the *pinus radiata*-lined office of the Premier. Bitsy tolerated few preliminaries. She pounded on the glass top of the Premier's desk with her fist and cried out, "I demand the immediate arrest of my husband. I want him charged with piracy, grand fraud, and grand larceny. He stole my father's yacht and sold it to a man no respectable person would be found dead with. I want that yacht impounded where it floats right now off Torrens Island.

I want everyone connected with such a foul transaction put under arrest and held behind bars. I want the person or persons who abetted the escape of my husband to be charged with criminal conspiracy and I demand that the forces of the Australian nation and the entire police community of this state be martialed into action instantly to drag that man off to a prison cell where his offenses against the civilized community dictate that he be held in chains."

"Seems like a reasonable enough, offhand request," the Premier said. "Where is your husband now?"

"That is *precisely* the question that my father, a key figure in the present American administration and the past six administrations, a career senior officer of the Department of State; my uncle James, Counsel to the President of the United States at the White House; my uncle Peter, a former governor and former United States Senator who is presently International Psychological Stress and Materiel Procurement Adviser to the Secretary of Defense and to the Joint Chiefs of Staff of the United States of America; my Cousin Gary, Assistant Secretary of the Department of Defense; and my Cousin Larry, Assistant Secretary of the Department of the Treasury, will be asking you and the federal government in Canberra twenty-four hours from now if my husband is not apprehended by you and shut up in your worst prison by that time."

Bitsy sat down. The Premier bowed his head slightly to her in appreciation of her performance.

Lord Harris took the floor. "Mr. Premier, my colleagues and I substantiate that which Mrs. Huntington has spoken. Grievous crimes have been committed. A dangerous criminal is at large in this country."

"It is a coincidence that such a case should be made," the Premier said. "Fifteen minutes ago charges which were almost identical were presented against the same man by the Japanese ambassador who flew in from Canberra. He was quite forceful —although, I must say, without such dire threats."

"*No threats!*" Three of the four lawyers cried out at once. Dr.

O'Connell shook his head, staring at the Premier.

"The fact is," the Premier continued, "I have had a rather highly charged call from our own Foreign Minister and, I suppose, within moments I shall be hearing from the Queen. One might say, I am beginning to twig to all this. Therefore, be assured that we shall search for Captain Huntington at every school crossing and in every barber shop. No straight line of investigation shall be left unturned. All available members of the South Australia police—Special Branch, Criminal Investigation, Armed Offenders—will be fanned out in pursuit of him. The Army will turn out the Army Reserve. The Air Force will black the sky with what I have been told are Bell Iroquois helicopters with Lycoming engines—which seems awfully nice of them—and our local system of Civil Defense, which is usually used only at times of flood, bushfire, and national disaster, will join the manhunt. I, of course, shall call out the National Australian Police, which is the equivalent of your FBI, Mrs. Huntington—one American agency, I presume, which employs none of your relatives—and the Australian Security Intelligence Organization, which is the same, in *every* way as your CIA. Measuring everything by the combined efforts of all these fanning out upon our streets, highways, and countryside, I should say we should have Captain Huntington under arrest, tried, and executed within the next twenty minutes."

"Very funny," Bitsy said bitterly. "Please tell your people I will provide the necessary photograph of my husband and will pay the costs for an all-points paper on him."

"Of course you will, my dear," the Premier said.

"And, if necessary, I will increase my offer of a reward to twenty-five thousand American dollars."

"Possibly not necessary," the Premier said. "Your father has already added fifty thousand dollars to the thirty thousand which you and the Fujikawa company have already posted."

27

Claire was sleeping when the doorbell rang. Yvonne had put heavy eyeshadow under her eyes to try to make herself look as depraved as her sister. She had her hair combed straight back, tautly, twisting it into a severe bun at the nape of her neck. She wore one of Claire's slatternly housecoats: hard red with large blue flowers and mustard stains. It was the kind of a costume issued to an actress who plays the failing tubercular prostitute in struggling theatrical road companies, except that her expression showed that she had refused the issuance of the standard heart of gold. She chewed gum. She wore shades. She blanked out her face and opened the door.

"Miss Bonnette?"

"Yes."

"I am Colin Huntington."

"Come in."

They spoke French. He wore the dark blue coveralls. The left side of his face was streaked with mechanics' grease. The false Claire shut the door and slouched across the entrance hall into the living room which had a ghastly odor; dolls with long legs jammed into overstuffed furniture, and a giant photo enlargement of Alice Cooper tacked on the largest wall. There were half-empty coffee cups on the tops of tables and sideboards. Cigarettes had been extinguished in them.

"Do you think my sister looks like me?" Yvonne said harshly.

"Not much, but there is a family resemblance."

"Sit down. What can I do for you?"

"Perhaps you've seen a newspaper this morning?"

"No."

"Television?"

She shook her head; chewed gum.

"They would have told you that I am—uh—in considerable difficulties."

"It happens." She blew a perfect gum bubble. It popped.

"Yvonne said you knew the—uh—the *milieu.*"

The false Claire did not answer.

"She told me you knew the opal business. That is what you can do for me."

"You have money?"

He nodded.

"How much?"

"Enough."

She leaned across to a television set and snapped it on. The news reader was coming to the end of a report on Dr. Kissinger's progress in the Mekong Valley where the Americans were insisting that Mother's Day be installed throughout southeast Asia as a condition of Vietnam entry into the United Nations. At the item which followed, the news reader said: "Rewards have reached a total of eighty thousand dollars for the capture of the retired Royal Navy captain, Colin Huntington, missing sportsman and gourmet, age forty-seven. Until yesterday he deposed in legal papers completed with an Adelaide banker that he was the sole owner of the largest yacht in the world. Charges of piracy, of stealing that yacht, and committing fraud have been brought against him in Adelaide by his wife and her family. The Japanese government, representing the giant Fujikawa Industries, have charged Captain Huntington with embezzlement, grand fraud, grand theft, and absconding. If captured and convicted, Huntington will face sentences of up to ninety-three years in prison.

"Huntington's brother, Lord Glandore, made a touching appeal to his brother on American television from his recreation center in Boise, Idaho. This appeal will be shown here at ten o'clock tonight. It urges Captain Huntington to give himself up."

"The bounder!" Captain Huntington roared, leaping to his feet. "The pushy, slimy, rotten little cad!" He rushed to the television set and forthwith kicked the screen in.

"Eh! What do you think you are doing, you big oaf?" Yvonne shouted at him. "What do you think that costs, a television like that one?"

"I am so sorry," the Captain said. "I lost my head. I will, of course, pay for the damage. I blacked out with rage." He counted out twenty $50 bills and placed them on the mantel.

As Claire, Yvonne walked to a radio which she turned on. A deeply portentous voice exhorted them, ". . . the Australian government, the Japanese government, the American government, the government of South Australia, the resources of the stupendous Fujikawa and Company, and the large rewards offered for Captain Huntington's capture all suggest that there must be far more to these charges than meets the eye." There was an abrupt pause.

"We have just received this bulletin from Reuters: The American banker, John Bryson of Pittsburgh, in the United States of America, has admitted to being the buyer of the yacht, the *Perfection*, from the fugitive, Colin Huntington. He now states that he will bring a suit for slander against Mrs. Huntington and her family for damages in the amount of three million dollars for derogatory statements they have made concerning him, and will sue for an additional ten million dollars if they prevent delivery to him of the yacht. Mr. Bryson added that he will contribute the sum of one hundred dollars to the reward pool for Colin Huntington's capture."

"He will offer it, as always, but he won't pay it," the Captain commented harshly.

"Sssshh!" the false Claire said sharply as the news reader's voice boomed on. ". . . by all available police agencies, by Air Force helicopters, by police and Army tracking dogs, by radar, and by a concentrated alert to all motels, restaurants, and public houses. It is estimated by authorities that Huntington will be behind bars within twenty-four hours. And now for a look at cricket news." Yvonne turned the radio off.

"You'd better have a lot of money, my friend," she said. "No one has been in this much trouble since the American people discovered Richard Nixon."

"The money is here. I'll need forged papers—a driver's license, an Australian passport, identity papers, and a Machinist's Union Card."

"What name?"

He thought. "Dick Richards. You can't get more Australian than that. Get me a little tweed fedora with a narrow brim, sunglasses, plaid slacks, and some hideously garish sport shirts."

"We could shave your head on the top. When the hair fluffs out at the sides it will change the whole look. And I'll try to get you a gold cap for your front tooth."

"No gold cap. Being bald is bad enough. I'll need suntan makeup for the baldness. How long will it all take?"

"At least three days."

He shrugged helplessly.

"Where will you wait?"

"I have a panel truck with a mattress and some food. I'll wait in some parking lot."

"Where is the panel truck?"

"Just outside."

"I'll move it. The police would pick you up the first day like that. You can wait in my cellar."

"What about opal?"

"We can do business."

I will lock him in the cellar and never let him get away, she told herself avidly. She will never see him again. I will lock him in there and he will be only mine. This is what I have always wanted.

28

Mr. Ikeda was able to sit up in bed by the afternoon of the second day. "Who would have thought an American woman with her breeding and privileges could be so vicious?" he asked.

"I don't think it was a woman, Mr. Ikeda," Bergquist said. "No woman can hit like that. I think it happened to be a transvestite—like a plant from Huntington himself to put us out of action."

"No. It is the woman. I have her picture and her dossier."

"What good are dossiers, Mr. Ikeda?"

"Evidence fits crimes. Evidence emerges from the essential characteristics of criminals. His dossier will find Huntington for us. It tells us that his business is opal, that his wife's passion is opal. He is so close to the source of great opal and is in such bad disfavor with his wife that he will try to take a prodigious opal out of Australia with him. I say he is on his way to Coober Pedy."

"That is pretty arrogant."

Mr. Ikeda shrugged. "Arrogance is in his dossier, as well. Privately, Commander Fujikawa deals in opal and he keeps two men in Australia to locate opal for him. You will go with these men to find Huntington until I can get back on my feet again."

29

When they got back to Andrews Air Force Base in Washington with Dr. Kissinger, who was being sneaked into the country to see his wife and to get a change of clothes, Daddy remained on board the big plane until his people had packed the Secretary under tarpaulin in the back of a half-track which then sped through the night without lights, out the seldom-used west gate. Daddy transferred to his own chopper and flew to his electronically guarded estate, named *Cerutti* by Thomas Jefferson after the gallant Luganese geographer.

Uncles Jim and Pete and Cousins Harry, Larry, and Gary were waiting for him in the vast Barmecide Room, named after the noble Persian family who came to power under the Abbasid caliphate. Many thought Daddy had chosen the name as a salute to Richard Helms when the former CIA Director had taken up duties as American ambassador to Iran.

"I had to order the house arrest of your Marine Duty Sergeant, Rogan," was the greeting from Uncle Jim. "She refused to turn off the goddam bug in this room without a direct order from you. The Marines shouldn't allow goddam women noncoms, anyway. Were we supposed to just sit here as silent as mummies until you got here?"

"Is it off?"

"Sure is."

"Good."

Uncle Pete said, "It's been confirmed. Bryson bought the *Perfection* from Colin for five and a half million."

"Five and a half?" Daddy said incredulously. "Bryson refused to pay us four for it."

"Colin walked with almost a million and a half," Uncle Jim said.

"He must have a good reason," Cousin Larry said. "Colin is no crook."

"The new charter rate could have raised the price," Cousin Gary said.

"What raised it is that Bryson's class reunion is almost on top of him. He needed that yacht," Uncle Pete said. "Hell, what's a million and a half to John?"

"Just his own blood in a soup plate," Daddy said. "John is one of the few really thrifty misers left." He shook his head. "I just can't believe he could ever have a school class to reunite with. He can't spell, and I've heard talking horses in vaudeville with better diction. But no matter—we finally got rid of that goddam yacht."

"Good for Colin," Cousin Larry said.

"I have put out an order to The Company's Chief of Base, Sydney, to eliminate Colin with extreme prejudice."

There was a babble of consternation as everyone tried to speak at the same time. Daddy lighted a Fancy Tale Cuban cigar and waited for everyone to calm down.

"Now hear this," he said. "Colin was given three hundred and fifty thousand Australian dollars by Fujikawa Industries with which to buy oil-drilling rights in the Great Barrier Reef where a field had been confirmed. He gambled the money away. He never showed to buy the leases. John Jackson got them."

They gaped at him tragically. Daddy wiped the palms of his hands with a silk handkerchief.

"Then, by Jesus," Uncle Pete said, "Colin is a good frienda

mine but the sumbitch *deezerves* to be eliminated with extreme prejudice."

"I think even Bitsy will agree with that," Cousin Harry said.

"She goddam well has to agree," Uncle Jim snapped. "The silly bastard must have blown his sanity."

"But, no, just a minute," Cousin Larry said. "Colin didn't know we were owners of Fujikawa Industries."

"Larry, what the hell is the matter with you?" Uncle Pete said. "He threw three billion dollars away if that was a confirmed field. You know he don't think for two millisecs before he fucks up. He's a dangerous human bean and I have thought many times about having Colin prejudiced extremely because that's the only way he'll ever learn to conduct hisseff rightly."

"When—uh—do they—uh—do it?" Cousin Larry asked.

"They can't even find the son-of-a-bitch!" Daddy shouted. "A little, underpopulated country like Australia with nothing but empty spaces between hick towns and the Central Intelligence Agency of the United States of America can't find him. The Japanese security forces and Fujikawa's Ikeda can't find him. The whole goddam Australian police force and their Army can't find him and there's an eighty-thousand-dollar reward on his head."

"I think you should turn the satellites loose on him," Uncle Jim said.

"I should have thought of that," Daddy said. "I'll do that right away."

"If by any chance he does make it out of Australia," Cousin Larry said, "I'll have him set up with Interpol. That's what it's there for. After all, it's just a privately owned French company Treasury leases services from."

"Good thinking, Larry," Uncle Pete said. "Interpol knows how to frame it to get Colin eighty to a hundred years in some Indonesian or Indian prison."

"Interpol will telegraph absolutely anything," Cousin Larry

said. "They do it for their clients every day. If you want, they'll plant evidence of narcotics or murder on him."

"God, how it takes me back to the old days," Uncle Jim said, "when the Nazi government owned Interpol and the old *Sicherheitsdienst* which ran the Gestapo called the tune. Doesn't have one goddam investigator, think of that. Just a gang of file clerks and telegraphers. Doesn't even have the power of arrest anywhere. It's as if some brokerage house called itself the FBI and everybody held still for it."

"You got to admire that kinda nerve," Uncle Pete said.

"We have just lost forty-seven percent of three billion dollars here," Daddy said harshly. "Let's move this thing."

"Say, what about the Russkies?" Uncle Jim said. "They owe you a favor or two."

"I've been mulling that over," Daddy said. "And the Russians are good on the large-area overtakes. They might enjoy the planning involved in an exercise like this. Climate problems, procurement, troop movement, water problems, total silence—all very interesting to the tactician."

"I vote to bring in the Russians," Uncle Jim said, "and to use the satellites."

"Who commands our undercover Australian tracking station, Gary?" Daddy asked.

"Jilly. One star. Used to be an attaché at Oslo."

"Oh, yaaaass. Good security man. Well—all right. Alert him. Get those satellites tracking."

"I'd just like to know who is going to tell Bitsy about all this," Cousin Larry said. "With all Colin's faults she is still very fond of him."

"That's my job," Daddy said. "And I know she'll understand. I'll get her back from Australia to London and we'll talk the whole thing over."

30

The false Claire Bonnette made Captain Huntington as comfortable as possible in the cellar room while she gradually made herself as horny as possible just looking at him, brushing up against him, and smelling him. There was a record player with one Delbert McClinton and one Phoebe Snow record, an Italian language edition of *The Tears of Autumn,* some commercial pâté de foie gras made from sheep's liver, and a half-gallon of local red plonk.

Upstairs again, Yvonne conferred with the real Claire.

"I'm going to be all right," Claire said, but she looked bad. She stared wanly at the black shadow applied under Yvonne's eyes, the taut hair, and the grim look Yvonne had acquired to convince Colin. "My God," Claire said. "Is that what I look like? I must remember to recycle my face. Does he think you are me?"

"Yes."

"This is very kinky, you know."

"He has to change how he looks."

"Easy."

"He'll need forged papers."

"If he has money, I can do it."

"He wants a big opal."

"The government takes a big tax. So when miners find a big

opal and they don't want to pay the tax, some of them go to a Dutchman named Van Hooch, some to a Pole named Susski— or they come to me. No matter who gets the deal, the opal usually goes out to Japan. It is a dangerous business."

"Dangerous?"

"If your friend is able to buy a big stone, how long do you think Van Hooch or Susski will let him keep it? Your friend will be in a boiling desert, a thousand miles from anywhere. They will kill him. That way it is all profit."

"He needs the opal so he'll take the risks. Can you find me the right opal, Claire?"

At noon on the third day, Yvonne knocked at the cellar room door and entered. Everything was as if he were expecting an admiral's inspection.

"Okay," she said. "Let's see some money. Here is an Australian passport with your new picture and name—costs three thousand dollars. Here is a driver's license, State of Victoria, five hundred dollars. The clothes, just as if you were an American androgyne—one hundred and nineteen, ninety-five. Just add a fifty percent commission for little Claire and give me a round fifty-five hundred." He counted the money into her hand.

"The suntan makeup for your bald head, when you shave it, is a present from me."

"Thank you. What about the opal?"

"We have to go to Coober Pedy for opal like that."

"Very well. The sooner the better."

"But after you get it, you have to keep it. Dealers for the Japanese would kill you to get it. You have to get it out of the country on the run across the outback."

He thought of Daddy's satellite staring at him, never blinking.

"You will be moving across an empty continent inhabited by wildlife you never imagined and strange, mystical aboriginal people. It is the driest place on earth. But you can come to places with more than eleven feet of rain. People drown in that rain. You will be trying to hide on the flattest place on earth with very little cover but which has snow-capped peaks, blazing red dunes, and dense forest. Most of it will be the bleakest wilderness you have ever seen, all of it beyond your experience. Are you sure you want that opal?"

He swallowed hard but he nodded. "I have plans for it," he said. "While I shave my head and put on suntan makeup and change my clothes, will you go down to Grenfell Street and rent me the largest air-conditioned Range Rover with water and petrol tanks?"

"You'll need guns."

He blinked. "All right. And a few grenades, please." He counted out more $50 bills. "Get some blankets and plenty of books."

"Books?" she said blankly. She had been thinking of sex. When she was beside him, she always thought of sex.

They left the Stanley Street house at 5:55 that evening. They drove due north through Gepp's Cross, then branched off to the right through Gawler. Yvonne, as Claire, drove while the Captain worked over the maps. He wanted to be able to continue driving when night came on, to go beyond Hawker up into the painted Flinders Range where they could safely take a few hours sleep below The Bowl, that massive synclinal undulation of pound quartzite, its escarpments enclosing about fifty-two square miles. To the aborigines it had been known as Wilpena, the place of the Bent Fingers, for as long as 570 million years.

Going north they were stopped by three roadblocks asking for identification and destination. They told each one they were on the way to bushwalk from The Pound to St. Mary's Peak and on to Edeowie Gorge. They were passed through each time without incident. When the dawn broke and the heat began to smite the outback, as it stretched out all around them in a valley which lay 3200 feet below them, they stopped the car and slept through the worst of the day in the cool of the high mountains between Glass Gorge and Parachilna, lying on air mattresses under the car.

At five in the afternoon they ate cold sandwiches from a freezer container and drank a bottle of fine, red wine from Coonawarra. Unknown to them, they were observed by walking parties of Unyamootha and Arkaba Tura aborigines; by hill kangaroos, stump-tailed lizards, bearded dragons, and sand goannas; by Rufous Whistlers and by gray butcher birds and wedge-tailed eagles as the car rested under the peppermint gum trees. Yaccas poised. Pink birds called galahs coursed across the mountainsides blending with brilliant colored pavanes of stratified rocks, yellow daisies, squash bushes, and acres of mauve Salvation Jane.

31

At the meeting among the South Australia police, the American CIA, the Japanese *Kokka Keisatsu Cho,* one representative of the Japanese Public Security Investigation Agency called *Koan Chosa Cho,* the Australian Security Intelligence Organization, the National Civil Defense, the National Australian Police, and the Australian Air Force, it was decided to call upon Scotland Yard, in London, to backtrack on Captain Huntington's origins based on the information that had been provided by his wife.

On the morning of the fourth day, Scotland Yard cabled confirmed information that not only was Captain Huntington's wife in Australia, but also his devoted mistress, Miss Yvonne Bonnette, whose twin sister was Claire Bonnette aka Maerose Carnaghi aka Gertrude Radin, both daughters of the late international narcotics import/exporter, Charles Bonnette. The Yard reported that Claire Bonnette was wanted by French, Algerian, and Senegalese police, was undoubtedly in Australia illegally, and was resident at 11A Stanley Street, Adelaide, South Australia. Claire Bonnette, the report concluded, was a criminal of violence who was further unstabilized by narcotics and who must be classified as dangerous.

Chief Superintendent Richard Gallagher of the South Australia Police immediately confirmed with Mrs. Huntington at the Hotel Australia, North Terrace, Adelaide, that indeed Miss Yvonne Bonnette was her husband's mistress, but Mrs. Huntington had no knowledge of Miss Bonnette's whereabouts in Australia nor had she known Miss Bonnette had a twin sister, Claire. When Mrs. Huntington hung up the phone on Chief Superintendent Gallagher she broke $726 worth of hotel furniture in her rage over admitting to such knowledge, then had the hotel move her to a different suite.

The Combined Task Force considered the Scotland Yard report. They took the decision to stake-out 11A Stanley Street at ten o'clock that night, setting up searchlights, clearing the street and the surrounding area of residents, and surrounding the house. They expected to arrest what would be their big catch, but the stake-out was made four hours after Captain Huntington had left Adelaide.

The Task Force commander spoke to the house through an electronic hailer, ordering all occupants out within five minutes or the house would be assaulted from all sides with tear gas.

Claire heard the enormous, threatening voice just after she had poured a small bucket of speed mixed with cocaine and heroin into the large vein on the inside of her left thigh. She was hallucinating at the speed of light squared, into induced, advanced paranoia. She knew instantly that the sound she heard was from certain Algerians, French, and Turks who had come to kill her and she knew she must defend herself, feeling rather sorry that none of those outside the house would have a chance against her.

She armed herself with two .38 calibre revolvers. She slithered along the walls at floor level like a hovercraft. She made it to the front door undetected. She worked the door ajar, then kicked it open and came sprinting out, firing both revolvers, killing three men and wounding two others critically before she was shot down by thirty-seven bullets, dying instantly before she could make the fence gate.

James D. Marxuach and Mr. Ikeda, who was armed with a

heavy sword, ran into the house ahead of the police. They searched it from cellar to attic but found no one. It was essential that police pathologists establish that someone had been hidden in the house recently so they photographed the cellar room in smallest detail and a policewoman named Jean Salvadore slipped the Italian edition of *The Tears of Autumn* into her purse, feeling that her husband would enjoy it.

James D. Marxuach began to work out what he was going say to Daddy when he got him on the phone wherever he was in the world that night.

After an intensive session with Mrs. Huntington, the Combined Task Force, now understanding the Captain's fascination for opal, reached the conclusion that he must be heading for Coober Pedy. Mrs. Huntington told the police almost in Mr. Ikeda's words, "Colin has never gotten himself into such trouble as he has done this time. It is my impression that he believes opals to be his lucky amulet, so he must be going wherever big opal can be found."

32

Daddy reached Bitsy at the Hotel Australia in Adelaide by satellite telephone one hour after the police meeting had ended. She was still trembling with overwhelming relief that Colin had not been in that raided house. Although she had no knowledge about the contracts which had been issued on Colin's life, she was a woman experienced in money matters and she knew that every time someone costs someone else three billion dollars that the entire community will cooperate to see that someone killed.

"I have something rather important to tell you, dear," Daddy said into the telephone. "We can't discuss it even on this phone. How soon can you return to London?"

"I might as well leave today. There is nothing more I can do here."

"Shall we say we'll have dinner at Farm Street at nine tomorrow night?"

They had a quiet dinner, cooked by Francohogar's *saucier*, Roja-Caza; a light, cold strawberry aspic followed by a soufflé made with Parmagiana *stravecchio*. They discussed a half dozen family business transactions in various stages of progress around the world. Then Daddy said, "You know, I suppose, that Colin had cost Fujikawa and Company three billion dollars?"

"Yes. I heard that."

"It forced me to reach a policy decision, dear. I called a family meeting at *Cerutti* and everyone voted affirmatively to what has to be done."

"What has to be done, Daddy?"

"Bitsy—even though Colin was able to stick Bryson with the *Perfection* for five and a half million—"

"Five and a half? Why, that's a stroke of genius!"

"It is what he has *cost* us which counts, dear. Forty-six percent of three billion dollars."

She felt herself turning to marble. She was afraid she was going to fall not out of the chair, but out of the room. "Oh?" she said calmly, for she was Daddy's girl. "What did you decide to do?"

"I did the only honorable thing there was *to* do, my dear," he said gently. "I ordered our Chief of Base, Sydney, James D. Marxuach, to eliminate Colin with extreme prejudice."

There was a smothering silence. Bitsy stared at the tablecloth. She could not move or speak.

"I realize that you were extremely fond of Colin and that he was, in many ways, an excellent companion, but—"

"Oh, I under*stand*, Daddy. Please know that I understand perfectly." Bitsy did understand how Daddy felt about power and money. She had been raised and tempered in that religion. She knew also that Daddy would never be able to understand how she felt about her husband, or even how normal people felt about each other. She wanted Colin thrown into a vile jail so he could know he had been punished; vanquished. Once he was caught she would put every known wheel to work to get him freed instantly. That was the extent of Bitsy's dream of revenge.

"I knew I could count on my little girl," Daddy said with enormous pride and pleasure. "And to make it up to you, I am going to send you the matched Titians from the New York flat." It was not only relief he felt. It was pride. He knew Bitsy would never oppose logical action. "The main thing is—don't sentimentalize over it. It will be all over in a jiffy and we'll all be the better for it."

33

The Range Rover's course turned west through the gibber on a track that cut south of Lake Cadibarrawirracanna toward Coober Pedy, 592 miles north of Adelaide. They were deep in the Never-Never, an indescribably lonely country. Purgatory was not as hot and had the advantage of being populated. In other great deserts there were always mountains in view. In the Alaskan arctic there was neverending scenery of majesty, but on the drive from Anna Creek to Coober Pedy there was nothing, not an object to break the monotony of shale and stone desert called the gibber, a place so flat that a railway train could be seen an hour and a half before it arrived. Water was so scarce only the aborigines could find it.

At 10:03 on the second night of the journey, the Captain unpacked his satellite telephone and reached Keifetz in Sydney.

"Have you heard from Juan?"

"Last night. He has the old man turned on to European food. Your case has been turned over to Ikeda who will be working with two opal dealers named Van Hooch and Susski and a man named Bergquist. They are all killers and they work directly for Commander Fujikawa."

"I've heard about them."

"Can you handle a grisly item?"

"Probably not."

"The old man ordered them to bring him your head. No kidding. How about that?"

"No comment. How is your project coming?"

"No, no! Wait. I got more stuff. Every newspaper and all the radio and television says there will be like a whole army of cops looking for you in the opal fields. You know where the fields are?"

"A few miles up the road from here, I hope. Now the good news. How is your work going?"

"Terrific. They are really going for it here. We are gonna turn this country upside-down."

From the instant Keifetz opened his mouth and his attaché case at the Australian Conservation Society's offices in Sydney the nation responded as though touched to its deepest being. With the announcement of an individual anonymous donation of $750,000 to save the Great Barrier Reef, money began to pour in from the Australian public from all over the country almost immediately, creating a fund of $1,620,000 within the first four days.

The mechanics of pressure had levered the result, but it was an astonishing response nonetheless. Within those four days Keifetz, working with a flying wedge of Conservation Society executives and an ever-increasing number of volunteers, had organized committees, platoons, and strike forces throughout the country. The emergency organization was most intense along the eastern seacoast from Sydney to Cooktown, an area that faced the reef itself. Keifetz set up the varied assignments: parades, citizens' committees, street banners, newspaper advertising, and petition-signing tables everywhere, outdoors under trees and in the shops of more than eighty-three percent of the merchants, in pubs, beauty salons, airports, and railway terminals. He sent out sound trucks, stump speakers, drew sermons out of pulpits, and sent out teams of champion athletes from all sports to make an appeal on television and radio while touring the country on transportation contributed by the airlines. They asked for and got more and more petition signatures. Within the first four days he had 400,000 signatures; then the school system threw itself into the battle. Doctors, dentists, barbers, bus drivers, zoo keepers, ferryhands, cab drivers, whores, and bartenders pushed petitions under Australian pens.

At the beginning of the second week a Keifetz-organized mass demonstration of about a million four hundred thousand people recruited in dozens of cities, towns, and villages marched upon the seats of local, state, and national government, each group bearing what seemed to be an endlessly long petition which demanded that the Great Barrier Reef be saved from murder by oil drilling. Rallies, concerts, mass meetings, and street demonstrations called out for instant action by lawmakers and politicians.

The State of Queensland, usually just short of one hundred years behind the other states, but the state which faced and depended upon the Great Barrier Reef, raced to capture the honor of passing the first law forbidding offshore drilling. South Australia and Western Australia followed with laws that not only banned oil drilling but barred eleven other means of spoliation of the ecological chains in the oceans off their shores. The national government then drove a stake into the hearts of the polluters by voting, by a 93 percent margin, to impose retroactive penalties upon those who had given notice of their intention to violate the reef. The carnage was heavy. John Jackson, the independent oil operator who had acquired the reef leases when Captain Huntington had failed to appear, had immediately sold them to a consortium of three of the largest American oil companies for $7,500,000. These companies had assembled crews and equipment and had moved two ocean-going oil rigs from the South China Sea. As these rigs crossed into the Coral Sea, the consortium was fined a total of $9,321,885. Lengthy, costly legal appeals began. It would take six years and four months before the final decision, which would uphold these penalties and which would cost the oil companies an additional $3,276,114 in legal fees, expenses, and impounded equipment, losses which brought about a suit for damages by the French stockholders in the American companies and which cost eleven highly-placed oil executives their jobs, causing the suicide of one public relations executive. Further stockholder suits would cost an additional $2,708,441 in awards and legal fees. Captain Huntington had blown the law of consequence again. However, perhaps the worst toll was measured in oil company effectiveness which in turn, because of Captain Huntington's insufficient grasp of the laws of consequence, sent the retail prices of gasoline and fuel oil into an upward spiral on the U.S. market. At a time when all attention should have been directed to vital exploration and development, at a moment when the best oil company minds should have been exploiting the growing division within the oil-producing countries of the Middle East (to squeeze them out of the entire "downstream" operation, to force a reduction in crude oil prices), instead the American companies lost tremendous potential gains to the Japanese oil industry, mainly to Fujikawa & Company, who darted forward into opportunities around the world, pulling oily chestnut after oily chestnut out of the fire.

As Bitsy Huntington finally demonstrated (perhaps a fortnight too late to save the lives of numbers of people), Fujikawa Industries, acting with almost clairvoyant speed following the miraculous, accidental salvation of their Australian investment, and spared the accumulations of fines and consequences, instead of losing three billion dollars through the loss of the Great Barrier Reef oil leases found it had quadrupled its world oil holdings by a gross volume of just under 4.8 billion dollars. The amount shared by Daddy, as Bitsy pointed out, was 47 percent of that figure.

34

Brigadier-General Gunther "The Dilly" Jilly, although in command of the most sophisticated satellite operations ever conceived in human communications was, at heart, still very much the cavalry officer with yearnings best suited to service at Fort Myer. He was a man who would have given up arms and legs gladly—even his nose (no inconsiderable gift if measured by the pound)—if it could have meant that Georgie Patton would walk the earth once more.

His head, like many a fighting general before him, was made of bolt-weighted ferro-concrete. His natural bent was to snuff people to maintain discipline, not in a kinky way but cleanly with his carbine or sword—but there were laws preventing that. He won his spurs as a military attaché. He had a flair for security because he had marched all espionage subjects to the public parks of Oslo, Pretoria, and Winnipeg by night—to name the three embassies which he had served—and had shot them. His effectiveness rating shone. No spy wanted to accept freelance assignments for any of the embassies to which Gunther Jilly was assigned. Being a cavalry man, and a diplomatic military attaché, he was, by Army logic, assigned to the command of one of the three most sensitive geosynchronous satellite stations.

His orders, issued by Daddy through Uncle Jim to Cousin

Gary at the Pentagon, were clear. To implement them he called in his assistant, the senior space specialist on the post, which was hidden 105 miles south of Coober Pedy. He slid Captain Huntington's ten-year-old photograph, in white tropicals with decorations, across the desk to Alan John Melvin. "Program the cameras to find this man in central Australia," he said.

A twelve-man expeditionary squad, a military unit of the KGB-USSR, was air-lifted out of Pinsk to Saigon where they were outfitted for desert operations. Their average age was twenty-four years with average intelligence ratings of 94 on a scale of 200. All were Stryne-speaking, taught by computer. They thought of little else but the possibility of screwing two or three hundred Australian women. Orders to their commander, Captain Ivan Ramen, were to return to the Pinsk base with a certain retired British naval officer. At Pinsk this naval officer would make a full confession to having been operating in Australia as an agent of the Peoples' Republic of China to foment an uprising of the Australian aboriginal people with intent to burn down all cities north of the Canberra-Perth line. The Kangaroo Commando, as it was called in File AUAGIT 543296–*Contra*, were dropped from 1100 feet at night 4.7 miles north by northeast of Coober Pedy.

The depth, strength, and extent of the forces pursuing Captain Huntington was formidable: 6 four-man squads of South Australia police; 5 four-man units from the National Australian Police and from ASIO; a 30-man platoon of CMF; 4 units of four men from the Australian Air Force helicopter service; James D. Marxuach from CIA/USA; 4 men from the Japanese *Kokka Keisatsu Cho*, acting on information received directly from the analytical security unit *Naikaku Sori Daiijin Kambo Chosa Shitsu;* 3 professional killers and 1 master of security from Fujikawa & Company; the American geosynchronous satellite system; a 12-man Commando unit of the Soviet KGB, and the inexorable energy and power of Daddy and Baron Fujikawa.

35

After her ordeal of understanding Daddy, after he had explained to her so patiently that the family's honor demanded the elimination of her husband with extreme prejudice, after Daddy had left Farm Street to board a fighter-bomber to rejoin Dr. Kissinger in Kamchatka, Bitsy had telephoned the president of the small Belgian bank she had bought to merge with the much, much bigger German bank, at his home in Brussels. She asked the banker a series of questions about related past incidents in Africa, particularly the Congo and Angola. He called her back in thirty-five minutes to say he had been able to secure the appointment she sought in Brussels for the following morning at 11:15.

The doorbell at Colonel Bocca's luxurious flat in the rue de Ste. Denise Grellou the next morning delivered a merry sleigh-bells effect. Beyond the door Nancy Sinatra could be heard singing.

The Colonel's batman, Starr, opened the door and bowed magnificently but carefully (he had a tendency to drink vodka in milk).

Colonel Bocca was one of the great shadow-figures of the world. He had deserted from the British Regular Army while serving as a regimental sergeant-major with the North Dorset regulars at Grove House near Semley. He joined Tshombe's legendary Six Commando as a private in 1961. By 1965 he was commanding officer with an army of more than 2000 men serving under him.

Between private wars, his supreme *métier*, Colonel Bocca worked in Brussels as a property dealer. Despite having invested in enough equipment to mobilize an army within two days (somehow he had stored everything: uniforms, mugs, transport, short wave radio, ammunition, rifles, grenades, and machine guns), he could still afford to buy diamonds and chinchilla for the three assorted young women, one white, one black, one yellow, who lived with him, *en plaid*, in the immense apartment.

Colonel Bocca was a mythical figure among mercenary soldiers. He had fought in the Congo, in Angola, in Rhodesia, in Lebanon, in Northern Ireland, in Chile, and in southwest Africa. He had assured opium deliveries on the Burmese sector of the Golden Triangle. He was responsible for finding pilots and technicians for the Nigerian government during their late disagreements and resisted a bribe of $500,000 deposited in a Zurich bank to persuade the pilots to land at Enugu. His enemies had accused him of everything from psychopathic killing to right-wing fanaticism, but no one had yet found him guilty of double-crossing. His secret was his desperate insecurity, which had him wanting to be tougher, harder, and more envied than anyone else.

Men who had moved under his orders were still on stand-by throughout the world. In each important staging area one full-time paid officer and one full-time regimental sergeant-major acted as Colonel Bocca's liaisons who kept in touch with men, governments, security networks, and revolutionary leaders. They reported to Bocca regularly, to Brussels. All bankers, throughout the world, fully approved of Bocca's work.

Colonel Bocca was enormously impressed by Bitsy's wealth and her beauty. He seated her cozily in the sitting room, so English it could have been decorated by Queen Victoria's gillie, offering her a choice of tea or Bovril. She asked for Coca-Cola, please. He lost control only for an instant to let her see how she had offended him, then ordered Starr, hovering at the doorway, to serve a chilled magnum of Dom Perignon '59. Bitsy had won the first round.

He returned to geniality. "How may I help?" he asked in his fluted voice as he undressed her in his mind. He was a short man with a tubby waistline—therefore more given to thoughtful, rather than active, sex. He had had a go at growing a stubbly Svengali beard.

Bitsy delineated in gravest detail, without interruption, omitting only that her father too had ordered the death of her husband, the forces which were being aligned against the Captain, the intent of some of these forces to murder him, and of others to arrest him to see him in prison for ninety-three-odd years.

"I must say I am not overjoyed at the idea of Australians, Japanese, Americans, *and* Russians all being in the game," Colonel Bocca said ruefully. "All of them are right nahrsty buggers on field maneuvers like these. They look at it like it were some kind of sports fing and they tends to kill too much. Oh, well. Not to worry."

"Do you accept the assignment, Colonel Bocca?"

"As I am in me orf-season, as it were, yes, I accepts. Cost you a packet though." He nodded to Starr to pour the wine. " 'Ow big a force was you finkinkov, Moddom?"

"You are the expert. I expect a battalion would be too many and a platoon too little. A company, I suppose."

"Yace. A commnee of hofficers an' men; sye a total dee-tyle of abaht fifty-two, all in. Lots a good lads oo likes a scrap."

"I would want all of them to have had commando experience."

"Oh, yus, Moddom. We'll give you an assortment of former Green Berets, British commandos, French legionnaires, American Rangers—all hand-to-hand and guerrilla people."

"Will you supply air cover?"

"Well—"

"It stands to reason that if they are going to be searching for my husband in that vast, flat, dry, hot outback, they'll be using helicopters. I am simply asking if these can be shot down if necessary."

"Indeed you can have yer air cover, Moddom. I got four gorgeous Starfighters off the Krauts when they got the wind up. Cost you a proper packet though. An' a bleddy forchune if we loses one."

"One Starfighter should be sufficient."

"Cahn't 'ave one of anything in a military operation, Moddom. The least I could allow would be two miv four pilots, four gunners, and ten men on the ground. We'll need a petrol dump and a ship to bring them in and lorries to truck the 'ole bleddy thing abaht three hundred miles inland to set up an airdrome."

"How much?"

"I don't like to say."

"Don't like to *say*?"

"I don't want to shock you."

"It is impossible to shock me, Colonel Bocca."

"Air cover alone will run you abaht a million two alone in U.S. dollars, Moddom."

"That's *shocking.*"

"Now—the matter of tanks. I 'ave two fine Russian T 34/76 tanks, but for this work I would recommend the British Chieftain because it's really got it miv its well-sloped thick armor and its hundred and twenty millimeter gun. It's got wet ammo storage and a multifuel engine miv a ranging set of machine guns. It's even got a schnorkle for deep wading if yer husband finds 'imself up a creek."

"Our family always liked the fifteen hundred horsepower Daimler-Benz the Germans put into their MBT 70."

"Not in the temperatures we are discussing, Moddom, I am afryde. But I can sye that the Swedish S tank—the STRV 103 —is a splendid vehicle to fight. No turret at all, you might sye."

"Then how do they lay in the azimuth?" Bitsy asked skeptically.

"They got a hydrostatic steereen drive, miv a clutch and bryke system for your very sharp turns. You can elevate or depress the 'ole vehicle. Guns load automatically. Commander has a gyro-stablized sight. Blimey, even flotation is possible."

"To go back to your first suggestion of the Russian 34. It does have night vision. It does have fin-stablized missiles, an infrared searchlight, and a really good schnorkle so, if you'll agree that we certainly do not need two of these, if you will supply fuel and manpower, then the T34 is the tank I'll have for my husband."

"Very good, Moddom. Will you wish any light-fighting vehicles? Perhaps an American XM808 Twister—eight wheels in a clever design what has an overhead cannon hung on bogies miv an engine on each which it is linked by pivot tokes to give movement on all three planes?"

"Now you are talking! Never mind the Russian tank or any tank. What will really do this job is the all-aluminum, armored British Scorpion—you know, the FV 101 with that wonderful power-to-weight ratio. It can cross soft ground and it has all the radar and image intensification we need. Oh, I am so grateful that you brought up light-fighting vehicles. How much?"

"Well—less than a tank. But you'd need two Scorpions to be well orf. Don't be half-safe."

"Yes. Good. How much?"

"Two vehicles. Six men to fight them. Three petrol dumps and base camps with four maintenance personnel at each. Spare parts depot, water, food, ammo, and the occasional young lady. Drumhead estimate six hundred and forty thousand."

"I'll take it. How much for the Commando company—and how many men?"

"Fifty-two men and officers."

"That seems much too many."

"I couldn't justify less than half of that strenff, Moddom. Wouldn't be worff my while."

"Twenty commandos including officers would do it."

"Moddom, do you not see what we will be fycing 'ere? Australian troops and air force. Russian military units. Paramilitary Australian police. American and Japanese assassins. My men look to me to give them every fighting chance to get back, you see."

"What is the minimum force you will rent?"

"Twenty-four men, six officers and noncoms."

"I have a few dozen samples of the new Rodman lightweight machine gun in London which I will sell to you, Colonel Bocca. This is the utterly new gun with such a simplified structure, soft-recoil, one half the weight of any other gun, including the Israeli. It has forty percent fewer parts than the standard M–60 machine rifle, and I can make you a really attractive price on it."

"That's beddy *maav*liss, Moddom. When our clients know we 'ave some Rodmans, the competition will melt away, I can tell you."

"How much for the thirty soldiers?"

"Well—I must fly them from all world points into Indonesia for mustering. There's supplies, ammo, explosives, gas cover, weapons, uniforms, a ship to take them in, airlift to Coober Pedy in two helicopter gunships, wear and tear, the occasional young lady—say one million, eight hundred seventy for the month."

"Do we have to have uniforms?"

"Uniforms is why soldiers enlist. 'At's where the discipline lives. My 'evvens, Moddom. Even the Chinese People's Republic Army wears uniforms. They don't have any ranks. They don't have any tabs or pips or markings, but they got the uniforms."

"What sort of style did you have in mind?"

"Oh, no brayettes or gay badges! No buckles, buttons, or brass! Drabbest battle dress in desert camouflage, I should sye.

Officers in your ordinary feldmutze caps. Depends on what I 'ave in the warehouse at the present time, you see."

"It would be awfully nice if the camouflage could be in my husband's racing colors."

"Very nice touch, Moddom," Colonel Bocca replied. "What are they?"

"Orchid and gold."

"I 'ave them! The very fing! I used them on both sides in Angola!"

"Shall we total?"

"Yace. Let's see. Two million for air cover, six fifty for light armor, a million nine for troops and transport, say two hundred and five for communications, three thousand for the occasional young lady, five percent for insurance, eight percent for pensions and retirement fund, eleven percent for rentals and six percent for Value Added Tax—makes a total of—ah—five million, nine hundred and fifty-two thousand, six hundred and fifty dollars. All in." He had not used a pencil and paper. It was mental arithmetic.

Neither had Bitsy. "You slipped a bit, Colonel. The total is five million, *seven* hundred thousand on that basis."

He reddened. "Next I know, you'll be ahskin' for Green Stamps, won't you? All right. That's the price."

Bitsy was pleased. After all, she reasoned, it wasn't costing her one cent. The bill would be paid out of the five-million-pound fund which Gash Schute had left to Colin and Colin had signed over to her. But even if it were now her money it was still a very good investment because it would bind Colin to her for years to come. If one could believe the police, the little French mistress was out there somewhere in Australia with Colin, but the little thing was only giving of her time, whereas Bitsy would be putting up a substantial amount of money to save her man. "We will deduct the price of the Rodman machine guns, Colonel Bocca," she said briskly, "and I will give you a check at once. When can you be operational?"

"Two dyes, I should sye. We moves fast because we always

has to. I have troops in southeast Asia and Ceylon; weapons and armor depots in Vietnam. We shall fly them to our staging area in Sumatra, fit out their kits, then airlift them to Coober Pedy. The air cover and the light armor will go in at Willamotta in northwest Australia. The enemy will have the advantage of satellite surveillance, computer tracking, and a large combined task force, but we shall have the advantage of surprise. If they should find your husband, we will get him away from them. If they can only locate his whereabouts generally, our fifth column inside their forces will pass the word out and we will find him first."

"Fifth column?"

"You are our fifth column, Mrs. Huntington."

"Oh. Of course."

"When we find him we'll take him out by fighter-bomber to our own armed camp in Sumatra where it would take all of SEATO to get him out."

"One small point," Bitsy said, "will I have any employer liability problems?"

"I am the employer, Moddom. You will be forever unknown to this operation. War is an all-risks job. About forty percent of the men buy it or get invalided out, but there is no employer liability ever. Now—my commander for these operations will be Captain Mitgang, my best officer in the field. It is essential that you return to Adelaide to remain in around-the-clock contact with the South Australia police. We will wire you up with recording devices. You will be informed how to pass that along to Captain Mitgang."

36

Juan Francohogar was received by the Fujikawa family in Tokyo with unabashed gluttony and no questions. As the Baron said to his son, "It isn't as though the man were some sort of confederate of your monstrous acquaintance. He is just a cook and cooks cannot be blamed for the sins of their masters. Engage him at once! For one month. I say one month because perhaps if I were to eat that sort of Western food for more than one month, I could be overdoing it."

"Very wise, sir," the Commander said.

"Settle him in my house. Get a Western bed and a chair from one of our export companies. Offer him a pleasant woman. Show him the kitchen there and at this office and in the Mercedes Mobile Home between here and my house," the ninety-six-year-old Baron said in Japanese while Francohogar towered over both of them in the Baron's office. "It is now eight-sixteen. Ask him when I may expect lunch. You must be my guest today. I hate to eat alone and this man's food is simply too good to be shared with anyone outside the family."

Francohogar replied to the Commander's question in English that lunch could be served at 1:15 PM.

"What will he make?" the Baron asked greedily.

Francohogar explained that, had he had more time, he would have begun the meal with some Jenny Lind quail consommé made with strips of quail meat and sliced mushrooms. However, under the circumstances, they would have soup *à la Crécy*. "Then I shall offer you filets of sterlet *à la Orloff*, cooked in the Russian manner, which is poached in white wine, fish stock, essence of mushrooms, and cucumber pickle. It will be garnished with cucumbers stuffed with sterlet caviar, simmered in butter with *vesiga*, the marrow from the backbone of this great sturgeon."

"Oh! How inspiring!" the old Baron cried. "What comes next?"

"I am thinking in terms of a *Schlesiche Himmelreich*," Francohogar said solemnly, "which means Silesian Heaven in German—a dish of pork chops simmered for thirty minutes, then fried in butter with mixed dried apples, apricots, pears, and prunes with a very special sauce and large potato dumplings."

"Marvelous!" the old man shrilled. "Go!"

During the ensuing eight days, Francohogar cooked four meals a day for Baron Fujikawa: an elaborate Irish country breakfast; a German or Alsatian lunch; high English tea, then a mixture of prodigiously low Balkan, Brazilian, Turkish, Swiss, northern Canadian, and Polish dishes which came with as many as six contrasting thick sauces, followed by four cheeses and accompanied by alternating wines. Baron Fujikawa believed that he was eating at the very peak of the greatest cuisine of France, which, in terms of skill and flavor, he was. The Baron was transported into an ecstasy of gluttony such as would never happen to him again.

The breakfasts were thick porridge served with butter, heavy cream, and refined sugar; Irish pease pudding, kippers, scrambled eggs with lashings of rashers of fatty bacon; thick, buttered toast, three jams, and strong black tea. The baron adored to eat everything Francohogar put before him. He always asked for more.

Lunch could be *choucroute garni* with slabs of ham, Schübling sausages and *rippenchen* artfully concealed under the great mounds of sauerkraut, with whole boiled potatoes served cold, as a salad, with heavy mayonnaise and capers; turnip soup with chitterlings in thick Chantilly cream; Scottish haggis; *serviettenknodel,* an extraordinary dumpling made with four ounces of semolina flour, a half pound of cream cheese, a bar of butter, and three eggs—all of it stuffed with stewed fruit and served sprinkled with powdered sugar and melted butter.

For high tea they might begin with Alpine tripe soup—made in simple congress of a pound of cooked tripe, bacon, two bars of butter, onions, garlic, and leeks; parsnips, turnips, and cabbage; dried pea beans and white kidney beans; tomatoes, potatoes, and one cup each of Sbrinz and Romano cheese with liberally sifted flour and two cups of *cappellini de angelo* added. The soup would be followed by four fruit jams; buttered scones, fried baps, York ham, and cervelats, topped off with hot black tea and Athole Brose. The Baron loved his little high teas.

He got sleepy from time to time. He did less and less work at the office. But he remained intently interested, almost hypnotized, wondering aloud throughout one course what the next course would be. At dinner Francohogar sent him a salmon soufflé served with East Indian mayonnaise, which is a pint of thick sauce mixed with garlic, curry powder, and eight jalapeño chilis; braised eel stuffed with breadcrumbs, and northern Pacific candlefish to be cooked in the manner of an oily smelt; *caneton Rouenais en chemise:* two ducklings with their breastbones removed, stuffed with duck livers and chicken livers with onions, poached inside a soaked pig's bladder (in veal stock), then garnished with fresh oranges.

There were desserts served with every meal except breakfast: pastries, tortes, tartelettes, and many sorts of shells and boats containing great amounts of nuts, fruits, custards, and flavored whipped cream. The cheeses and fruits came from as far away as Mexico. A special (personal) import department had to be set up within Fujikawa & Company so that delectables could be flown to Tokyo by air express.

Commander Fujikawa withdrew from the feastings after the second meal with his father "in order to facilitate more greatly the importation of gastronomic necessities." He seemed to regard Francohogar with a new, warier, and far more respectful eye; with an almost wistful, wondering expression which seemed to be cast in gratitude. "Oh! I say!" he remarked carefully to Francohogar at the end of the second meal. "You must tell my father about that most famous of famous French dishes, *le Pot au Feu de Didon-Bouffant.*"

"Ah! Yes!" Francohogar breathed.

"What is it? What is it?" the Baron shrilled. "Tell me. I must know. I must have it." The Commander withdrew from the room as if he could not bear to hear a description of the dish again.

Baron Fujikawa died at lunch on the eighth day. He had gained thirty-one pounds. He expired over an utterly cleaned platter of *le Pot au Feu de Didon-Bouffant.* He was smiling in death.

The fifth, sixth, and seventh days had been extremely hot and the Baron would not tolerate air-conditioning. After the autopsy, which Commander Fujikawa demanded, to establish beyond doubt that the Baron had not been poisoned, it was shown, if it were to be put in non-medical terms, that the Baron had simply exploded. Due to his hallowed age, the walls of his stomach were paper-thin. Into it he had introduced great weights of solids, fluids, and resultant gases to stretch those gossamer walls still further. With the accumulation of fluids there was a corresponding loss of chloride so alkalosis, dehydration, and tenany occurred. The legends which sprang up said that the explosion of the Baron's abdomen could be heard throughout the Ginza district.

The Baron's protean intake had also triggered his ischemic heart disease. His body had needed to deliver volumes of blood to the peripheral circulation to cool itself. His heart was simply starved to death while he shoveled in such plenitude, and the inevitable myocardial infarction had occurred simultaneously with the awful detonation.

Commander Fujikawa took over absolute control of the operations of worldwide Fujikawa Industries and, as a measure of his enormous respect for the late Baron, Daddy requested permission from the President and the Chairman of the National Republican Committee to leave Dr. Kissinger temporarily in Montevideo, capital of Uruguay, to fly to Japan to attend the funeral and to acquaint himself with his new partner.

37

Coober Pedy was about 150 miles north of the Trans-Australian Railway, which ran west to east from Perth to Sydney. Names shown on the map of the area were not towns or villages, but homesteads, sheep stations, and dry creek beds. There was only the same gibber everywhere: flat, hot rocks and sand on a tracklessness of blistering monotony.

Opal was discovered at Coober Pedy by gold prospectors. Opal mines were the world's most desolate places: no wood, no water, no shade. Every drop of water had to be hauled in by railway tank cars and distributed with strictest rationing. The daytime temperature rose to 120 degrees but the nights were "cool." The miners and shopkeepers lived in dugouts, which were often multi-roomed apartments dug into hillsides and completely underground. Coober Pedy was an aboriginal place name which meant "man in a hole." The town was several small stores and a post office, three underground motels, and the miners' cave-homes. There was an airport, which connected with Alice Springs, at the center of the continent, and Adelaide, served by Opal Airlines. The town had restaurants, a pharmacy, a supermarket, and an opal shopping complex, all underground: FARID KHAN "THE OPAL PRINCE," ABDULLAH CHAN "THE LUCKY BUYER," and one firm ever-willing to rent Suzuki 4-wheel drive vehicles. Opal found at Coober Pedy was seam-opal, which occurs to a depth of seventy feet where the stratum slopes under a ridge which forms thin veins of the finest color.

When the Captain sighted the town, he and Yvonne, as Claire, suddenly stopped talking as if the danger were as apparent as beasts in a dense forest. They had not spoken at all during the first day and a half, then the false Claire had asked him to tell her of his feelings about her sister, Yvonne.

"I love her," he said simply.

"Really? Deeply? Truly?"

"There is no other way."

"You wouldn't marry her, I hope?"

"How could I? I am married."

"I meant—if you were not married."

"I cannot even imagine that."

"I would expect you to say you would not marry Yvonne."

"Why?"

"Would you or would you not?"

"No."

"Good."

"Why good?"

"You have become a criminal and besides marriage is bad."

"It is not bad."

"Why wouldn't you marry her?"

"It simply would not be right. It would not be fair to her. She is a gloriously young woman. She could have any man in the world. She is one of the three most beautiful women I have ever seen and she has an incomparable mind. I am well past middle-age. If I were to claim I were middle-aged right now, I would have to die at ninety-four. That she is willing to enjoy what I have left to give her is all to my great, good fortune. But when she marries—if she marries—she must marry a young and stable man."

"She will never marry. I know her. She loves you. She doesn't need to marry you, she loves you so much."

"I hope she is happy."

"She is happy."

38

Australian opal is so distinctive because the host rocks that surround it along the seam are not volcanic but sedimentary. Most gemstones are large, single crystals. Opal is not crystalline. It is an amorphous form of silica. Precious opal is a mineral than can exhibit sparkling colors which may range across the entire visible spectrum from violet to deep red. Opal is unique, unlike other gemstones. The fire of the diamond is produced by the facets of the stone. A well-cut diamond provides the longest light path within the stone by arranging the facets so that the rays are internally reflected several times before they emerge. The iridescent color of pearls comes from selective interference between several light waves, reflected from regularly spaced layers of calcium carbonate separated by organic films.

The color that flashes out of precious opal has very little relation to the color displays from other gemstones. The opal fire does not depend on the size of the gem or on faceting. Opal is essentially an amorphous, hydrated form of silica which normally has the same optical properties throughout. Opal color originates with three things: small, irregularly shaped color grains in the texture, the way the colors of the grains change as the orientation of the stone is changed, and the spectrally pure colors of the opal fire.

They could see Coober Pedy in the distance. The Captain got out of the car to walk to the town alone. "There are three motels," the false Claire said. "Van Hooch stays at the Desert Cave. Susski stays at the Opal Inn. I always stay at Grace Wherry's. That way the miners know where to find us if they need us."

"Therefore, I go into Wherry's."

"They will have a room for you in the name of Dick Richards. When they assign the room don't rush off. Chat and trade gossip. Ask for mining news. I will be in my own apartment called Shady. No one can see you go there because the way is turning, narrow tunnels. When you get there I hope I will have news of the kind of opal you want." She was beginning to sweat out the worry of whether Claire's message to Tomas Buckley had gotten through. Leaving him on the track, she drove off to Coober Pedy.

Tomas Buckley was a Portuguese national who had once, in the early years, played on his country's Davis Cup team, reaching the quarter-finals. He was a legend as an opal miner, not only in Australia but in Queretaro, Mexico, where opal is quarried rather than mined and where the cherry opal is found; at Heppner, Oregon; at Red Rock Canyon in Kern County, California, and at Erandique in Honduras. Most importantly he had made black opal history at Rainbow Ridge, Nevada, and at Lightning Ridge, New South Wales. Luck had not had a great deal to do with Buckley's success. He earned more from opals than any other miner in the world and everybody in the business knew he was deeply into smuggling opal out without paying tax, but no one had been able to prove it. Buckley had taken out precious opal where all other miners thought only milk opal existed. He refused to deal with Van Hooch or Susski. He worried about the kind of settings his stones would eventually find and he was convinced he would get better settings in Zurich or London, the markets served by Claire Bonnette. Unknown to him, they all went to the

Fujikawa Collection in Tokyo anyway. Claire Bonnette had been one of the Fujikawa trinity in the Australian opal fields from the beginning.

When Yvonne checked into Wherry's under the short bluff in Coober Pedy she was photographed by hidden cameras planted by the South Australia police. When the Captain, calling himself Dick Richards, checked into the motel two hours later, he and his baldness and his dinky tweed fedora with the half-inch brim, his Samoan shirt, and his three-day growth of beard were photographed by the same cameras which had been planted in all three motels. The exposed films were picked up at six o'clock each night, and flown to Adelaide by Opal Air for processing in police labs each morning at 7:00.

The Captain and Yvonne slept in their separate rooms for six hours, as they had planned, awakening at 4 PM. Their rooms were far back in the tunnel and were entirely lined with wood which had been assembled at Port Pirie, then sent north for construction. The Captain found his way through the dimly illuminated passageway to the door marked Shady. The false Claire let him in and locked the door. "It is best to do opal business in a hotel," she told him. "The bad element can't locate what room you are in, if you bribe the room clerk regularly. That way they can't keep an ear to the air pipe to find out your business. Even better, the worst element, the thieves and murderers like Van Hooch and Susski can't drop a gelignite bomb down the air pipe if they can't figure out what room you are in. Never take chances out here. When I am forced to go to a miner's dugout, I bring a man with a rifle to sit on the surface and keep people away from the air pipe."

There was a light tap on the door. She spoke through it, then opened it and a slip of a man with a nose like an aubergine came sliding into the room as if walking on sand skis.

"Hello, Claire." It was like a voice from Sesame Street.

"Did you bring it, Tomas?"

"Who is he?"

"My buyer."

"London?"

"Huntington Opals," the Captain said. "In Farm Street."

"Good. Very good settings. I admire your settings. Who brought all the action to town?"

"What action?" the false Claire asked.

"Ain't you been outside? It looks like Andamooka crossed with Surfers' Paradise and King's Cross. All strangers and mostly cops."

"Captain Huntington sold his yacht in Adelaide and it has everybody all excited."

"No kidding? This the same guy? Why that's terrific. You beatin' the sytem. Now we got to keep up the good work and make sure you keep beating the system."

"Quite an articulated system, I would say, old boy."

"Where's the opal, Tomas?"

"You know I wouldn't bring it."

"How big is it?" the Captain asked.

"Units of mass?"

"Please."

"Twelve thousand, five hundred metric carats."

"About five and a half pounds weight."

"That's it. Two and a half kilos of flawless, precious, uncut, black opal."

"There will be four and an eighth pounds of single stone when it's cut and polished."

"The chips and cuttings alone will pay for the world's finest jeweler," Tomas Buckley said softly.

"How much?" the Captain asked.

"I know how much to the last cent, my friend. I'm my own appraiser and my cousin is a government appraiser. This opal is two hundred thousand Australian dollars—right here, in the fields."

"It couldn't have come from here."

"No."

"Lightning Ridge?"

"Yes. And when you take it into the market place in London or Zurich it will be worth two million dollars."

"But I must see it."

"Can you get out of here without getting arrested or shot?" he asked sardonically.

"Count on it," Yvonne said.

"When?"

She looked at the Captain who said, "I think tomorrow morning at about four o'clock."

"I'll go out with you."

"Where to?"

"I'll show you the way," Buckley said.

At 10:15 that night, from his room under the hill, the Captain called Keifetz in Sydney on Daddy's satellite telephone.

"Captain? Terrific. We had two tremendous days here. I got a million, four hundred thousand signatures so far. The Queensland parliament sits to vote on the whole thing tomorrow morning in an extraordinary session."

"I don't know how to thank you," the Captain said.

"That's just openers. Western Australia votes on Friday and South Australia goes on Monday. The whole country is jumping. You got crowded off to page twenty-eight."

"What about Juan?"

"Solid. He says he cooked every dish you told him to cook for the old man and whatta you know?—the old man is dead. He overate. The son now runs everything. Hey, how about you? How you doing?"

"It's hard to say. Tomorrow will tell the story. If I'm going to get out it will start tomorrow."

The film exposed from the camera plants in the three motels went to Adelaide by Opal Air. A police despatch rider took it to the photo labs where it was developed and printed by the police. Chief Superintendent Richard Gallagher did not see the prints until after 9:15 that morning, after they had sufficiently puzzled the commanders on the case. They were baffled as to how Claire Bonnette could be laid out in an ice locker in the City Morgue in West Terrace, South End, Westside and yet be photographed checking into a hotel deep in the outback at Coober Pedy three days after she had been shot to death.

"This is the twin sister," Gallagher said. "Give me the shots. I'm going to see Huntington's wife at the Hotel Australia."

Bitsy spead the shots out on a coffee table. "My God," she said. "Jesus, he looks awful. I can't believe it. He looks six years younger when he's bald. And he's so much more svelte than in London. It's terrific. I mean—except for the shirt it's really terrific. No wonder you couldn't find him."

"You identify the man in that photograph as your husband?"

"I'd like to negotiate with you, Chief Gallagher," she said.

"Negotiate?"

"Wherever he is he will not allow this little French mistress to stay with him. I know him. He is too gallant. It's true. He's too generous and courteous to expose her or anyone else to danger. When he gets away from her and begins to try to get out of the country, she is going to have to travel on some fairly public transportation, then she is going to try to fly to wherever she thinks he is going. If you promise me to stake out airports at Coober Pedy and Adelaide and to pick her up as Claire Bonnette when you get her, I will make positive identification of that photograph."

"I think you already have, Mrs. Huntington."

"You think so. Then go ahead. Arrest her."

"I can't arrest her as Claire Bonnette. Claire Bonnette is dead."

"Then arrest her for abetting the escape of a fugitive. I don't care what you hold her for. I want her in prison here for at least three weeks."

"Why?"

"I don't want her to get to my husband first, trying to prove that it was she who saved him. I want to be there when he comes out. It's as simple as that."

Gallagher sighed. "Okay. We have a deal."

"That man," Bitsy said, tapping the photograph, "is Captain

Colin Huntington, Royal Navy, retired."

He got up. "We'll take him today."

"Maybe you will, maybe you won't. Gallagher?"

"Yes, Mrs. Huntington?"

"There is quite a large pack of hunters after my husband, and I think I know that in that pack there is at least one man, and maybe more, who intend to kill him when he is found."

Gallagher remembered the big automatic pistol in James D. Marxuach's hand and the heavy sword Ikeda carried into the Bonnette house in Stanley Street. He shrugged. "I wouldn't know about that, Mrs. Huntington."

"My husband will be your prisoner, Gallagher. No one else's. It's your turf."

He stared at her. "When we get him, he will be brought to trial, Mrs. Huntington. He will have my full protection."

39

The Nigerian flag freighter, *Jemnito*, brought the mercenaries' planes and materiel into the short harbor at Willamotta on the northwest coast of Australia, a place uninhabited since the planet had been formed. The Commando unit had been flown in long ahead under the command of Captain Mitgang, not only leading the commandos, but in charge of the Combined Operations Task Force. He had been a professional soldier for twenty-three years, since the age of fourteen. He had been corporal to Sergeant Bocca with the North Dorset Regulars at Grove House.

After deserting with his sergeant, he had served under him for Tshombe's money in Africa; with the American CIA's private *Waffen SS* of 30,000 men in Laos, where he won a field commission; then he transferred to North Vietnamese forces as a breveted Major in Operations Plans under General Giap.

Mitgang had freelanced in the Philippines (once again an Area Commander for one of Colonel Bocca's armies of instant convenience). He had risen to be Bocca's Asiatic Operations Commander at a fixed salary of $97,000 a year with expenses and six weeks of paid R&R annually, plus thirty percent of all booty and ransoms. He was also made president of the Mercenary Soldiers' League Fund, to which all members of Bocca's various armies were required to contribute. The Fund's proclaimed intention was to confer pensions upon all mercenaries who reached the arbitrary retirement age of sixty-five after a minimum of ten years of service, not necessarily consecutive. No one ever made it. Two who had come within weeks of making it had been shot through the head by Captain Mitgang during fierce combat with adversary forces. Colonel Bocca permitted Captain Mitgang a share of thirty percent in the proceeds from the Fund, a share which was enhanced by Colonel Bocca's practice of lending money in the form of mortgages on Las Vegas hotels and gambling casinos.

Colonel Bocca had been so impressed with Bitsy's wealth, power, and beauty that it had been his pleasure to interrupt Mitgang's R&R to take command of her requirement. It had not been convenient for Mitgang to do so. He had been crossing Switzerland by lake steamer, riverboat, canal vessel, punt, motor launch, kayak, barge, and flatboat with his fiancée of twelve years, the Italian film actress, Signorina Rosa Cacciatore. Colonel Bocca had reached him at Bad Ragaz, had disallowed Mitgang's outraged protests, and had ordered him back into the line in Asia.

At 22:27 hours of the second day after Bitsy had met with Colonel Bocca in Brussels, Captain Mitgang had his assault team assembled at the Sumatran staging area. He issued his order of battle:

"Combat troops will board air transport in zero point thirty-three minutes to be dropped at the rally point near Coober Pedy. You have been briefed. You will be able to identify, then capture and defend our objective, Captain Huntington. When he has been overtaken the Signals Officer will request best transport to get him out. If available, I will accompany him. It is to be expected that Captain Huntington will be messing with us, at base in Sumatra, within the next seventy-two hours.

"Seaborne units will shove off from this beach in zero forty-one minutes," Mitgang rasped. "Your lorries are loaded. The air cover code name is Tinkerbell.

"The two gunships which will transport troops will bear the markings of the Australian Air Force. When they drop troops at Coober Pedy, they will deliberately become a part of the official police search for Captain Huntington. When our objective is overtaken, gunship two will shoot down any official Air Force helicopters that attempt pursuit.

"The three mobile units of our reconnaissance will move up thusly: Unit One to Coober Pedy, maintaining cover at all times. Unit Two to area twenty-one miles north of Alice Springs. Unit Three will stand by for rescue detail twenty miles south of Darwin to be available should Captain Huntington get through our screens. Mobile units will take direction from air reconnaissance, which will take orders from me."

The assembled task force wore orchid and gold camouflage, black berets and face paint, and jump boots. The commandos carried new Rodman light machine rifles. Grenades dangled from each belt. Each man was chuted. Compact radio equipment, ammunition, rations, and medical issue was packed in cases with chutes and with television cassette recorders and sound units. Bitsy had expressed an interest to Colonel Bocca in having a motion picture record made of Colin's rescue. Lieutenant Fairfax, the Signals Officer, had produced and directed three TV commercials in civilian life which had won awards at the Montreux Festival for three years running, so, with this innovative idea of Bitsy's, Colonel Bocca (and Captain Mitgang) was to earn a seventeen percent increase on all war budgets because, when he showed other clients duped footage of Bitsy's taped cassette production, everyone buying wars from him wanted their own reality-oriented souvenirs.

Before the troops filed into the gunships, Captain Mitgang outlined targets for the final time. "In order of their elimination," he barked, "the twelve-man KGB Commando, a vicious bunch who will have no idea we will be there. No problems. Intelligence has all KGB sector identification at Coober Pedy.

"Two, the Japanese. These poor chaps are reacting badly to the local food, the frigidity of the beer, and the extreme heat.

They should never have left their embassy at Canberra. Kill them quickly, they are dedicated men.

"Three, the single American presence: a CIA geek named James D. Marxuach. His photograph is in your kit. When you see him, pop him a burst.

"At no time are you to engage Australian forces—other than the choppers which we may need to shoot down. They are there merely to arrest Captain Huntington, not to execute or kidnap him. If we do not engage the Australians, they may never know we fought a war in their country, it is so vast and deserted. That means fewer explanations in high places for Colonel Bocca.

"Lastly, but importantly. Keep a keen eye out for civilians representing Fujikawa and Company. In other times and situations this company has been our client. The group is in charge of Mr. Ikeda, a good worker, whose photo is in your kit. Mr. Ikeda has four assistants. Kill all on sight, please. No survivors."

40

At ten minutes after three that morning, six hours and fifty minutes after Bitsy and Chief Superintendent Gallagher had their photo identification meeting at the Hotel Australia in Adelaide, the false Claire Bonnette through circuitous tunnels, following diagrams given her by the real Claire Bonnette, led Captain Huntington to the car park which stretched out in darkness twenty-nine yards from the motel. The Captain made it safely and relatively unobserved to the floor at the back of the Range Rover. He covered himself with tarpaulin and went to sleep.

The geosynchronous satellite twenty-two thousand, three hundred miles over Port Moresby recorded his movement across the lot and into the car and transmitted the photographs to the U.S. secret tracking station at Maccarri where it was analyzed at 6:10 AM and placed in General Jilly's IN basket to await his arrival at 8:59 AM.

At 3:58 AM the false Claire Bonnette and Tomas Buckley left Wherry's through the front lobby, chatting noisily as they paid their bill. They took their baggage to the Range Rover which the false Claire asked Tomas Buckley to bring around to the front of the motel. They got into the car, waving good-byes to Grace Wherry and the assorted miners who were out to enjoy the cool of the morning. Buckley driving, the Range Rover turned into the track going northwest. The car moved out of Coober Pedy through what appeared its entire population and those of two other towns; all soldiers, police, and paid assassins. While the car was still in sight a pursuit was mounted.

They could hear the helicopter tracking them. As it radioed the Range Rover's direction to the ground units, the signals were picked up by Captain Mitgang's Signals Officer, seated behind the driver in a passenger bus which carried twenty-six armed mercenaries. The bus was four miles north of the helicopter and seven miles northwest of the Range Rover, so the helicopter did not bother to report its presence. The signal was also received by James D. Marxuach waiting beside a Honda 300 motorbike four miles ahead of the oncoming Range Rover's path. The directions from the chopper were recorded by Captain Ramen, the KGB unit commander, seated with eleven Soviet commandos in the back of a covered truck one mile south of the crossroads which the Range Rover would have to traverse. At points of the compass, in desert personnel carriers, four units of South Australia police took the signal and began to move in, broadcasting to James D. Marxuach and the Van Hooch/Susski unit to maintain a parallel course with them on the one side while the Japanese forces and security agencies kept an identical course on the other, everyone remaining out of the sight of the Range Rover until it had reached its destination.

As the Range Rover crossed the perimeter of Coober Pedy, Tomas Buckley said over his shoulder, "Stay right there on the floor until I tell you to get up, no matter how long it takes."

An answering grunt was returned.

Buckley directed the Range Rover into an evasive action over a widely circuitous route. It took over six hours to travel the eighty-two miles to Buckley's dugout at Scorched Ridge. Before they got halfway, the information had been passed from General Jilly to the Sydney base station of the CIA that Captain Huntington was in the car. Characteristically, James D. Marxuach's lifetime of training with The Company did not permit him to share that news.

Twice Buckley's wide-roundabouts which followed a compass course of the instrument set into the car's dashboard had confused the pursuers except for the radio-knowledge from the Air Force helicopter.

"Don't worry about the chopper," Buckley said confidently. "They got a very short range. We'll just keep circling and traveling and that helicopter is going to have to turn back to base to refuel; then we'll lose them all and head for the hideout." Within twenty minutes the chopper had disappeared and Buckley began to maneuver the Range Rover bewilderingly until, after an hour and fifteen minutes, they were on higher ground at the center of the desolation of the outback. The pursuit, excepting the KGB assault team and Captain Mitgang's Commando, began to run into each other, causing traffic jams at the middle of nowhere. James D. Marxuach began to worry about what kind of a story he could tell Daddy to explain how he had forgotten to fix a beeper under the fender of the Range Rover in the night so he could have found it wherever it went.

Buckley stopped the car at the side of a hill. He got out of the Range Rover, removed branches and other cover from a hillside area, revealing and opening two doors set into the ground. He motioned Yvonne to drive the car through the opening; then Buckley closed and bolted the door behind them.

"Ain't nobody goin' to find us now," he said, scratching his elbow of a nose with pleasure. "We got food and good tea and the world's biggest opal to keep us company. Now who could ask for anything more?"

Yvonne had to shake the Captain to wake him up as he lay on the floor of the wagon.

41

Bitsy saw it on television, heard it on the radio, and read it in *The Advertiser.* The parliament of the State of Queensland had outlawed drilling for oil on the Great Barrier Reef. Everything else tumbled into place within her mind. Colin's extraordinary, even superhuman, adeptness at eluding his self-inflicted troubles through creative coping had become the single most characteristic attribute of her husband, even surpassing his sexual prowess.

She remembered as clearly as if she were actually hearing Mr. Zendt tell the police that Colin had handed $750,000 to a man named Keifetz in Mr. Zendt's presence to be taken to the Australian Conservation Society. Until the moment of knowledge of the action of the Queensland parliament she had not made the connection between what Mr. Zendt had told the police and the sudden avalanche of Australian public opinion against drilling for oil on the reef. She knew Colin had engineered this sudden legislation with his wits and her money in order to convey to Fujikawa & Company that they had not only not lost anything by not acquiring the oil leases which Colin had presumably lost for them, but that they had actually been saved enormous sums in public fines for any attempt they would have made for drilling on the reef had not Colin saved them! She felt a surge of pride for her husband. Colin had thought he was waylaying Daddy's anger by getting five and a half million dollars for the *Perfection*. Colin could never have known that the area at which Daddy had taken greatest offense would be the loss of the oil to Fujikawa & Company, because of Daddy's ownership in that company, which now didn't matter at all because Colin had solved it by organizing the Barrier Reef sanctuary legislation.

The main thing was he had saved himself! He was saved! Daddy could now call James D. Marxuach and Commander Fujikawa could call Mr. Ikeda, and they both could call all Japanese and Australian authorities to stop the murder, prosecution, and revenge to be taken upon Colin. They wouldn't need to kill him now and they would easily be able to understand that. Colin could come back to her out of the oven of Central Australia.

She rushed into her bedroom at the hotel and unpacked her satellite telephone. She dialed Daddy's number. She had not called Colin from the moment he had gotten into such terrible trouble because that would not have been fair. But in a very, very, very short time she would be able to call him to tell him that he was out of danger and free to come home.

Daddy's telephone answered instantly.

"Daddy?"

"Bitsy?" It was a dark, heavy German voice.

"Yes. Oh! Dr. Kissinger?"

"How nice to talk to you, Bitsy."

"It is very nice to talk to you, Dr. Kissinger, but actually it is rather important that I talk to Daddy."

"He isn't here."

"Not there! But—"

"It's all right, Bitsy. I have no intention of trying to escape back to Washington."

"But where is Daddy?"

"He had to fly to Tokyo to the funeral of Baron Fujikawa. He will represent the President and the National Association of Manufacturers there."

"Oh."

"He will be back here in Montevideo in two days."

"Thank you, Dr. Kissinger. Please give my love to Nancy."
Each one hung up.

Bitsy strode to the hotel telephone and chartered a jet to take
her to Brisbane, Manila, Hong Kong, and Tokyo. She went to
the writing desk and dashed off a cablegram to Commander
Fujikawa expressing her deepest sympathies and asking him to
inform her father that she would be arriving to see him on a
matter of utmost importance and that he must wait for her.

She began to pack a suitcase hurriedly.

42

Buckley's dugout, far in the desolate gibber, was the most luxurious ever seen in opal mining history. "I bought this entire underground apartment at the World's Fair in New York in 1939 when all the rich folks knew they was goin' to get bombed," Buckley said. "We got everything here they got in them penthouses except we're under the ground. We got six big rooms. We're air-conditioned. We got electric cooking and refrigerators, hi-fi, and a piano. I bought all this fine furniture at R. H. Macy and my sister, Beanie, made them curtains in Weehawken, New Jersey. Sit down. Have some tea."

He wandered off to the kitchen. Yvonne and the Captain sat facing each other.

"Remarkable man," the Captain said. "I think he lost all of them back there."

"But how will we get away from here?"

"You and Tomas will ride out in the Range Rover. You have nothing to get away from. I'll stay on here for a while."

"I stay with you."

"You are my broker, Claire. You did your job and I am grateful to you. Now you must go back to Adelaide."

Buckley came back with an electric tea kettle, china, and all the makings. "This is a mixture of Chinese tea and mint tea," he said. "I am kind of a tea freak."

"How very pleasant," the Captain said.

"He wants to stay here, Tomas. He thinks if we go back to Coober Pedy and he stays here that they will lose him and he can get out."

"Pretty good thinking. But sooner or later you'll have to get out, Cap'n, so we better talk about that." He poured the tea. "Can't walk out, you know."

"If we take the Range Rover, how does he get out?" the false Claire asked urgently.

"I need to make it to Alice Springs. I'll be all right if I can get there."

"Alice Springs? That must be hundreds of miles!" Yvonne said. "How can you get to Alice Springs?"

"What happens when you get there?" Buckley asked. "You think you can take a bus or a plane out of there? No way."

"Delicious tea," the Captain said. "What a marvelous flavor!" He sipped it again. "The fact is, I keep a balloon in Alice Springs."

"A—what?" Yvonne said dumbfounded.

"You fly balloons?" Tomas Buckley asked admiringly.

"Yes. It's a family sport, actually. Before I left London, we made the arrangements to send the equipment out here with a professional balloonist in case my wife and I decided—or if we had the time—to do some ballooning under these ideal conditions."

"I am so happy! You are so marvelous at coping!" the false Claire said, throwing her arms around him, then suddenly remembering who she was supposed to be. She drew back. "But you still have to get to Alice Springs. So—we must drive you to Alice Springs in the Range Rover just the way we brought you here."

"No," Buckley said. "We got to draw them off by going back to Coober Pedy without him."

"But how will he get to his balloon?"

"Come on, Claire," Buckley said with irritation. "Enjoy your tea."

"Then let's have a look at your opal," Captain Huntington said.

43

A Fujikawa-stretched Rolls-Royce met Bitsy at the Haneda airport in Tokyo. It sped her into the city to the Fujikawa building. A senior executive of the company was waiting to meet the car in front of the Fujikawa building. He took her to the forty-first floor where Commander Fujikawa now presided in what had been his father's office. All had been transformed into a flawless reproduction of a living room in an English country house, an effect greatly enhanced by the presence of many original Chippendale pieces.

Daddy was waiting for her with the Commander. Bitsy expressed her sympathies. The Commander acknowledged them gravely.

"I came to meet with both of you," Bitsy said. "You see, the Queensland parliament has outlawed any drilling for oil on the Great Barrier Reef forever. The fines for anyone who is planning or who had planned to drill there are not less than staggering even for oil companies—as a clear warning that the Australians mean business about this."

"They can't do that!" Daddy expostulated. "That oil is worth three billion dollars!"

"I knew it!" Commander Fujikawa said with satisfaction. "I warned my father that this was coming."

"It's all over," Bitsy said. "They can appeal and appeal for ten years before they find out that it is all hopeless and useless."

"Of course! Absolutely!" the Commander said. "Much better to put our money elsewhere and let the others take the losses. I have startling news from our explorations in Brazil."

"What I want to talk about right now—don't you see, Daddy —please listen carefully, Commander Fujikawa—is that the way it has all worked out hasn't cost the company any money at all. In fact, Colin may have saved us millions and millions of dollars."

"Oh, yes," the Commander said. "I agree. I quite agree. Not only that—he has returned all the money he lost at gambling which was intended to secure the leases and he returned the salary we paid him."

"And I shall return the amount paid for the charter of the *Perfection* because Colin has more than made up for it by the price he was able to get for the sale of the yacht," Bitsy said.

"Your husband is a fine fellow," the Commander told Bitsy with great pleasure.

"Oh, Colin is a first-rate man," Daddy said.

Bitsy felt able to breathe again. "Then—I mean—don't you see?" she said. "Don't you think you should withdraw all the charges made to the Australian authorities and instruct the various people here and there that they are not to—uh—continue to *harass* Colin any longer?"

"Oh, yes!" Commander Fujikawa answered. "By all means! At once!"

"I find myself in complete agreement with both of you," Daddy said. Deep within his devious mind, Daddy thought about having to ask his friend the Russian Premier to rescind direct orders given to the rival institution within the Soviet government, the KGB, to ask them to withdraw just this one little mistaken operation. He knew he could withdraw James D. Marxuach. He knew he could withdraw the reward. He knew he could persuade the Australian police, in concert with Fujikawa, to withdraw the charges and give Colin safe conduct out of the country, but he knew that no matter what he said the Russian Premier would not inform the KGB that the Commando operation was a mistake and ask them to call it off. He felt sharp regrets for Bitsy's sake, but the die was cast. Colin was hoist. He was going to spend the next few years in a Russian prison until elaborate arrangements could be made either to have him released or to let him escape.

"I am proud of you, Bitsy," Daddy said, "for coming all the way here to tell us all this news before serious mistakes could be made. By God, yes, we've got to put every wheel in motion to see that Colin is relieved and delivered to you safe and sound. We've got to get your husband back for you."

"Oh, yes!" Commander Fujikawa said, floating directly to a battery of telephones inside a Chippendale cabinet. He struck an intercom switch and said, "Call the Foreign Ministry, please, and ask Mr. Ikeda's assistant to come in."

"While you are doing that," Daddy said cheerfully, "Bitsy and I will go into my office and call our Chief of Base, Sydney, and the Prime Minister of South Australia to call a halt to— uh—all activities."

"While you are both so busy," Bitsy said, "I wonder if I might have a small reunion with my cook."

"*Your* cook?" the Commander asked blankly.

"Juan Francohogar."

"Yes," the Commander answered softly. "He is your cook. To me he stands for so many things, that I think of him as being part of the House of Fujikawa." He summoned a guide to take Bitsy to the executive kitchens as the telephones began to ring.

Bitsy and Francohogar were alone in his small kitchen office. They greeted each other with all the warmth of people who meet far away from home. Then, as a Japanese waiter came into the office to bring an elaborate tray of tea, Francohogar said, in English, "What is going to happen?"

Bitsy looked from him inquiringly across the room to the attendant and raised her brows questioningly.

"It's all right," Francohogar said. "He doesn't understand English."

"To be safe," Bitsy said, "we will speak French. Captain Huntington is safe. He has saved himself. All is forgiven. Commander Fujikawa and my father are on the telephones right now to the Japanese Foreign Office and the Australian authorities and our own American agencies to withdraw all charges and to obtain a safe conduct for the Captain out of the country."

"So that is why you are here, Madame. To tell them to do it and to make sure they did it."

"I brought information to help them make a decision, yes. But Captain Huntington forced the decision. And I am sure that is not all he did to influence that final decision, because I find you here in Tokyo."

"Yes," Francohogar said. "I am here by the Captain's design."

"If the Baron were still alive, his pride and his honor would have forced him to redouble all efforts to kill Colin. No doubt about that. Did the Captain ask you to cook specific meals for the Baron?

"At every meal. Meal after meal."

"Oh, Juan! What a happy day this is!"

She called for a guide who took her to a private office. She telephoned Colonel Bocca in Brussels. "Oh, Colonel Bocca," she said happily into the telephone, "I am delighted to inform you that an armistice has been negotiated in Australia and peace has been declared."

"How is that, Moddom?"

"All charges against the target have been withdrawn and all the forces are—right now—being dispersed."

"*All* the forces, Moddom?"

"Yes."

"What about the Russians, Moddom?"

"The Russians! Oh dear, I had forgotten about the Russians, but I'll take care of that."

"But you want me to send your troops a withdrawal signal?"

"Yes. Yes, I do."

"And suppose the Russians do not withdraw, Moddom? Will you still wish your troops to cease operations?"

"Well—no. Of course not. But why shouldn't the Russians withdraw?"

"Because they are different from you and me, Moddom. Their reasons for doing somefink are never what are the syme as ours. You sye they'll withdraw. I sye it ain't bloody likely."

"Oh, I assure you, Colonel Bocca that—"

"The way I looks at it, Moddom, is this: Your troops ayn't there to do the target no 'arm, you see? Therefore, they should stye right there until the objective is syfely out of that country, if you sees what I mean."

"I accept that. It is logical."

"It's not as though it's going to cost you any more, is it, Moddom? Best to think of your troops as a peace-keeping force, and to myke sure they is the very last to leave the field."

Bitsy hurried to find Daddy.

"All set," he said as she came into his office. "I've talked to all of them and I am happy to say that Colin is free to come and go as he pleases."

"The Chief of Base, Sydney?"

"Oh, yes. I talked to Base. They have passed the word to Chief of Base who is now in the field and he called me back to confirm."

"And the Russians?"

Daddy had made a science of dissembling when he discovered how much money there was in it. He had trained himself to keep all of his reactions at normal no matter what surprising disclosures were turned on him suddenly. He didn't color. His irises tightened slightly, but Bitsy didn't notice that. "All handled," Daddy said. "I just hung up on Mr. Brezhnev. The KGB operation in Australia against Colin is now entirely cancelled."

Before Bitsy could cross-examine, Commander Fujikawa

came bounding into the room. "All settled!" he crowed triumphantly. "At this moment our embassy in Canberra is nullifying all action against Captain Huntington, and Mr. Ikeda's assistant is on his way to Haneda to fly directly to Australia by company jet to pass my orders to Mr. Ikeda personally. What a relief to know that it is all over and that my friend and colleague is utterly safe."

Mr. Ikeda's personal assistant security chief at Fujikawa & Company was a secret policeman from World War II and earlier, who had worked with Mr. Ikeda most of his life. His name was Kaneko Surogacho. He met with Mr. Ikeda in the house near the sea, north of Sydney. Although Mr. Ikeda had forced himself to go to Claire Bonnette's stake-out raid in Adelaide, that had been done under conditions of deepest pain and physical inconvenience. He had returned to bed, turning over the search for Captain Huntington to his three paid representatives. He was now tentatively out of bed and able to hobble about if he walked carefully, and with the help of several painful exercises he felt that he was going to recover ultimately from Bitsy's terrible kick.

He sat while Surogacho stood before him to report. He was preoccupied with the worry that he might have lost his manhood.

"Commander Fujikawa, now head of the House of Fujikawa, sent me to you to bring to you his orders that your mission to return with the head has been cancelled."

"Cancelled?"

"I only know that Commander Fujikawa has instructed me to inform you that it is all now unnecessary. Those are his words. He ordered me to tell you that since it is no longer possible, by law, to take oil here and that since all proper recompense has been made, that he no longer wished you—or any of our people here—to pursue Captain Huntington."

Mr. Ikeda was stunned. "I didn't expect to hear anything like that from you, Mr. Surogacho, or any other person who ever had the honor to serve Baron Fujikawa. I know only one thing. The Baron would never have forgiven what this man has done to our house. The Baron would never have done you the dishonor of sending you to dishonor me with such orders."

Surogacho was silent.

"But the son is the head of our house now. We must obey. So we must live with our dishonor—to ourselves and to his great father—and obey."

"I have more to report to you."

"Tell me."

"The family of Huntington were with the Commander for a long time before I was given my orders. The wife of Huntington then held a meeting with the cook. They spoke in French. I was in the room. I stood beside them and heard with my own ears that Huntington killed Baron Fujikawa."

"What are you saying?"

"Huntington sent the cook to the Baron. Huntington knew the Baron's weakness for food. As I stood in the room with them, the wife asked the cook if Huntington had told the cook what dishes to make for the Baron and the cook said every dish, everything he cooked and had placed before the Baron, had been ordered by Huntington."

"There was an autopsy, Surogacho! There was no evidence of poison!"

"Poison did not kill the Baron. Food did it. Heavy, heavier, heaviest food. He ate and ate and ate until he burst, because Captain Huntington knew that would happen. That was how the old Baron died."

They stared at each other expressionlessly and silently.

"You have returned my honor to me, Mr. Surogacho." Mr. Ikeda got out of his chair resolutely, forgetting his injury. He began to dress. "You will return to Commander Fujikawa at once and inform him that I received his orders gratefully. You will tell him that I will return as soon as I have assured myself that all the Australian agencies have dropped the case."

"You will return?"

"I will return as my Lord Fujikawa ordered me to return when he chose me to avenge the dishonor upon his name. I shall return with the head of Captain Huntington."

44

It was the most magnificent precious black opal he had ever seen; the largest, the heaviest, and the most perfect. It reflected every color in the spectrum. He estimated that it could not contain more than three percent water, which made it the most durable. He could visualize how the large rock in his hand would take its final shape, into which he would cut and polish it. It would be the finest jewel for any queen. In all of Bitsy's collections of diamonds, emeralds, rubies, and sapphires, this gem would be the foremost because it was the most thrillingly extraordinary gem that had ever been found. Nothing could have such beauty and such mystery. It would stand alone above all the jewels in the world because it was impossible to imitate it in the most remote form. It was a precious stone whose beauty and value towered over even the Southern Cross, owned by a khedive of Egypt, or the King Midas, which was held by Czar Nicholas II of Russia, or the Bird of Paradise, found for J. P. Morgan after a years-long search by a dealer who had been sent from New York to Australia to find a perfect opal. He decided to name this opal the Baron Fujikawa because it was so filled with everything.

He hefted the stone. He studied its grain. He stared at it through a loop. His cheeks became flushed and his eyes brighter. He did not speak for more than ten minutes while he worked with the stone. The false Claire Bonnette and Tomas Buckley sat on either side of him, but he did not seem to remember that they were there. At last he placed the stone on the table in front of them and leaned back. "I would like some tea now, Mr. Buckley, if you don't mind," he said.

Buckley swung up the teapot. He refilled their cups. "We drink to that opal," the Captain said. "And to you for finding it. And to you, Claire, for finding such a miner." He sipped the hot tea thoughtfully.

"I'll drink to your money when I see it," Buckley said.

The Captain took off a money belt. He removed wad after wad of bills. "Two hundred thousand, you said?"

Buckley nodded. "No tax."

The Captain counted out the money. Yvonne recounted it. Buckley took each stack as it came to him and counted more deliberately. When he finished he packed it all into a haversack. "Here's to money," he said, lifting his teacup. "It never stops traveling, does it?"

"Okay—how does he get out?" Yvonne asked.

"I have a tunnel. It leads to an underground shed about a half mile away, on the other side of the hill from the way we came in. There's a right handy little car in the shed which I am going to sell to you if you agree to leave it with an old geezer name of Willie Richert who runs a photo shop in Alice Springs."

"Sell?"

"If you leave her in the right place you can call it a lease. It's the only one between here and civilization after we leave in the Range Rover. Cost you five thousand dollars."

"What kind of a swindle is this?" the false Claire asked belligerently.

"It's worth every penny," the Captain said.

"Betcher boots," Buckley said. "It's a light hovercraft that's a combination of an airplane, a power boat, and a snowmobile. It'll cruise nine inches above that gibber or over water and it gets along at over twenty-five knots. It can go sideways and backward and do three-hundred-and-sixty-degree turns like a helicopter. A big rear-mounted fan and two hundred and ten ceecee engines move her and she gets two hour of travel for each gallon of fuel. Nothin' like her. Goes anyplace. Ordinary car couldn't be no use where you're goin'."

"Maps?" the Captain asked.

"Maps and a compass. Best way to Alice from here would be through Kulgera and on past Angas Downs. Just make sure you pack plenty of water. You can go light enough on food, and it's only a four hundred mile run, but lay on the water. It's a bad, mean old stretch of ground. And hope with all your might you got a balloon waiting for you at Alice."

That night, as Yvonne reshaved the top of the Captain's head, she had to call upon all her talents for agonizing self-control to keep herself from throwing her arms around him and telling him who she really was, begging him to take her with him. But she knew he could not get out with his life unless she did exactly as Buckley told them to do. She turned her back to him as she lay in a sleeping bag in the darkness. She would not speak. She wept silently, thinking of being alone, thinking of her life ending in a retreat into a closed room in the Charles Street house, never to see him again.

The Captain did mental exercises as he lay in the darkness to free himself from the negative thoughts of Australian prisons, or being shot, or his bored and yawning head upon a plate being presented to Baron Fujikawa. Instead he tried to think of all other things: of how much Rogier von der Weyden's *Portrait of a Lady* from the fifteenth century looked like the actress, Faye Dunaway; of how the Master of St. Giles' painting *The Baptism of Clovis* resembled Ralph Nader, and of how the child in Dürer's *Madonna and Child* resembled Edward Heath. He thought of Yvonne safely back in London exceeding all melancholia upon the soprano saxophone, sweeping away all threats of reality with the strains of the terrible anguish and regret of Lucifer in *Night on Bald Mountain*. He remembered the masses of her soft, golden-red hair and he compared it with

Bitsy's beautiful deep blue hair and Kimiko's incomparable black, black hair. He thought of Bitsy and how, if he were not shot down by police or hacked into two neat pieces by Mr. Ikeda, if he were not shut up in a prison, she would do nothing else until she had moved all the power at the family's command to have him set free.

He could not have done that for her. Yvonne couldn't do that for him. He couldn't, nor could anyone else, do anything to return Kimiko to life.

He wanted to call Bitsy to feel safe just by talking to her. He wanted to call Keifetz and Francohogar to find out how far the pack was behind him, but he had left Daddy's satellite telephone with all of his baggage back at Grace Wherry's in the black of night when they had gone through tunnels to get him into the Range Rover. If he had called Keifetz, or if Keifetz could have called him, he would have known that the chase was over and that he was free to proceed to any Australian airport to fly out of the country or remain—as he pleased. He believed he was still a hunted man and he thought with the sharp panic and instant reactions of a trapped animal. He had to get out. He *had* to get out.

As they separated the next morning, while Buckley was opening the camouflaged doors which folded into the side of the hill, the Captain asked the false Claire Bonnette to promise to pick up his telephone equipment at Wherry's and to send it on to her sister in London. Yvonne agreed, as she would have agreed to anything which could help him, and it reminded her that she had to go back to Claire's to get her own copy of the satellite telephone.

As they had slept fitfully in Buckley's underground apartment that night, all Australian police and Army units, all Japanese units, and James D. Marxuach had withdrawn from their confused positions out in the gibber and returned to Adelaide. As Yvonne and Buckley left the hideout, only the unit of Soviet commandos and the half-company of Bitsy's mercenaries were waiting out in the desolation.

The Captain kissed the false Claire good-bye, on the forehead. It was a famous first he would never know about. He had kissed Yvonne everywhere else upon her body excepting her forehead. She got into the car silently, weeping. The shed doors were open and Buckley backed the Range Rover down the track. The Captain shut the doors and secured them from the inside.

As the car drove away, it was watched through binoculars by a scouting party of the Russian commandos.

The Captain lost no time inside the apartment. He finished the pot of English breakfast tea, found the trapdoor into the tunnel. He closed the door after him and moved the light carpet over it from below with the magnet as Buckley had shown him to do, and began to feel his way by patting the wall of the tunnel along the half-mile walk in pitch blackness to the underground shed which held the light hovercraft vehicle.

The Russians were aware that all police units had withdrawn. They had never known that Bitsy's mercenaries were in Australia. They stopped the Range Rover three-quarters of a mile along the track. Two men with machine rifles appeared in front of the car. Two other soldiers with rifles ordered them out.

The Russians searched the car. They looked for hollow compartments, they ripped off fenders, they examined the understructure carefully. They took up the floor boards; then they spoke for the first time in flawless Stryne. "Where is he?" the sergeant asked.

"Who?"

The sergeant swung the butt of his rifle into Buckley's face. He went down like a dropped anvil. Yvonne tried to kneel beside him to help him but the soldier took her brutally by the hair and jerked her to her feet. "Where is he?" he snarled.

"I don't know what you mean," she said. The sergeant slapped her heavily. "We have twelve men," he said. "They haven't had a woman for a long time. You tell me where Huntington is or all of us will have you."

"You'll try to do that anyway," she said. The sergeant hit her with his fist, slamming her into the side of the car. "When I get through with you no one will want to mount you," he said. "We will go back where you came from—and I will show you the way."

Yvonne and the unconscious Buckley were dumped into the back of the car. The sergeant drove. The three soldiers sat quietly, ignoring the prisoners. The sergeant drove the car to Buckley's hill. "You came out of this place," he said, "so it has a door. Open the door."

Yvonne and Buckley's limp form were pulled out of the car. Two of the soldiers found the door. One of them fired a burst into it. Yvonne screamed.

The sergeant stared heavily at Yvonne. "Rip her clothes off," he said to the men.

Captain Mitgang and his troops, twenty-seven yards away, formed into a half-moon which went around the Russian unit in a semicircle. He nodded an order to his marksmen to fire. Bullets from six rifles took the Russians in the backs of their heads. Captain Huntington heard the fire as he emerged in the light hovercraft a half mile away, on the concealed side of the hill. He thought the Australian police had reached the hideout. He panicked and started the vehicle going north toward Alice Springs and, in blanking out, forgot to load the stone jugs of water aboard.

Two of the Russians fell dead on top of Buckley. Mitgang ordered his men to move in to search the dugout area behind the hill doors and to search both Yvonne and Buckley. Yvonne was staring in shock at the burst heads and the blood. She could not comprehend what was happening. Captain Mitgang liberated the $200,000 from Buckley, pocketed it carefully in both front pockets of his tunic, giving him a more than Raquel Welch-effect, then he poured a canteen cup of French cognac for Yvonne to bring her round and into clearer comprehension again.

"It's all right," he told her. "Is your friend dead?"

"No! He mustn't be dead. He must get away!"

"I meant this friend," Mitgang said, gesturing to soldiers to pull the Russians off Buckley. They brought Buckley around. "He's okay," a soldier said. "He just got a whack on the head."

"Put him in the car."

"You know who they were?" Mitgang asked Yvonne.

She shook her head.

"They were a Soviet commando patrol who were sent out from the main body to find Captain Huntington."

"Who are you?"

"We are troops hired by Mrs. Huntington to rescue him and get him out. Where is he?"

"At Coober Pedy."

"Let's save time," Mitgang said sympathetically. "The satellite tracked him here. I don't think you heard me and we don't have time. The main body of Russians will be out soon to find out what happened to their mates. We are Huntington's men. Mrs. Huntington hired us."

Yvonne thrilled suddenly. "She did that? She spent her *money* to save him?" Yvonne was made ecstatic by the knowledge that Colin's wife really did love him and had proved it with the supreme sacrifice of her money to save him. She must really and truly *love* him, Yvonne reveled. It was so wonderful for him! She loved him even more than she loved her money!

"Where is he?" Mitgang asked in a kindly way, made softer and more empathetic by the $200,000 he had just liberated.

"There is a tunnel in the dugout," Yvonne told him, "which goes to a shed on the other side of the hill. Tomas Buckley kept a special hover vehicle there. Captain Huntington is, by now, in it, on his way to Alice Springs where he has a balloon waiting for him to take him out."

"A *balloon*?"

She shrugged. "That's the sort of chap he is."

At that moment, Captain Huntington was moving the light hovercraft along map lines at twenty-eight miles an hour, already wishing he had brought water.

45

General Jilly studied the prints that had just come in from the satellite transmission.

"What are they?" he asked belligerently.

"The analysts say they are two sets of troops, sir, with two different sets of markings, operating about ninety miles northwest of Coober Pedy."

"What kind of troops?" General Jilly asked. "Australian police and Army?"

"No."

"No? How can it be anything else?"

"For one thing they are in combat against each other. For another, one side is wearing Soviet-issue uniforms and the other side has on the uniforms worn by the mercenaries who fought in Angola."

"What the hell is this?" Jilly said with fright. "Where are the police? Where is the Australian Air Force? How the hell can foreign troops fight each other on Australian soil?" How he wished he had taken the course in analyzing these crappy little pictures, fahcrissake.

"During the night," A.J. Melvin said, "the Australians withdrew. Our Intelligence people say that it was announced by all Australian media that all charges against Captain Huntington have been dropped."

"I don't give a goddam what the media says. It doesn't mean a goddam thing until Washington tells me that officially. Where the hell is Huntington?"

"Captain Huntington is moving between the combat area and Alice Springs, sir, aboard a hover vehicle."

"Are those goddam troops connected with Huntington?"

"Have to be, sir."

"Well, if the goddam Australian police and Air Force and Japanese have withdrawn from the area because Intelligence says the media says all is forgiven, what the hell are they still staying out in that God-forsaken place in those goddam uniforms and shooting at each other for?"

"They have to have other reasons, sir."

"How can there be other reasons except the charges which were brought against him and which are now supposed to be dropped? He's a simple multimillionaire civilian. What would Russian troops—if they are Russian troops—want with him? And how the hell did Angolan mercenaries get into this thing, no matter how we look at it?"

"There were twelve Russians, sir. Now there are eight. There are thirty mercenaries."

"Does Intelligence have any conjectures?"

"They say Captain Huntington doesn't know that the charges have been dropped, that he is probably making for Darwin, on the north Australian coast, 1200 miles away, and that he thinks both the Soviet troops and the Angolan mercenaries are Australian police."

"Keep me filled in," the general said. "Dismiss. I got to get on the pipe to Washington."

He unlocked a drawer of his desk. He removed a satellite telephone, and reading from a directory, dialed Daddy's number.

When Daddy hung up on General Jilly, he was in northern Greenland with Dr. Kissinger on a sound-out of Ronald Reagan's potential strength, and he was also in a dilemma. He had ordered Jilly to keep him in touch with the troops' action—he was baffled by the presence of the mercenaries—and to keep tracking Captain Huntington. It was a difficult quandary for Daddy. There were Bitsy's personal interests in this thing and there were The Company's relationships with the Premier and the KGB. If he were to allow Jilly to report the Russian presence to the Australian government, his own credibility with the Russians would be seriously threatened. If he were to allow Jilly to report the presence of the mercenaries, the Russians would be immediately uncovered. And, after all, he reasoned, he had had every guarantee from the KGB that when Colin was taken by the Soviet Commando he would not be (physically) harmed and he decided to depend on that because to doubt it would violate Russian credibility. Bitsy would have Colin back because he would be released (eventually). Therefore, all things considered, Daddy decided not to report the Russian presence to the Australian authorities. He decided to sit tight upon the classical historical position of allowing a natural flow of violence to establish a true course of events, as all rulers before him had so disposed.

46

As the camera watched from twenty-two thousand, three hundred miles above the equator, the pawns confronted various aspects of their situations.

Captain Ramen, unit commander of the Russian squad, sent a coded radio message to Pinsk, reporting the loss of four men in combat with Angolan mercenaries eighty-eight miles northwest of Coober Pedy, the escape of Huntington, and his need for replacements, more and different materiel, and requested air transport to North Australia.

The reply signal stated that a fifty-man Commando was airborne to Harromatso, the rendezvous point north of Alice Springs, bringing mortars, night-sighting machine rifles, amphibious vehicles, and mobile radar. The relief unit would also bring direct communications equipment to talk to Pinsk via the Soviet satellite hung geosynchonously above Singapore and whose cameras would be reporting enemy troop movements and engagements. A Gelbart 690SCHM would pick up the eight Soviet commandos where they were in the outback to fly them to join the new force at Harromatso under the command of Major Axelrod. Ramen read the message with awe. He was to fight under the command of the most victorious commando leader in the Red Army! He knew the operation was being mounted for Soviet military history books.

As Yvonne drove the Range Rover to Coober Pedy, Tomas Buckley returned to consciousness. The first thing he did was to search and check for his money. He groaned. "They rolled me, Claire. They got the loot."

"Oh, my God!"

"There goes your twenty percent commission, too. Jeezcrist, they looked like Russian troops, Claire!"

"The troops you saw are all dead, Tomas. It must have been the other soldiers who took your money."

"Other soldiers?" he repeated dully.

"Are you all right?"

"Just some loose teeth," he said. "Who the hell are those people?"

She told him she didn't know. She didn't want him jumping on Bitsy with lawyers to get back his $200,000 until she knew Colin was safely out of the country and back in her bed in Charles Street.

"By Jesus," he said, "I hate to do it but I'm goin' to have to pay some taxes on my opal to get me a stake to get us back to Adelaide."

Captain Mitgang and twenty-six men rode in the large school bus at fifteen miles an hour over the gibber, sweating out the buckets of water they were pouring into themselves in the heat while Mitgang raised his air base in North Australia and fixed the map intersection pick-up point for the gunship to come in to fly them to a drop area near Alice Springs. He called for a close aerial reconnaissance of the area between the Buckley dugout and Alice Springs and ordered that the base camp of the Russian assault force be located.

Captain Huntington was two hours out and three hours away from Alice Springs when he was sure he was going to die if he didn't get water. He had never felt so much heat so unceasingly; he had never before been able to imagine what it was like to burn eternally in the fires of Hell. He wore a black broad-brimmed hat which the false Claire had insisted upon jamming upon his head before he left and although he knew it was probably saving his sanity he felt keenly the indignity of dying from exposure while wearing women's millinery. His sweat dried as quickly as it poured out of him, dehydrating him. Mile after mile after mile passed by unnoticed as he began to hallucinate. He thought he saw kangaroos off to his left but when he looked directly at them nothing moved in the vast nonscape of loneliness. Buckley had meant him to travel by night. He should have stayed in that beautiful apartment with all that water and all that cool. This ride to Alice Springs would merely have been a pleasant adventure by night. Age had reached him. He had panicked for the first time in his life. He had run away into this giant oven.

He rubbed the moisture from inside his hatband across his cracking salt-covered lips. He wanted to urinate badly but he knew that whatever moisture he could keep inside himself would keep him conscious just that much longer. The hallucinating got worse in the waterless, wasting heat. He began to think that he was standing upon the bridge of the *Henty* on the high seas, spray flying, messman standing at his left with a high glass of chilled orange juice. He made himself come back to the hover vehicle. He made himself remember that if he had not been diseased by gambling he would not be standing here in torture. He would still be in command of the *Henty*, and spending his life rolling across the world with cold, lovely water on every side of him. How cold and blue the sea was! He crashed his hand into the side of his head to hammer himself out of the mirages. He must keep the vehicle moving forward along the map lines. He must teach himself to absorb the heat and to welcome it and he must measure the time and the distance which would tell him how much farther it would be before he had crossed this lost and wasted antilife to Alice Springs.

47

Uëli Münger was waiting at the place where he had been asked to wait, in a small house that Bitsy had rented for an enormous sum to persuade the tenants to move out for a few weeks until she and the Captain could make up their minds whether they wanted to go ballooning. He was unhappy. Alice Springs was unlike Zurich.

The Captain looked worse than the young child's drawing of a man that is framed in every home when the child reaches four years old. He brought the vehicle to a slow stop in front of the house, which was six hundred yards beyond the Alice Springs perimeter. As he climbed out painfully, Münger, who had rushed out of the barn, yelped with fear. The Captain was forty pounds lighter than Münger had ever seen him, which was when he had been eating and drinking with such pleasure in the restaurant of the Hotel Ascot in Zurich on an icy cold, wet winter's night.

The Captain tried to enunciate the word water but neither his throat, his tongue, nor his lips would move. He was able to summon up the strength to help Münger recognize him by pulling off the wide-brimmed black hat of Yvonne's. He fell down twice on the way to the house, Uëli trying to hold him, but he made it to the water and leaned into it to let it run across his face and head while Münger stood ready to pull him back should he try to drink too much of it. He went to sleep in a bathtub filled with glorious water. Münger put a pillow under his head. He slept stretched out in the bathtub for six hours. When he awoke the danger returned to him. The town of Alice Springs must by now be filled with waiting police. He yelled for Uëli, who appeared instantly as if he had been worrying outside the bathroom door.

"Start the burners," he said in a strange rusty voice. "Get the bag filled. Uëli?" The great Swiss skier-balloonist turned at the door. "It's not for sport this time. Either that balloon gets me out of here in the next hour or two or I will be arrested or murdered."

The Cameron balloon had forty gores, each gore having thirty panels of high tenacity nylon in alternating stripes of pink and green. Four sets of stainless steel cables passed from under the burner frame through the sides of the basket as the support arrangement for the double burner system that heated the air, which was fed in from two master tanks and by which the balloon was not only filled but replenished with air after partial descents and when higher rises were required. The basket was solid-weave willow with oak skids bolted through the woven floor, and it could carry the highest certifiable load of any balloon made. Bitsy had had the basket woven in green and yellow. The basket contained a compass, a chart desk, a 20,000 feet altimeter, and a thermistor-type temperature indicator, as well as a 2-scale electric variometer with a zero-adjust potentiometer.

The Cameron was an English hot-air balloon that held the absolute altitude record of 45,839 feet, which was two miles higher than had ever been reached by any other hot-air balloon. Because it would be flying close to the equator at such heat, Münger had had it fitted with a vertical flap-type vent, which would increase vertical control.

He had kept the balloon half-inflated for the past week, expecting to receive flying orders at any moment. Within two hours they were ready to take off. Captain Huntington loaded three times more water, in stone jugs, than would be required for a trip to Jakarta; three one-pound tins of Persian caviar, and three boxes of Chocolate Olivers.

He had changed to a floppy khaki safari suit that had walking shorts and many pockets. He wore a beige Australian bush hat padded on the inside with newspapers. He put on white wool knee socks and stout shoes. The shoes no longer fit because his feet had lost so much weight. He loaded the basket with his rifle and his shotgun, two eight-inch hunting knives, and a .38 calibre long-barreled revolver.

He said good-bye to Uëli, bewildering him. "This is not your fight." He pressed four $1000 bills into Münger's hand. "This balloon is expendable and it is my one chance to get out. I will call you in Zurich, at the Ascot Bar, in a few weeks." He swung into the basket. "Cast me aloft, please."

The Captain turned to the burners. Uëli raced to release the staying ropes. Abruptly, the balloon soared into the air. As the Captain watched the ground recede, he patted the opal in his left side pocket.

The juncture of the two Russian forces north of Alice Springs was almost simultaneous with the Captain's lift-off. They were so busy congratulating each other on the efficiency of the operation that no one noticed the pink and green balloon sailing at 4500 feet and climbing, over their heads. Major Axelrod and Captain Ramen were toasting each other, Mother Russia, the first eight astronauts, the entire Bolshoi, and American wheat farmers, with 120-proof Lithuanian potato vodka when the first call came in from Pinsk. The call was to alert them that the satellite over Singapore had reported that Captain Huntington was no longer in Alice Springs but had departed in a large pink and green balloon and was at the moment heading north by northeast at an airflow rate of forty-one miles per hour and that the Angolan mercenaries were now flying into North Australia.

Pinsk expected that Georgi Axelrod would execute one of his classical operations, models for Russian textbooks, which would dispose of the mercenaries and overtake the target in one beautifully executed plan, because the War College at Dianalevinsk would be watching, via the satellite, and Pinsk understood that the Guerrilla Command at the Pentagon in Washington, other high senior Army and Air Force officers, and the highest military sector of the Central Intelligence Agency would also be watching. "Give them all a great show, Georgi!" the KGB base at Pinsk cheered their field commander.

Axelrod gloried in the vision of twenty or thirty Red Army generals sitting in comfortable chairs, sipping and chatting and enjoying the greatest sport in the world, but mostly he was thrilled to his knuckles to know that the American brass would be watching his work with the intensity that Grand Dukes had once watched ballerinas.

Supremely confident, and quite drunk, he set out his ambush of the Angolan mercenary force at an intercept point eighteen miles northwest of Alice Springs. He transported men and mortars by helicopter to wipe out this interference with his overtake of the objective. He despatched a Commando of twenty-four officers and men to overtake the balloon, to bring it to earth with judicious awareness that the objective needed to be overtaken alive. Once taken, Major Axelrod, with characteristic elegance, would be flown to the objective, greet him in a courtly manner which would impress his entire international audience, then fly him out through Saigon to Pinsk as just one more gloriously achieved day's work.

Captain Mitgang and the gliders carrying his troops reached the rendezvous point with his own air support twenty miles southeast of Alice Springs, at the very center of Australia, and loaded them aboard a gunship. The Russian position estimator had somehow gotten turned around and had mistakenly placed this force, however temporarily, as being northwest of Alice

Springs. Mitgang learned from the gunship pilot that Captain Huntington's balloon had been observed moving at 5100 feet and climbing and that the encampment of a military force had been photographed on Polaroid film at Harromatso, twenty-six miles due north of Alice. Captain Mitgang decided at once to wipe out the encampment before proceeding northward to overtake the balloon.

As Mitgang was meeting with the mercenary pilot of air transport, one of the viewing admirals seated in front of the large ADVENT screen in the war room at the Pentagon tinkled the dark brown Scotch and soda in his hand and said, "What do you infantry guys think he'll do now?"

"I wish I knew who he was," General Gordon "Ginko" Manning, Chief of U.S. Guerrilla Counter-Operations said. "I could tell you better then."

"The hell with that, Ginko," the admiral said. "What would you do if you were the man on the spot? You're the guerrilla expert."

"A water-logged binocular man like you probably thinks there is a choice here," General Manning said. "Or that this cat ought to keep his eye on the ball and go get the man in the balloon."

"Never mind what I think," the admiral sang out. "What do you think?"

"I think he's got to kick the stuffing out of that Russian base camp and then go get that balloon."

The sixty-three generals, admirals, and their aides laughed heartily at that. The Army representatives applauded Ginko Manning and the messboys circulated among the audience to check that all glasses were filled.

The one hundred and twenty marshals, generals, and admirals at the Soviet War College at Dianalevinsk glared at the huge black-and-white television screen intently and belted vodka. "This is a very peculiar operation," a Red Army marshal growled. "What is Georgi Axelrod doing? The Angola mercenaries have linked up with their air transport and we don't even know if Georgi is sober."

"Look! Marshal Martonovitch!"

The Soviet ambush troops left Harromatso and began to move northeast just as the mercenary air transport began to move north on almost the same axis.

"Where are they going?" the marshal demanded. "There is nothing where they are going."

"I think some idiot has given them the wrong directions again," an admiral of the fleet said.

"Mareki!" the marshal yelled. "What would you do if you were in command of the Angola mercenaries?" Mareki was the ranking counter-guerrilla fighter in the war room.

"My orders would be to bring the man in the balloon out of Australia, comrade. To get him out I would want to feel that I had neutralized any force which would try to prevent that. So—first I would wipe out the base at Harromatso, then I would proceed north to take the balloon without diversion."

"Good, Mareki," the marshal said. "Let us see how this mercenary thinks."

"I will bet you five hundred rubles that the Angolan mercenaries continue north after the balloon and do not attack Georgi's camp," an admiral said. "Mercenaries are just commercial soldiers. They do not fight for any motherland. They are not interested in defense depths and classical military history."

"Mareki takes the bet," the marshal said. They all watched the screen with absorbed interest.

"A—ha!" Mareki said with admiration. "This man is a soldier!" They watched the mercenary gunship put down two miles behind the Red Army task force camp. They watched the mortars come out and go into the jeeps to move up silently.

"Shall I telephone Georgi, Marshal?" a lieutenant-colonel of KGB commandos asked nervously.

"No! If this were a war we would call him. If the motherland had anything at stake here, we would call him. But this is a simple field exercise in the center of Australia, and he has done nothing to protect himself when he was ordered not only to produce a magnificent result for the Red Army but with his skill and daring to set terror into the hearts of the high command at the Pentagon. Say—these satellite pictures are really very good. I am pleased. I am entirely delighted."

Mitgang's three mortars began their fire, destroying the camp. Troops placed near the perimeters of the camp cut down all survivors in a crossfire. With sixty-three minutes of touching down to mount the attack, Mitgang and his unit were airborne, heading north to find Captain Huntington.

"All right!" the marshal said. "We will now show them how we can snatch victory from the jaws of defeat. Telephone the Ramen Commando and send them north to intercept that balloon."

"Very strange how that Russian commander just sat there after he had split his force," Captain Mitgang said to the pilot of the gunship. "Anyone would have thought he would have gone north on the double."

"Russians have a very low attention span," the pilot replied.

"That fucking Russian commander must have been drunk out of his skull," Ginko Manning said at the Pentagon.

"Georgi was drunk," Mareki told the assembled brass at Dianalevinsk. "He became overexcited thinking about the quality of the audiences watching him across the world."

48

Mr. Ikeda was reasoning out his plan, which would place Captain Huntington's bleeding head inside the Mossbros leather hatbox already arranged to be cleared by the right, cooperative customs officer at Haneda. It was well known to Mr. Ikeda, privy to South Australia police information through the Japanese embassy, that Mrs. Huntington anticipated that her husband would make his way to Alice Springs where, in happier days, they had thought to have their sporting balloon available to them.

Mr. Ikeda sifted through Captain Huntington's options. He apparently had no way to receive communications from the outside world or he would have known that there was no longer any reason to flee the police and all other pursuit. He would most probably have taken commercial air transport out of Alice Springs to Adelaide or Sydney, would have been photographed and interviewed by newspapers, TV, and radio and Mr. Ikeda would have known about that. Therefore, Mr. Ikeda reasoned, he was in his balloon heading north in the hope of escaping through Darwin.

Because Mr. Ikeda was a first-class security chief by any standards, he had asked the embassy to get all information possible about the balloon at the time Mrs. Huntington first mentioned it. He knew where it was. He knew the name of the man in whose charge it rested. He sought linguistic counsel at the embassy to solve how to pronounce the name Uëli Münger and had been delighted to discover that his first name was merely a Swiss version of an old Chinese name: Yew Lee.

Mr. Ikeda bound his wounded testicles loosely in the softest muslin obtainable, chartered a small plane at the Sydney airport, and was flown to Alice Springs. He arrived in the early afternoon after the morning Captain Huntington's balloon had taken him northward.

Mr. Ikeda strolled, attempting to appear as much like a tourist as possible with a Polaroid PRONTO camera slung around his neck, toward the pretty little house which was considered "out of town" in that small place. He introduced himself to Uëli by offering his two-sided card marked Fujikawa & Company. Uëli had known the Captain was in the Orient on business for the Japanese but, marooned in Alice Springs and uninterested in newspapers other than the *Zürcher Zeitung,* he had no idea that the Captain was in trouble with the police and multiple other agencies.

Mr. Ikeda told Uëli that he had been sent out by his company to convey messages and instructions to Captain Huntington.

"He isn't here," Uëli said.

"He isn't *here?* Where is he?"

"Well, for one thing, I have every reason to believe he was in trouble. He didn't look at all well and he said right out that the police wanted to arrest him and that someone was trying to murder him."

Mr. Ikeda laughed. "You know Captain Huntington, always teasing. He picked up a bit of a tropical bug along the way and he got a pretty bad case of Kangaroo's Revenge but I was with him two days ago and, far from being in trouble, he was sitting on top of the world. Where is he now?"

"He left in the balloon about four hours ago."

"Where is he going?"

"To Darwin."

"Can a balloon pinpoint a landing that exactly?"

"Oh, yes. We do it all the time. The Captain is an expert."

"How long does it take for a balloon to get to Darwin?"

"It is eight hundred and fifty miles. If the winds are constant —this is flat country—it should take twenty to twenty-two hours."

"At what time did he leave?"

"Just after ten."

"Then it is possible that he could arrive at or near Darwin by nine tomorrow morning."

"Oh, yes."

"Thank you, Mr. Münger. You have been very helpful."

Because Münger was Captain Huntington's man, as Mr. Ikeda had been Baron Fujikawa's man, Mr. Ikeda was forced to kill him. He broke his neck in two simple movements, then dragged the body into a closet and locked the door after he had removed his business card from Münger's pocket.

Mr. Ikeda returned to the Alice Springs airstrip. He gave instructions to the charter pilot, and the helicopter flew north. All the pilot needed to know was that they were searching for a large pink and green balloon that was sailing on a direct course from Alice Springs to Darwin.

The 1961 WSK-built SM-1WS of the Soviet Air Force was the steady, ready workhorse of the Soviet helicopter fleet. It had a Polish Ivchenko radial piston engine that could move it no faster than ninety-six miles an hour, but it had a roomy thirty-nine-foot fuselage that could carry either a lot of men or a lot of blinis. It moved in dangerously close to the pink and green balloon nineteen miles south of Birdum in the Northern Territory, about 125 miles from Darwin. The chopper pilot waved the balloon down but the Captain pretended it was merely a greeting and waved back as joyously as he was able to do.

The aircraft gained altitude in a directly vertical line, then it hovered twelve feet over the balloon. The pilot slid open the window at his left side. He lifted a Van Itallie compressed air rifle—the highest velocity, gas-operated, smooth-bore weapon ever developed—made deep in the Thuringer Wald, near Suhl, by Engelson & Schrader—which fired a 6.3mm precision steel dart. He shot directly downward into the balloon, reloading deliberately after each shot, driving six darts into the bag of hot air and forming a jagged hole five inches wide across it.

The balloon was sailing at 1500 feet to allow the Captain to maneuver it in the almost still air. He was far below the stronger air currents at higher altitudes. He felt the effects of the escaping air upon the balloon instantly as it began to drop toward the lightly forested area that edged toward a great rain forest below. He started the burners to force more hot air into the bag, but the input could not compensate for the air loss and the balloon kept descending steadily. To slow the rate of descent he began to jettison everything of any weight in the cabin. The heaviest objects were the many stone jugs of water.

One of these jugs, falling with power, landed directly on the head of a taipan, one of the world's deadliest snakes, which had been poised before the horrified eyes of a walking party of Djingili-Wambayan, at a split second before it was about to strike into the ankle of the venerable chief of the walking party.

Immediately upon the death of the taipan, the basket of the enormous pink and green balloon descended to earth, the light wind took the colored nylon to stretch it out along the ground to the rear of Captain Huntington's tall, shiningly bald, bushily dundrearied figure in loose shoes dressed by Abercrombie & Fitch, so the walking party of aborigines was in no way to be blamed nor to be thought of patronizingly for casting themselves face down upon the ground before the basket or for worshiping the Presence which climbed out of it wearily.

"Am I going right for Darwin?" Captain Huntington asked. The venerable leader got to his feet. He approached the Captain fearlessly and with dignity. He handed his weapons to the Captain. He took off ancient body decorations and pressed them upon him. Other men stood. They came to the Captain and loaded his arms with clubs, boomerangs, spears, amulets, necklaces, and one small dingo puppy.

"How very kind of you," Captain Huntington said.

The old man answered in one of the family's three languages, which was complicated enough to have tied down a team of three Protestant missionaries from the Summer School of Linguistics for four and a half years, so the Captain, who only had English, super-French, good Italian, and fair German stood baffled.

The old man touched one of the supine women with his foot. She stood.

"I went to English school," she said. "You saved our father's life. The family believes you are supernatural."

"Please don't tell them otherwise until I am able to get on the road to Darwin," the Captain said. "But do ask them to accept the return of these gifts, and this small dog, perhaps hinting that I have blessed them all, making them extremely lucky for the user."

The girl nodded. She spoke to her family in the 6000-year-old, prodigiously-suffixed language. She was a very, very handsome girl, Captain Huntington began to think, also knowing he must not. He began to say to himself over and over in the ensuing silence, "When the chambermaid begins to look good to you, it is time to go home," the only homily his father had ever passed along to him.

The men of the tribe agreed to receive back the blessed weapons and the holy dog. They were greatly cheered. The Captain retained an extraordinarily woven bracelet to give to Yvonne as a souvenir of his visit to Australia.

"Please tell your family to get me to some safe cover," he asked the girl. "Please tell them that several evil spirits in many various forms are trying to destroy me."

The girl made a short speech, translating this passionately. The old man made a long speech in reply. A younger man seconded the reassurances of the old man in a definitely pronounced speech which took just under twelve minutes. The girl translated to tell the Captain that the family would protect him with their lives and take him to impenetrable cover in the rain forest.

As she was finishing, Mr. Ikeda's helicopter landed seventeen feet away from the group, making enormous noise but, because the Captain did not flinch, the family did not flinch. Mr. Ikeda had been able to spot the great pink and green balloon envelope with ease as it stretched out across the savannah. Mr. Ikeda descended from the helicopter carying a large sword. He stood nine feet away from Captain Huntington staring at him without expression. The Captain was unarmed. Rifle and shotgun had been jettisoned from the falling basket.

"My master, Baron Fujikawa, he who was the head of the ancient house of Fujikawa until you brought death to him, commands me by his death, as my honor commands me, to take your head from your body and to bring it back to the son who has succeeded him."

The young girl translated this for her father in a soft voice.

Mr. Ikeda stepped two paces closer to the Captain. "Prepare to die!" Mr. Ikeda said, lifting the great sword.

The old man threw a stick into the air at random. The family watched it go. The Captain wished he could watch both the stick and the sword. The stick went high into the air behind Mr. Ikeda; then, suddenly, it made a turn and started back in the direction from which it had come. The captain forgot the sword and watched the stick.

As Mr. Ikeda leaped forward with a screamed battle cry, wielding the sword, the stick struck him a violent, cutting rabbit punch at the back of his neck. He went down heavily. The sword fell from his hand. The old man leaned forward, picked up the sword, and with one deft and powerful stroke cut off Mr. Ikeda's head.

"Farkin' 'ell!" the chartered helicopter pilot yelled in purest Stryne. "Strike me bluddy dead, wot the bluddy 'ell is goan-on 'ere?"

Two young Djingili-Wambayan males moved to either side of Captain Huntington, took him under each elbow and, lifting him, ran with him ahead of the family toward the rain forest.

49

The South Australia police picked up Yvonne at the Coober Pedy airstrip, arrested her, and flew with her to Adelaide. She was booked for conspiracy, abetting the escape of a dangerous criminal, and for suspicion of dealing in illegal opal. She was put into a solitary cell where Chief Superintendent Gallagher came to see her the following morning.

Yvonne was crumpled.

The Chief Superintendent knew that since the case against Captain Huntington had collapsed he had no grounds for Yvonne's prosecution, but he had made a bargain with Bitsy to make sure that Yvonne could not rejoin the Captain and, grimly, he was carrying it out.

"Please send for my sister," Yvonne asked the moment the cell door closed behind him.

Gallagher had not known that Yvonne had not been told that her sister was dead, but he was a direct policeman. "I regret to inform you that your sister is dead, Miss Bonnette."

"Claire? Dead?" Her eyes were wide with horror. "But— how could she be dead?"

"She killed three police officers when we surrounded her house, believing Captain Huntington was inside and calling him out."

"Oh, God. Poor Claire. But I am glad. She was so unhappy."

"Miss Bonnette, I am here to tell you that I can offer you a choice. You can take the next plane from Sydney airport to London or you can face trial here on the charges brought against you."

"Aren't you going to question me about Captain Huntington?"

"This does not concern Huntington."

"But you charged me with abetting his escape, with conspiring with him, with dealing in illegal opal for him."

"This does not concern Huntington."

Yvonne was certain that, for whatever reason, a reason which she would soon know when he got back to England, Colin was safe. The police were no longer interested in him.

"Thank you," she said. "Please send me back to London."

When he left she lay face down upon the prison cot and remembered Claire—all the many Claires from all the many years before the slow, slow stain of Claire's life had blotted her away.

50

Nine minutes after the band of Djingili-Wambayan had carried Captain Huntington into the rain forest, the Ramen Commando of the Soviet forces in Australia put down in a large gunship twenty feet away from the balloon basket and its scattered, exotically colored envelope. As the troops came out they hit the ground, rifles at the ready. Ramen wanted a textbook operation done with style and dash because he had just been awarded a spot field promotion to major by telephone from the War College at Dianalevinsk. He knew that every move his men would make would be studied and evaluated in Moscow and in Washington. He knew that if he played his bullets right he could have his own regiment within a year and take over Georgi Axelrod's place in the Red Army history books, so he watched his performance carefully—careful not to speak vulgarly and offend lip readers, cautious not to overgesture. He did not want to play his part too broadly and yet he would be working on big screens across the world and knew that a certain amount of bravura would be expected to get the best reviews. He managed to swagger with exactly the right degree of emphasis as he got down from the gunship, giving his boot a smart crack with a riding crop as he stepped from the gunship, and was killed instantly by a fusillade from Captain Mit-gang's force.

"I'm a son-of-a-bitch, it's another ambush," Lt. General Gor-don "Ginko" Manning drawled at the Pentagon war room. "Don't those Russkies ever learn *any*thing?"

"Whut would yuddah done, Ginko?" the admiral who was General Manning's straight man asked.

"I sure as hell wouldn't have brought that goddam gunship down next to that goddam basket," Manning said. "Shit, that's elementary. Goddam thing coulda had a massive booby in it. And I sure as hell wouldn't have exposed my whole force, that's for sure. All but two men should still be in that fucking gunship. Now look at them."

Nine of the twenty-nine in the Soviet Commando made it back inside the gunship and covered four remaining point men who were setting up gun emplacements at flanks of where the hidden force in the rain forest was imagined to be. The gun-ship opened with its cannon, spraying .50mm shells along ninety yards of forest. The attack silenced suddenly.

Captain Mitgang slewed slowly through the forest on his stomach to count his losses. There were six dead, two wounded. He shot the wounded through their heads out of kindness. He pulled a lieutenant and a sergeant into the almost-darkness of the dense forest. "Very easy this," he said. "You keep pounding at the men who are trying to emplace the heavy machine guns while I go round and lay a few grenades under that gunship. Lay in six minutes of free fire, then give me all the noise you can make so I can get out and back."

"And they tell the kids that Errol Flynn is dead," the ser-geant grinned.

The gunship exploded seven minutes later. The two gun emplacements were cut down, but two guns and two flame-throwers had gone far around through the tall bush grass to the mercenaries' right flank and, as the Soviet emplacements went out firing wildly, the flanking power shot up and burned the entire remaining mercenary force from the right side.

Mitgang took the remaining Russians out with two tossed grenades. No one but Captain Mitgang was alive, seventeen minutes after the action had started. There were twenty-nine dead Russians, and twenty-nine dead mercenaries, three of them eligible for pensions from the Mercenary Soldiers' League Fund within five months.

The radio post began to sound. Mitgang tottered over to it and slipped on earphones.

"Hello, Captain Mitgang. This is Mrs. Huntington, your employer."

"Good afternoon, Mrs. Huntington."

"Have you overtaken my husband yet?"

"Not yet. But I am close behind. I should have him soon."

"How will you take him out?"

"One of our gunships or the Starfighter will fly him out."

"The Starfighter, I think. Where will you take him?"

"To our Sumatran base. Colonel Bocca's orders."

"I am so glad. I shall telephone you tomorrow. Thank you so much."

"Not at all, Mrs. Huntington."

When he hung up he called the Mobile Base and gave the map coordinates to have one of the Scorpion vehicles come to pick him up with some infrared personnel detecting equipment and three armed men.

"Ginko" Manning said, "Say—who *is* this guy? This is one very classy commander here. Never mind his one hundred percent losses—he knocked out the target."

"The target is the guy in the balloon," the talking admiral said.

"Listen, I'd like to hire this commander on our side. He is real talent."

"It's probably Mitgang, Bocca's topside honcho in Asia," the Chairman of the Joint Chiefs of Staff said, "so you can forget what you're thinking, Ginko. If it's Mitgang, he's one of the top paid military executives in the world."

"*ГОВНО!*" the marshal of the Red Army yelled, throwing his vodka glass against the wall and stamping out of the room at Dianalevinsk.

51

Captain Huntington was deep into the rain forest with the Djingili-Wambaya walking party that night. As they ate a dinner of small white slugs that the old man had discovered under a rotting log, and which the Captain thought were simply delicious, he asked the handsome young girl her name.

"Wirri."

"Lovely name. Wirri, does the old man understand that I must be put on my way to Darwin tomorrow morning?" He thought she had absolutely super breasts. And such a darling little arse.

"Yes." She paused, then she said, "He will do it if you will leave something with him."

"Of course. Anything."

She became animated. She called across the fire to the old man and the others in the family. She spoke gaily and rapidly in the enchained, agglutinated language.

"What were you telling them?" the Captain asked.

"I told them how kind and willing you were to do as my father wishes."

"Do?"

The family was wildly happy. They were striking sticks upon tree trunks and singing with happiness.

"Put a baby in me," the handsome girl said.

"My dear girl—where on earth would I get a baby?"

Her face fell. "My father wishes me to have your child because that child will bring the great spirits to us."

"You mean—have a child with you?" His face was shattered by incomprehension as if he had never associated sex with manufacturing progeny. "But I am *Ir*ish!"

"We do not care. We want your child anyway." She took his hand and stood up. Gently she eased him to his feet. By God, the Captain thought, she is a *beautiful* girl. She led him off into the forest saying, "My family has never seen a balloon before."

They found a soft, dry place. Wirri took off her skirt. The Captain stepped out of his smart safari trousers and removed his shorts. They lay beside each other, touching each other. The Captain, immensely aware, rolled over upon her and entered her, and began The Enormous Pleasure.

"As you were, Captain Huntington, sir," Captain Mitgang's voice said as the four armed men ringed the tiny glade. "I am here as your wife's representative and I am ordered to take you out of Australia."

Dazed, the Captain was lifted to his feet and, under rifle bores, got into his shorts and trousers with mechanical numbness. "Take him out to the Scorpion," Captain Mitgang ordered, and the three men, in a triangle around the Captain, moved him out into the darkness. Captain Mitgang was out of his trousers and shorts in an instant. Wirri smiled up at him. Her father would never know the difference. Mitgang descended and rose, descended and rose, and so left behind him a remarkable future chief of the Djingili-Wambaya.

52

When the Starfighter touched down at the mercenary Sumatran base, only Captain Mitgang, Captain Huntington, and one pilot were aboard. The Captain was relaxed into euphoria at his salvation, having no way of being aware of, or of counting, the 117 men and women who had died because he had spent such an unlucky night at the Denbigh Club.

They stood at the center of an elaborate compound of buildings at Fort Bocca in glorious tropical twilight. When he had finished describing the layout of the military base, Captain Mitgang said he had had a hard day and thought he would turn in early. He pointed out Captain Huntington's quarters across the compound. The lights were already on in the small elegant building, so it was an easy thing to find the way.

Terribly weakened, forty pounds lighter, almost unrecognizably bald and moustached but elated and ready for twenty or thirty hours' sleep, the Captain opened the front door and walked into the living room, to face Bitsy, Daddy, Uncle Jim, Uncle Pete, and Cousins Harry, Larry, and Gary. His legs buckled. Uncle Pete grabbed him for support and led him to a chair facing the semicircle, as they all sang "For He's A Jolly Good Fellow."

Bitsy's own satellite telephone buzzed. She picked up, said

hello, and listened. "I'm sorry," she said, "I'm afraid you have the wrong number."

"Who was that?" the Captain asked.

"I believe it was your little French mistress calling from Hong Kong," Bitsy said. "Darling! Oh, my darling, welcome home!" She rushed across, lifted him from the chair, and took him in her arms.